The Ghost Files

Volume I

By Apryl Baker

The Ghost Files

Limitless Publishing, LLC
Kailua, HI 96734
www.limitlesspublishing.com

Formatting: Limitless Publishing

ISBN-13: 978-1-68058-059-4
ISBN-10: 1-68058-059-0

Dedications

For Granny –
You are missed every single day.

Part I: Secrets

Chapter One

Cherry blossom lipstick applied to full, pouty lips to perfection, check. Smoky eyes, check. The hazel color does throw off the smoke effect, but they still look pretty darn good. Dark brown curls flowing down white fleece in a flirty style, check. Kid with the hole in her head, check. Skinny jeans…hole in her head?

My head snaps around and I stare at the kid. She can't be more than eight or nine. Her blonde hair is pulled back in a ponytail. The sundress is adorable, little daisies everywhere with blue slippers to match. She's as cute as a button if you can ignore the pasty skin and the hole, which looks like a bullet hole. Not that I've ever seen one up close and personal in my sixteen years, but I do watch *Law and Order: SVU*. Stabler is hot for an old guy.

"Mattie, you done in there yet?"

I roll my eyes at the whine in Sally's voice. She's *so* jealous about not getting invited to Megan

1

Johnson's party. Not that she'd go, mind you, but that's not the point. It's the invite that matters.

"Can you help me?"

It's the kid. My eyes flick back to her. No. I'll ignore her and she'll go away, just like always. Yep, that's been my rule since I was five. It's one thing that I actually see ghosts, but I don't want *them* to know that.

"Mattttiiieee!"

"All right already!" I yell. Sheeze, can't she chill for five more minutes?

"Please."

"Yeoww!" The dead kid touched me, and it hurt. It felt like a knife had sliced through me. I shudder. It's never pleasant if they touch you. It's not *my* pain I feel, but hers, mostly pain and confusion. And I hear...things. *"Mommy, Mommy, where's Mr. Bear?"* The kid doesn't know she's dead?

"Mattie, you see a roach or something?"

I can hear the worry in Sally's voice. She has a thing about roaches. The dump she and her mom used to live in was infested. She'd told me once she'd woken up with one in her mouth. So gross.

"Please, please, can you help me?"

Don't look at her, Mattie. Don't say a word. She wants to touch me again, but I scoot backward and run for the door. I can feel her behind me. She's confused because I won't talk to her. Too bad. Then I open the door. "Bathroom's all yours, Sally."

"Is there a roach in there?" she asks, eyeballing the room with fear.

"Just a mouse," I say and slide down the hall, stopping to grab my coat. That was mean, even for

2

me. Sally's scared of mice too, but if the ghost stays in there…can't chance it. Sally can't see her, but who knows what the dead kid might do?

That is my screwed-up life in a nutshell. Yup, Mattie Louise Hathaway—the foster kid who sees dead people. Not something I'll ever talk about in casual conversation, mind you. No way will I end up in the loony bin. Nobody—and I mean nobody—knows my secret. And that's exactly how I plan on keeping it—very, very secret.

I'm outside, and there are no ghosts. Excellent.

When my ride shows up a few minutes later, I'm all smiles. Oh, yeah. Jake Owens is a major hottie, the absolute cutest guy I ever drooled over. Every girl in school goes all gooey around him. Who can blame them? He's the tall, broad-shouldered football captain with big brown eyes, and a smile that could defrost even Mrs. Wynn, the stuck-up English teacher trapped in the seventies. And he's all *mine*.

"Mattie, you're looking great tonight," he says in his deep voice that makes me warm all over.

I wink and settle into the car. It's cold outside and I'm frozen, but I won't act cold. This girl didn't dress for warmth, but to flirt. Why we girls torture ourselves to look good, I'm not sure any of us can really answer. Guys don't go through half as much trouble as we do to impress. All they do is throw on just anything and look good. It's so unfair.

Meg's party is at an abandoned mill—not at her house, like last time, when the cops got called and her parents grounded Meg for a month. She had to do community service, too, which had to suck. They said it'd help her build character and learn responsibility. Yeah. Whatever. When that day comes for me, I'll sprout wings and fly.

All Megan cares about is spending Daddy's money and keeping her boyfriend, Tommy James, happy. Megan is hands-down the most popular girl in our school—head cheerleader, with perfect hair and skin. I can only wish to look half as good. Anyway, back to Tommy. He has roving eyes that often land where they shouldn't. Megan can do much better, but she's hooked on the guy. Stupid, but not my business.

The party is in full swing by the time we get there. Everyone is milling around, laughing, talking, and drinking. Jake lays an arm around my shoulders and I snuggle close. It's freezing! Why Meg decided to have a party outside in the dead of winter is beyond me. We make a beeline for the bonfire raging out back. Jake grabs a beer, but I decline.

I never, *ever* drink at parties. The only thing I'll drink is water I run from the tap myself. I'm not stupid enough to set myself up to get drugged and raped. Jake is a pretty decent guy, but I've only known him a couple of weeks, and have no idea what he's like when drunk. I'm a smart cookie. I never take chances.

"Mattie!" Meg waves her beer bottle at me. She's already buzzed; her eyes are a bit glassy. See? Not a smart cookie. She'd be an SVU nightmare. Don't get me wrong. I really, really like Meg. She's one of the first people who accepted me when I got here last month. That girl's got a closet full of clothes I'd sell an organ for, but her personal choices are not always the best ones. She's the town's sweetheart, the golden girl expected to do great things. I guess she doesn't think anything bad could ever happen to her.

"Hey." I smile and shake my head when Tommy offers me a beer.

"Aw, come on Mattie, have a drink, loosen up a bit," Tommy wheedles. His eyes are on my chest. Such a jerk. Meg hasn't noticed, and I'm grateful. I'd hate for her to get mad at me because of her idiot boyfriend.

"Leave off, Tommy." Jake glares. He *has* noticed where Tommy's eyes are. "You know Mattie doesn't drink."

"Chill, man. I'm only trying…"

I roll my eyes at the rising testosterone. Time to change the subject. "Meg, didn't I see Ava over there wearing knock-offs?"

"I know! Can't believe she thought she could pass those boots off as designer. I mean, really." Meg nods. "And that handbag…O-M-G!" Nothing upsets her more than a knock-off. She's a fashionista in the worst sense of the word. She plans on going to a New York design school after graduation.

"The stitching is all wrong on the bag, too." I am *not* a fashionista, but I've heard that stitching can prove if something is original or not.

"It's atrocious!" Meg laughs. "I can't believe she thinks anybody will buy that nonsense."

"Maybe her folks aren't rich and it's all she can afford?" Jake asks, voice dripping with sarcasm. Jake's parents are pretty close to poor. His dad is often out of work and his mom's a housekeeper for the local hotel. Jake will work part-time this summer to help pay the bills. It's one of the reasons I liked him to begin with. He's not like the usual high school boy. He understands life is hard, and you do what you have to do in order to survive.

Meg's catty remark did sound a little snarky, I must admit. Not everyone's father is the mayor and can afford to dress in high fashion. Look at me. I wear Wal-Mart clothes. I don't pretend to be anything I'm not. That's probably why Meg and I get along so well.

Meg sighs. "That sounded really bitchy, huh?" She's one of the nicest people I've ever known, but when she's drunk, the girl can get a little mean.

"Just a little," I tell her, "but I started it." I'd *tried* to stop a potential fight between Tommy and Jake, but ended up dissing someone else. I felt bad. It's a new feeling for me. I typically don't let myself get attached enough to people to feel anything for them, but being around Jake and his family made me start rethinking my whole me-myself-and-I mentality. Not that I don't have reason to keep people at arm's length, but Jake is thawing me just a bit. I don't know if I like it or not.

"Know what you're gonna do for your public speech on Friday, Mattie?" someone asks behind me. I turn around. Oh, joy. Sam Jenson. She and I are competing for the only junior spot on the debate team. I need it for scholarship purposes; she wants it only because *I* do.

Since day one, Sam and I disliked each other. She's a snob and I'm a smartass. Put us in a ring

6

and I'd knock her on her snotty arse in two seconds flat. Does she honestly think I'm gonna tell her what I'm doing? But...considering that I'm standing with people who are nearly drunk or well past that state, she probably assumes I am, too.

"Sure I do," I tell her, "but *you'll* have to wait until Friday to hear it." I smile sweetly at her and snuggle under Jake's arm. Sam has a huge crush on Jake. This I discovered from her friend Mimi. The snuggling only makes her mad and she stomps off. Good riddance. I so don't want to get into a cat fight tonight.

"You know that spot is yours," Jake whispers in my ear. "I've heard you practicing. Don't worry about it."

"Do I look worried?" I breathe in Jake's rich scent. He smells clean and woodsy. I'm not sure what kind of cologne he uses, but it's addictive. I could stand here forever basking in the warmth of the fire, enjoying Jake's arms around me. This is as close as I've ever come to being, well—*not* so much happy, but I guess maybe content is the right word. It's another new feeling for me, but it's one I sorta like.

"No." Jake grins down at me. "But you do look very, very kissable."

I smile as he lowers his head and kisses me until my toes curl. Jake kisses better than any boy I've ever met. Not that I'm a slut, mind you; I don't sleep around. I'm still a virgin, but I do enjoy the whole kissing aspect of dating. Jake's kisses make me want to rethink the whole not-sleeping-around thing, which worries me. Not that he's said anything, but if he did, I'd have to think really, really hard, and I don't know what my answer would be. It's always been 'no' before, but I've never met a guy I liked *this* much, either.

"Get a room," Tommy grouches, breaking up our little interlude.

Jake and I both laugh at Tommy's obvious disgust. He'd hit on me not more than an hour after I'd arrived at school my first day. Tommy has never understood why I didn't jump at the chance to let him in my pants. Why does Meg put up with his crap? Again, not my business.

The joke rattling on my tongue dies as a girl steps into the firelight. She's turned away from me, dressed in a bummy-looking gray nightshirt, hands bound behind her back. Long, stringy brown hair is matted with a dark sticky substance.

Not here. Oh, please, oh please, oh please, not here.

I want to avert my eyes, but can't. She's turned to face me; her eyes are so lost and scared. There's a small bullet hole in her head, almost exactly where it was on the other dead kid I'd seen earlier. Her mouth is covered in duct tape, so she can't speak, but I don't need her to. I know her.

It's Sally.

Chapter Two

"Take me home. Now."

Jake and Tommy stop their sports talk mid-sentence and stare at me.

"It's only been two ho–" Jake shuts up when he no doubt sees the shock, worry, and anger in my expression.

It's wrong for Sally to end up murdered, and I couldn't care less if Jake's upset about leaving early. I gotta get home.

"Mattie..."

"Now, Jake," I cut him off. "You either drive me home or I'm walking." He frowns and I stalk away. I hear his sigh behind me and then a muffled "Sorry," before he hurries to catch up.

"What's going on?" he demands.

"I just gotta get home." No way can I say I've just seen my foster sister's ghost, bound and gagged. My face is stone; I suspect my eyes are, too.

"Fine," he sighs. "I'll drive you."

Yeah, he's irritated. Too bad. He's nice and all, and I *really* like him, but he'd best not be thinking I

9

owe him anything. If he insists, he'll learn Mattie-move number one: hit first, ask questions later. But when I wanna go, I just go. He'll deal or move on.

The ride is tense and I can feel Jake's stare. He's no doubt sure I've gone nuts...but I refuse to explain. I turn my attention to the more serious problem—what will I do at home? It's not like I can say, "Hey, I just saw Sally's ghost!" I have to *do* something.

As we pull up, the house is quiet and dark. No lights, no movement. Nobody knows Sally's gone, maybe? Not good. I don't even give Jake time to stop the car before I'm out and running up the porch steps, yelling, "I'll call you tomorrow!" I guess he drives away, but don't bother turning around to find out.

I fumble my keys, but finally open the front door. My feet pound up the stairs, thumping in concert with the rapid beating of my heart.

"Mrs. Olson!" I bellow and burst into Sally's room. The door bounces off the wall.

The bed is rumpled, like she's just gotten up to go to the bathroom or the kitchen for a snack. Her shoes lay haphazardly in front of the bed, and her robe is in a puddle on the bedspread. The lamp is still on. Sally always sleeps with it on so she'll know where she is when she wakes up *and* that she's safe. But not this time.

Where is she? I rip open the closet door, half expecting to see her there. There's no way she could have gotten far. I'd only been gone a little over two hours. I circle the room looking for anything to tell me where she is. Nothing is out of place here. I want to scream.

"What is it?" Mrs. Olson staggers into the room, wiping sleep from her eyes and blinking like an owl.

"Where's Sally?" I demand. My voice is a little too shrill.

"She went to a party." Mrs. Olson yawns and pulls muddy brown hair out of its elastic band. "Why all the fuss, Mattie? She said she was going to meet you."

"No way. She wasn't invited, and had no way to get there, even if she was crashing it." My mind flitted anxiously. Sally had been wearing her night clothes! That means whatever happened to her started *here*. "We have to call the police," I mumble, still trying to see something in the room that could give me a clue.

"The police?" Mrs. Olson groans. "Mattie, she's at a party. Why would we call the police?"

"Because I already told you she wasn't at the party!" I shout.

Mrs. Olson stares at me like I sprouted horns. "If she's not home in a couple hours, then we'll call the police, honey. You need to calm down."

I growl through my teeth. Why won't she listen to me? Just because I don't have the magical number eighteen attached to me doesn't mean I don't know what I'm talking about! Arghhhh.

Mrs. Olson is shaking her head at me and I throw up my hands. To heck with this. I stomp down the stairs and pick up the phone.

"Mathilda Louise Hathaway, just what do you think you're doing?" She thuds down the steps right behind me.

"I'm calling the cops since *you* won't."

She takes the phone from me. "No you *won't* call the police. Sally went to a party, and whether you saw her there or not, that is where she is. I am sure she'll be home soon."

"Really? So when she doesn't come home and we end up calling the cops, what are you gonna say when they ask you why didn't you call sooner?" I spit out. "You're supposed to be taking care of us!"

Mrs. Olson's pale gray eyes turn steely. *That* hit a nerve.

"I *do* take care of you—better than most, Mattie. You have no right to say that."

"Then call the cops! She's not at the party! She's dressed in her night clothes for crying out loud!"

Mrs. Olson's eyes turn sharper. "I thought you said you didn't see her, Mattie. How do you know what she's wearing?"

Fudgepops, I shouldn't have said that. Think fast, Mattie-girl. "Because…when I left, she had on her nightshirt and her fluffy gorilla house shoes. She was getting ready for bed."

"Then she changed her mind," Mrs. Olson replies. "Sally told Larry she was going to a party."

Wait, *Mr. Olson* said Sally went to the party? And just where is *he* now? Why isn't he out here to see what the shouting's about? Everybody else is up; doors are opening and closing upstairs. "Where's Mr. Olson?"

"He got called in to work." Mrs. Olson runs a hand through her hair again. "Mattie, I promise you if she's not home in a few hours, we'll call the police. Can you wait that long?"

"Okay." I hold back a sigh. She really believes Sally is at the party. Sally's already dead, so technically finding her won't help, but I don't want her to be just another kid marked as a runaway. She deserves better. She deserves justice.

Mrs. Olson smiles tiredly at me. "Go fix yourself a cup of tea, dear. There are plenty of cold-cuts in the fridge if you want a sandwich." She heads back upstairs, cordless phone in hand.

Great...what to do now? There's only one thing to do—the one thing I swore I'd never do. I can talk to the dead kid in the bathroom. Sally can't talk even if she shows up. Her mouth is taped over, but the little girl in the bathroom can.

I so don't want to do this, but it's not about me, it's about Sally.

I steel myself and head toward the bathroom.

Time to talk to the dead kid.

Chapter Three

My insides churn like I'm gonna upchuck at any second. I've worked so hard to deny this part of myself. It's terrifying to own up to it now, but I have to. It's for Sally. I can speak for her; I can find out what happened. My best chance is the kid. She had a wound similar to Sally's, and even if the same person didn't kill them both, maybe she saw what happened to Sally. It's a place to start.

The door to the downstairs bathroom beckons me, but I hesitate. What if this starts something I can't stop again? What if they never leave me alone? This could be the beginning of the end of my sanity.

Stop, stop, stop, I say to myself. *It's not about you, Mattie Louise.* Sure, Sally and I have only known each other a month, but foster kids are different. We know what it's like to be dumped and abandoned. We're tough as nails, but we stick together to survive. Finding her body is important to me, and maybe her too.

I take another step and stop again. I really, really don't want to do this. The cold is what bothers me the most. I've never been able to get warm, not really. And the cold I'm feeling really hurts—it burns through me. Especially right now. Deciding I should talk to the kid opened a door I'm not sure can be closed again. I feel the locks opening and the cold is already snaking into my bones. By the time I reach the door, I'm shivering. But I can't back out now. Time to own up to my weirdness. This is for Sally.

Resolved, I push open the door and go in. The light switch is beside the door and I waste no time flipping it on. The harsh white tile greets me, but there's no dead kid. But I've never tried to find a ghost before, either. They usually find *me*. *Well, Mattie, do something,* I think. *Standing here like an idiot isn't helping.* "Um... hello?"

Silence.

Nada. No surprise there. I close my eyes and think of the kid, picturing her the way I remember from before and concentrate really hard on that image. "Look, kid, I'm sorry I ignored you earlier. Will you come out?" How stupid does that sound?

Well, dang it. Maybe I need to concentrate harder. I close my eyes so tight they hurt and whisper, "Come out, come out, come out." All I need now are red shoes, a blue checkered dress, and a little dog named Toto. I feel *really* stupid.

A giggle breaks the silence behind me. I whirl around, but the only thing that greets me is the towel rack over the toilet.

"Hello? Little girl?"

"You're silly."

It's not my dead kid from before, but a little boy.

15

He's sitting on the bathtub and looks about nine. Floppy brown curls tickle his ears, and eyes as blue as a cloudless summer sky stare at me from a bruised and smashed face. Dear God, it looks like someone caved in half of it. The left side of his face is sunken in, bones sticking out of the skin in a random pattern. His clothes are torn and muddy, and he only has on one sneaker. His shoeless foot has been butchered. But it's the bullet hole in his head that catches my attention.

"Hello," I whisper.

"You can see me?" He jumps down and moves closer, forcing me to back up until I hit the door. My hand grabs the knob, ready to bolt if he gets too close.

"Yes."

"Can you help me?" Those big blue eyes bore into me and the cold intensifies.

"What happened to you?"

"I don't know."

He sounds so lost and alone. I remember sounding like that after the whole Mom incident. It's the worst feeling in the world. I probably looked about as bad as this kid too. I'd been scared and alone with no one to tell me everything was gonna be okay. It's a lesson we all learn, but to learn it like *this* is cruel. He's just a little boy.

"Do you know the little girl who was in here before?" I ask him softly. After all, I don't want to scare him.

"Can you find my mommy for me?" he asks. *"She's gonna be so mad. I wasn't supposed to leave the playground, but I did, and now I can't find her.*

16

Please, can you take me to my mommy?"

Oh, crap. I feel his pain and fear inside me. Why can't the kid just shut up? I don't like feeling sorry for him. It makes me vulnerable, and I don't do vulnerable. Ever. Best defense is always a good offense. *Focus, Mattie.* "Look kid, I'm trying to find my friend Sally. Have you seen her? She's tall, about my age with brown hair and brown eyes? She's wearing a Mickey Mouse nightshirt."

He backs away from me, his eyes going round with fear and horror. His poor face becomes even more bruised-looking, if that's possible, now taking on a purplish hue.

"It's dark there," he whispers. *"And cold."*

"Where?"

He shakes his head no. *"I can't tell,"* the little boy says. *"Not ever."*

The lights in the bathroom dim, almost going out, and the temperature drops to freezing.

"Why not?"

"Janey tried to tell," he whispers. *"She got caught, and now she can't never tell no one."*

Who is Janey? Another victim maybe? "Will you tell me where the cold, dark place is so I can find my friend?" Holy crap. I can see my breath. Frost appears on the mirror, working its way up like a vine, and then splinters to cover the entire surface in white.

"No!" the little boy yells. *"We can't tell!"*

"Please…"

"Not ever!" he screams, and the lights go out.

I plunge into an icy black abyss. Terror chokes me as I slam open the door behind me and flee into the hallway. I stand there shaking. *Calm down, Mattie,* I tell myself. *It's just a ghost, it can't hurt you.* Then I concentrate on evening out my breathing and letting my heart rate fall back to normal. Whew. The fear is still there, but at least I'm not biting my knuckles to keep from screaming.

Well, *that* didn't turn out the way I hoped. The kid disappeared on me. I probably scared him as much as he scared me. What now? I could go looking for clues in Sally's room, maybe. But even if I find something, I can't do anything. Mrs. O has the phone…wait.

Duh, idiot. Can you say *laptop*?

I run up the stairs to my room, lock the door, and hit the power switch on my one-and-only possession. While waiting for it to boot up, I grab a new shirt and kick off my shoes. In the time it takes for me to pull the shirt over my head, the room turns into a freezer.

Well, fudgepops.

I hear a choked gurgle, and that's when the lights go out.

Chapter Four

I nearly break my neck trying to dodge my desk chair as I fumble for the lamp switch. Bright light blinds me while I search the room. I *knew* this was going to happen. Talk to one ghost and the whole lot of them come out. *So* not fair.

Nothing. Absolutely nothing. I'm creeping myself out for no reason. It takes me a second to remember what I was doing. The laptop. That's what I was going to do. I need to contact the police, and I'll do it via Google Talk. Thank you, Google.

Shaking my head, I turn around and come face-to-face with the little girl I'd seen in the bathroom earlier tonight. She's sitting on my bed! *On my freakin' bed!*

Come on! This is my *room* for cripes' sake. Can't they stay in the bathroom or somewhere that's *not* my room?

"Can you help me, please?" Her puppy-dog eyes plead with me. Why am I sucker for puppy-dog eyes? She looks so normal compared to the little boy. At least she isn't mangled, just shot.

They all have a bullet wound in almost the exact

19

same place. I know, I know. That doesn't signify a lead, but it's all I have to go on. Detective Stabler wouldn't dismiss it, and neither will I.

"Look, kid, I don't know if I can help you or not."

"I just want my mommy," she says. *"She told me to stay by the swings and I didn't. I wanted to see the balloons."*

"The balloons?"

"They were floating," she whispers. *"Red balloons just floating in the wind. They were pretty and I wanted one. I asked Mommy to buy me a balloon and she wouldn't. I just wanted a balloon."*

"Did you get a balloon?" I ask her, afraid of the answer.

Hmm...lured away from her mom with balloons? The kid is at least nine or ten—old enough to know better than to go off by herself. I knew that even before entering the foster care system at five years old. Really, how stupid can you be?

"I don't remember." She shakes her head. *"I woke up and it was cold and dark and...and..."*

"And what?"

"I don't know!" she wails. Tears, real tears, make wet tracks down her face. *"It hurt and then I was in the dark place. Please, please, just find my mommy! I want to go home."*

The pain and confusion in her voice twists my stomach. I know how that feels. No, no—can't go there. Just push those feelings aside. I need her help. "Do you remember my friend Sally? She came into the bathroom when I left."

Her eyes go wide, and she nods.

"Did you see where she went?"

The room takes an even worse temperature dive, and I start to shiver. The kid is shrinking in on herself. She's drawing away from me, fading, I guess you could say. She looks terrified.

"She's in the dark with us."

That much I already know, but I need to know the location. "Where is the dark place?"

"Can't tell." She shakes her head again. *"Can't ever tell."*

"What's your name?" I change tactics, not wanting a repeat of what happened with the little boy. I don't want her running away from me just yet.

"Emma."

"That's a pretty name," I smile at her. "You want me to find your mommy and bring her to you, Emma?"

She nods, her face brightening.

"I can't do that if I don't know where you are. I need to know where the dark place is so I can show her where you are."

An ugly rattle floods the room, and the little girl jumps off the bed, terrified. *"No, no, no, no, no, no, no..."*

The lights flicker and the temperature plummets past freezing. Oh, this can't be at all good. The rattle seems to be everywhere, coming from nowhere, but surrounding us in its awful gurgles. Emma is crying, and I almost feel like doing the same thing. I haven't been this scared since that awful day with my mom. I hate the feeling, and as

21

usual, when I get scared, I get mad.

"Emma, what is that?" I demand.

"I won't tell," she whispers. *"I promise I won't tell."*

Something's not right. The kid's not talking to *me*. That much I know because she's not even looking my direction. She's looking in the mirror. My eyes focus on the mirror, and I fall backward trying to get away from the image there. Bloody, broken bits of flesh make up what I think is a face, but it's hard to tell. It looks like someone carved it up with a cleaver. I don't even know if it's a boy or a girl staring at me, and I'm not sure I want to know, either. The bullet hole in its head is there, but it blends in with the sticky black and red of the shredded face. Whatever got Emma got this... person too. But why is it stopping her from telling me where they are?

"Look here, buster," I fume, working hard to sound confident and angry, "I'm trying to help. I can't do that if I can't *find* you!"

I blink, and that bloody mess of ragged flesh is now standing in front of me, breathing heavily. I can smell its hot, putrid breath. For the first time in ten years, I know true terror. If it touches me, all bets are off. I'll scream like a girl and run.

"No."

The sound of its voice is painful; the screech is soft, but intense. Cold grips me and I want to run, but can't. This broken mess of flesh, one eye missing, and the other bloodshot-blue, now towers over me. I feel so much anger rolling off it. Anger at me, anger at whoever hurt it, and anger toward everything in general. Oh, crap. If a ghost *could* actually hurt a person, it would be *this* one. Not that I begrudge it the anger part, I just don't want it this up close and personal with *me*.

"Back off, ghostie," I snarl and hope my anger masks my fear.

"You first."

Pain explodes in my head, and my hands automatically cover my ears. As I fall to my knees, the screeching intensifies with the cold burning all the way to the bone. Make it stop! The screech is even louder, like a power saw cutting through a wall of nails, each one twisting and screaming as they die. It's what I'd imagine a banshee to sound like. I can't see and can't breathe past the pain grinding away at my ears. My mouth opens and I'm screaming, but I can't hear it over the noise in my head.

Somehow I feel the vibrations of feet thudding on the floor, but that's it. Shapes blur as I try to blink away the tears. It hurts *so* much! I just want it to stop. Please, please make the pain stop. Hands shake me, but I can't talk.

The mutilated mess of flesh swims up in front of my face, and it's the only thing I can see clearly. Its death rattle is the last thing I hear before a white-hot pain rockets through my head and I fall into a dark pit, screaming as I go.

Chapter Five

The steady beep, beep, beep wakes me. My eyes slam shut as soon as I open them. The bright light shoots pinpricks through my head, and the slightest movement causes spirals of fresh pain to ripple through my skull. My stomach rolls and bile rises up into the throat. I don't ever remember hurting this much. Holy crap. If *this* is what a hangover feels like, I swear I will never again even contemplate sipping a beer.

It takes a minute for my fuzzy mind to remember what happened. What exactly did Mirror Boy do to me? At least I think it was a guy. Anyway, I didn't know ghosts could physically hurt people. Scare them, sure, but actually cause harm? That's new to me. First order of business when I feel better is to do some intensive research into ghosts. Even if I never speak to one again after this, I want to know what they can and can't do.

There's that antiseptic smell—and the beep, beep, beep. It's a big indicator, at least to me, that I'm in a hospital. Hospitals are a haven for ghosts. It's why I never willingly go into places like this.

They badger me with questions, and it's all I can do to pretend I don't see the little buggers. Usually, it doesn't bother me. They're background noise like a TV or radio playing, just to eat up the silence. But since my encounter with Mirror Boy, I'm more than a little bit terrified.

Fear is an emotion I'm not used to feeling. I've made myself fearless over the years—but when that ghost got in my face, all my defenses scattered to the wind. Blind terror was all I'd felt. I didn't like it then and I certainly don't like it now. Nothing has been able to make me feel helpless since the Mom incident. Being here, I can't help but remember that day.

We were in yet another run-down motel in New Jersey. I was five. The walls were an ugly shade of burnt orange, and the stains in the carpet only added to the stink of the room. Mom gave me Spaghetti-O's to eat and then turned the TV to the only cartoon channel the motel's cable service offered. I remember watching SpongeBob and laughing as he and Patrick irritated Squidward.

Mom came in and sat down next to me a little while later. She stroked my hair absently. It was odd because she hadn't done it in a while. She was usually jonesing for her next heroin fix, and this was nice. I didn't see the knife at first. I was too caught up in the fact she was acting like my mom again. I remember she started to hum, and I smiled. Mama could sing like nobody else I'd ever heard.

"Don't worry, baby girl," she'd whispered. "It's all going to get better now." She raised her hand, and that's when I'd seen the knife. By then it was too late. I pitched forward off the couch when she ripped the knife out of me. Pain lanced through my chest, and I screamed. She brought the knife down again and again, her eyes calm and peaceful the whole time.

She kissed my cheek and told me to go to sleep. Raising the knife once more, she pushed it deep into her own throat before pulling it out. She collapsed beside me, her face inches from mine. I had to lie there and watch her die. The last thing I remember seeing until I woke up in a hospital room was the life bleeding out of her eyes.

Something snapped in me that day. I broke in ways I'm not sure I can explain. It's also when the ghosts started showing up. I still secretly wonder if I'm not just a little insane. Mama was crazy, or so they told me. Paranoid schizophrenia. She heard voices. Ghosts maybe? Did they drive her to do what she did? I want to rationalize it, to find a reason why she'd try to kill her own daughter, but I can't. Maybe I never will. I just don't know.

Since then, I haven't ever really been afraid of anything. Defense mechanism, that's what the psychologists called it. I was closed off with trust issues. Yeah, well, let their moms try to kill them at the ripe old age of five, and then tell me if *they* don't have a few emotional roadblocks.

But Mirror Boy? He scared the bejeezus out of me. I'm lying here in a bed, afraid to open my eyes for fear of what might be standing next to me. I so do not like this feeling, but I'm not sure what to do about it yet. It's new to me, and I hate it!

"There *has* to be something wrong!" I hear Mrs.

Olson shout. "She was screaming her head off and her nose was pouring blood!"

She's near enough I can hear her shouting, but not so near that she's close. Hallway maybe? I can't hear what I presume is the doctor's response, but I hear the door shut. My irrational new fear raises its ugly head, and my muscles tense up at the sound, Oh, no, please, not another ghost.

"Hey, kiddo," a soft voice whispers tiredly.

Nancy. Thank God. I relax and start to say something, but am interrupted when the argument in the hallway moves inside my room.

"Her tox screen is negative," a male voice says. "She has no alcohol or drugs in her system. The CAT scan showed no abnormalities. There's nothing physically wrong with her that we can find."

Well, that's good. Thanks for that, Doc. The ghost didn't do any permanent damage. Kudos for me.

"Doctor, I understand." Nancy sighs. "I saw her clothes from when she came in, though. They were bloody. I have to agree with Mrs. Olson. Something is wrong."

"And I agree with you both, I just don't know what *is* wrong." Even the doctor sounds frustrated. "We are going to keep her a few days for observation and more tests."

Oh, just great, leave me here in the ghost hang-out. Not what I want to hear.

They move away, still arguing, but that's okay. The loud voices are making my head hurt worse, anyway.

Fingers smooth my hair and I flinch. The memory of the mutilated ghost breathing on me is hitting fast. *Please* don't be a ghost. And no, I still can't open my eyes.

"Mattie?"

Whew. Nancy, just Nancy. My breathing slows and I calm down a bit. Man, I hate this. I will not let this fear-stuff control me. I am stronger than this. Taking a deep breath, I open my eyes. Nancy's worried blue eyes stare down into my hazel ones. She looks tired, much older than her early forties tonight.

Nancy Moriarity. She was and *is* my saving grace. She's the social worker who got stuck with my case when I landed in North Carolina. She and I had a long talk about what I'd been through and what I needed to make things better. Nancy is the reason I'm not just another statistic. I don't know where I'd be without her. She's awesome.

"You're awake," she says and smiles. "I swear if you scare me like that again, kiddo, I'm going to beat you black and blue."

I wince, and hope she's kidding. Right now, even her soft tone feels like knives stabbing me.

"What's wrong?" Her voice takes on a worried tone.

"Head hurts," I whisper, and she leans over and dims the lights, which brings a small amount of relief to my aching noggin. "Thanks."

"What happened?" she asks softly.

That question makes me remember what I need to do. The ghost had caused all other thoughts to flee. Sally! Oh Lord, how could I forget Sally?

She's the reason I talked to the stupid ghosts to begin with. "Nancy, you have to call the cops."

"The police? Why, honey? Did someone do something to you?" Anger creeps into her voice. I love Nancy. She's the only person who's ever fought for me. She fights for all her foster kids.

"No," I say. "It's Sally. She's missing. Mrs. Olson was supposed to call the police, but I don't know if she did."

A chair scrapes, and I yelp. The sound reminds me of that awful noise. This has to stop. I refuse to go around jumping at noises.

"Sorry, honey," Nancy soothes. She must think the sound made my head worse. True, it hurt like nobody's business, but that's not why I yelled. "Let me go check with Mrs. Olson to see what's going on."

I'll bet the old lady forgot about Sally, especially if she had to rush me to the hospital. It's only a minute before they are both back, and yup, I'm right. She *didn't* call the cops. Nancy, being Nancy, makes her call home to see if Sally came back from the party. It only takes a few minutes before she comes back with a worried expression to report Sally never came home. Why couldn't she have just listened to me to begin with? The cops would already be looking for Sally, and I wouldn't be here suffering from a headache worse than death.

"She's supposed to be at the same party Mattie went to," Mrs. Olson frets.

"I told you she wasn't," I snap and wince. Ow. I need to learn to not yell when I have a sledgehammer pounding away inside my head.

There's a hurried whispered conversation and they disappear out into the hall. It's a good long while before Nancy comes back in, a frown marring her features. She sits back down, and her frown makes me nervous. Questions I can't answer are coming.

"Mattie, Mrs. Olson said you came home adamant Sally was missing. How did you know that if she wasn't at the party?"

See? Stupid questions. It's not like I can say I saw her ghost.

"I just had a feeling."

"Mattie…" She stops speaking when a knock sounds, and then two uniformed police officers come in. One is older, in his forties, the other very young, barely twenty if he's a day. The older cop who introduces himself as Officer Rogers asks me the same question Nancy did.

"Look, I just had a really bad feeling something was wrong," I tell him. "Then when Mrs. Olson told me she was at the party, I knew I was right. Sally hates those kinds of parties, and I know she wasn't there."

"A feeling?" The officer's eyebrows shoot up and I sigh. "Was there a lot of drinking going on at this party?"

"I can tell you for a fact, officer, that she's not been drinking," Nancy says in a clipped, warning tone. "They ran a tox screen on her for drugs and alcohol when they brought her in earlier. She's clean."

He gives Nancy the stink-eye, as I like to call it. It's a look meant to cower people into shushing, but

30

that won't work with Nancy. She glares back at him.

"I'm just trying to get the facts," he says in his most deadpan voice. "Now, aside from this...*feeling*, what made you think Sally was missing?"

I sigh in frustration. I knew this was going to be hard. "Well, the fact that she wasn't home when I got back seems like a big indicator she's missing, don't ya think?"

"Let me tell you what I think," he says. "I think you knew that your friend was going to run away."

"What? No!"

That makes Nancy turn thoughtful. I don't want them to peg Sally as another runaway. She's lying somewhere with a hole in her head, for crying out loud. I just don't know how to tell them that.

"Mattie..."

"No, Nancy," I interrupt her. "She did *not* run away. I swear."

I can tell she doesn't believe me. This is so not how I planned this.

"Can I speak to you for a moment in private, Ms. Moriarity?" Officer Donut Hole gestures for her to follow him. I want to scream in frustration when they leave.

"You're really worried about your friend, aren't you?"

My attention snaps to the other officer, the young one. Warm brown eyes shine with sympathy from a face made for smiling. His wavy brown hair falls loosely around his face. He takes Nancy's seat, and I sigh. Here we go, good cop, bad cop.

"Well, duh."

"You always this sarcastic?"

I snort and wince. Dang it, my head hurts.

"What landed you in here?" he asks me.

"Headache." He sighs and looks down. Yeah, I know I can be a smartass, but I really don't like cops. The uniform brings out the mouth in me.

"My name's Dan Richards. Mattie, right?"

I give him my best how-stupid-are-you glare, which he ignores.

"I know you're worried, but if your friend *did* run away, pretending she's missing isn't the way to help her. I know you don't want her to get into trouble, but…"

"Look, Officer Dan," I say, hearing the sarcasm rolling off my tongue. "I know you don't believe me, and I don't care. She's missing, and the longer you guys stand here making the wrong assumptions about her just because she's a foster kid, the more time her killer has to cover his tracks."

"Her killer?"

Holy crow. Why did I say that? It has to be this freaking headache. Officer Dan is staring at me with speculation now. Dang it.

"Look, she's gone. Last I saw her she was in her nightclothes getting ready for bed. When I got home, her bed was rumpled, and she's wasn't there. Something happened. She didn't run away. Someone had to have taken her."

"What makes you so sure she didn't run away?"

"Because she wouldn't do that!" I shout and then shrink back into the pillows, hands gripping my head as streaks of sharp pain cuts through it. Ohhh, crap, crap, crap. Soften it up, Mattie. "Sally has never had a decent place to stay. The Olsons aren't perfect, but at least the place is clean and we get enough to eat. That's more than Sally's ever had. She wouldn't run away from that. I know you don't understand. You probably grew up in a good home, but to us, that's something pretty special. None of us would throw it away."

"What do you think happened to her?"

"Somebody shot her." Fudgepops. My eyes go completely round and my hands cover my mouth. What in God's name is wrong with me? It has to be the drugs they have me on. This is not helping. Now he's going to think I'm jerking him around.

"What aren't you telling me, Mattie?" He leans forward, his eyes searching. "Why do you think she was shot?"

"You won't believe me," I tell him with a sigh of my own. "It's crazy." What's crazy is that within five minutes of being alone with Officer Dan, I've come close to telling him my secret several times, when I'm usually very good at hiding it. I am a professional liar, have been since I was five. *Drugs, Mattie*, I tell myself. *It's the drugs.*

"Try me."

I'm saved from having to answer when the nurse comes in and shoos him out. I ask her if she can give me anything for my headache. She isn't paying too much attention to me. Her eyes are on the machine I'm hooked to. I look over at it, but can't figure out what has her so freaked. It's just numbers to me.

She leaves and gets the doctor, who comes in

and declares all visitors for the night are done. He has the nurse shoot something into my IV, and I start to get sleepy almost immediately. I hear him mumble something about my blood pressure.

My eyes droop, and as they close, I can hear the screaming nails in my head again, but before I can freak, I'm out.

Chapter Six

The musty, damp smell assaults me. My nose crinkles in disgust. I hate anything that stinks. I religiously clean my room and invest in air fresheners. When I was little, we lived in a rundown apartment on the ground floor of a decrepit old building in New Orleans. Whenever it rained, we got flooded. The place would stink like stagnant water and mold for days. It made me sick to my stomach on a daily basis. It's a smell I never forgot and *that's* what I smell now.

My eyes blink open and there's very little light in the room, only the slightly-cracked-open hallway door. At least the headache has eased up a bit. The smell is killing me, though. It's gathering at the back of my throat and I want to gag. It's so bad, my eyes start to water. I reach out, looking for the switch to the lights above my hospital bed. The minute I turn them on, I can see what is causing the smell.

Sitting in the chair beside the bed is a girl about my age. Blonde hair, matted with blood, hangs limply down her back. Her jeans and t-shirt are

35

caked with mud and splattered with blood. She smells of dirt and stale, standing water, and she's blindfolded.

Fear claws its way up my spine, fast and hard. I keep expecting the pain to come back, but it's just a dull ache now. I'm afraid to move, afraid she'll do something. My hand searches for the nurse's button, but I freeze when she turns her head in my direction. What's she gonna do?

"Am I dead?"

"I…guess, maybe. I don't know," I whisper. And I *don't* know. She still has color in her cheeks, and her complexion isn't pasty or waxy. She doesn't really look like a ghost, but I get the same cold feeling from her I get from the others.

"I'm scared."

No kidding, I almost snort aloud. It's something I'm getting used to myself.

"I thought when you died you were supposed to see this bright light, and then you'd go to Heaven. I didn't see it. Does that mean I'm going to hell?"

Do I look like Dr. Phil? I have no clue.

"No one else can see me," she says. *"I'm cold, so cold."*

"Where are you?"

"I…I…don't know."

"What's your name?"

"Mary," she says. *"I just wanted to go see Jimmy, so I snuck out of the house. My mom worked a fourteen hour shift, so I knew she'd sleep all night. Jimmy and I got in this huge fight, and I needed to tell him I was sorry. He only lives a few minutes down the block, and I took my bike instead*

of the car so I wouldn't wake Mom. I remember it started to rain, and then I saw headlights coming when I turned the corner. I tried to get out of the way, but it all happened so fast I couldn't stop."

Aw, man, she died in a hit and run? That sucks. No, wait. Why does she have a blindfold on if she got hit by a car? It makes no sense.

"Why are you blindfolded?" I ask her softly, my finger firmly attached to the nurse button. She seems nonviolent so far, but I'm not taking any chances.

"I woke up and tried to open my eyes," she tells me. *"I couldn't. I couldn't move at all. I think I'm sitting up, but I can't be sure. I'm scared. He hurts me."*

She got nabbed by a killer, maybe even the same one who got Sally. Then again, maybe not. Time to find out.

"How did you find me?"

"I'm not sure. They were talking about you..."

"They?" I interrupt her.

"I can hear them talking softly, whispering. They leave me when he comes. They said you could see them, and I don't know, I just thought about you and...and here I am. I don't know how."

Well, dang. She thought about me, and poof, here she is? So very, *very* not good. Mirror Boy can just pop in whenever he wants to? The fear, which had been subsiding, hits me full force and before I can stop myself, I hit the page button. The beeping on the monitor goes a bit crazy the more I think about that mutilated ghost. My heartbeat is going into overdrive, and it makes me a little dizzy.

The hallway door pushes open and the night nurse hurries in. She takes one look at my monitor and then my face and hurries right back out. I have no clue what it must look like, but I feel very bug-eyed and my breathing is a bit labored. Shock. I think I'm in shock.

I blink rapidly and look again at the chair where the girl sat not more than five seconds ago. She's gone. That doesn't mean I'm safe, though. She or Mirror Boy could pop in whenever they want to. How are they finding me? How do any of them find me?

The nurse comes back and shoots something into my IV. Ten seconds later, I'm drowning in darkness, scared and fighting to stay awake. It's a battle I can't win.

The next time I open my eyes, sunlight streams through the windows. I furtively search the room, but don't see any ghosts. Okay, good. I'm a little shocked I haven't seen more of the little buggers. Hospitals are a breeding ground for them, but I've only seen the one girl. Not that I'm complaining, but I don't know why they're leaving me alone.

Ghosts are just *one* reason I hate hospitals. My first experience with hospitals traumatized me beyond repair. I woke up hooked to more machines and tubes than I could count. I remember it hurt to take a breath. They said one of my lungs had been hit when Mom took the knife to me. Anyway, I associate hospitals with that awful day. It's not something I think about, but being here, surrounded and hooked up to machines, the memories of that…that attack really haunt me today.

Five. I'd been five freaking years old, and my mother tried her best to kill me. And not just kill me—she'd done it in a way that caused lots and lots of pain. There are hundreds of ways to kill a person with little to no pain. Trust me—I checked. I don't know why she did it. Typically, a woman kills by way of poison or overdoses. But not *my* mom. She went into the kitchen, found the biggest butcher knife she could get her hands on, and proceeded to plunge it into my little body not once, not twice, but eight times. The doctors said it was a miracle I'd survived. If it hadn't been for the nosy woman next door, I wouldn't have. She'd heard me screaming and called the cops. I was lucky there happened to be a patrol car close and an ambulance even closer.

It was a cop who told me my mom was dead and I'd survived her attempt to kill me. I'd been devastated, and all he'd done was stand there like it was nothing for a parent to try and kill their child. To me, it *had* been something. It shattered me. I was alone. No one had come to hold my hand or tell me it was okay, that it had been a mistake. I'd spent several weeks in the hospital before being shipped off to my first foster home. To me, hospitals and cops are a glaring reminder of the worst day of my life.

Speak of the devil, and so shall he appear...

In walks Officer Dan, and in street clothes no less. He was more cop-ish in his blues, but he looks so normal in regular jeans and a t-shirt. What's he up to? The bag he's carrying is giving off heavenly aromas that have my mouth watering and distracts me. I'm starving. I eye his Starbucks cup with just a little envy. I can't afford the darned things, but their caramel macchiato is my secret passion. It makes my taste buds understand the word lust. Oh my gosh, if that's what he has, I am going to tackle him, wires and all.

Mrs. Olson comes in right behind him, looking worried. As startled as I am to see Officer Dan, I'm downright shocked to see Mrs. O. She's wearing the same clothes she had on last night, and I can't stop the question from stumbling out. "Did you stay last night?"

"Of course I stayed, Mattie," came her tired reply. "You were sick and needed me. I wasn't leaving you here by yourself."

Wow. No one has ever done that for me before. Mrs. Olson spent all night here with me? Because she thought I needed her? I feel so bad for yelling earlier.

"I'm sorry I didn't believe you about Sally," Mrs. O tells me. "I should have listened to you."

Well, duh, but I'm still feeling all warm and tingly from her caring enough to stay, so I keep my smart reply to myself.

"I'm sorry too," I say instead. "I shouldn't have accused you of being a bad parent." There, I apologized.

A smile breaks out across her face and she smoothes hair away from my forehead. "That's okay, Mattie. You were just worried. I forgive you. Now I have to call and check on the kids." She turns to Officer Dan, the warning clear on her face. "Do not upset her."

He nods and takes the same seat he'd been in last

night. Breakfast rolls in on a cart, and I make a face at the runny eggs and toast on my tray. The only salvageable item is the orange juice. I give him a nasty look when he bites into his steamy pastry. My stomach growls and I scowl. He laughs at me and takes a sip of that wonderful coffee.

"What, you decided to torture me today?" I snarl, eyeing his goodies with severe envy. He has yet to say a word. What's he doing here anyway?

"Possibly."

He says it so dead-pan. How do cops do that? Develop a voice with no emotion? It's wrong, that's what it is. And evil.

"Then you can just march yourself right back out of here."

"I thought you might like to know what's going on with Sally's case."

Well, that's the one thing guaranteed to make me keep a zip tie on my notoriously smart mouth. I need to know what's going on with Sally. He won't meet my eyes, and my small spark of hope plummets. They aren't going to look for her, not really.

"Runaway, right?" I ask sourly. "She's just another foster brat who ran away because she couldn't appreciate what she had."

He sighs heavily. It sounds odd coming from him. No one his age should know how to make that kind of sound.

"Yeah," he nods. "That's the official report. Your friend has a history of running away from her foster homes. The Olsons are her third one this year."

"Well, thanks for nothing, Officer Dan." My voice drips with sarcasm.

"You said last night…"

"I don't remember what I said last night." I cut him off. No way do I need him asking me questions that might make me look crazier than I already do. "The joy of drugs, ya know?" At least I hope it was drugs that made my lips loose.

"You said she was shot," he continues stubbornly.

"Did I?"

"Why did you say that, Mattie?" His eyes burn into mine, daring me to lie to him. Which I happily do.

"No clue."

"Since you have no clue, then I guess she's gonna get classified as another bratty foster kid who ran away. Happens every day." He stands and gathers his things.

Dang it. He called my bluff. "Wait. Did you check to see where Mr. Olson was?"

"I did this morning. He went in to work a little after seven last night, and left when your foster mother called him to stay with the kids so she could come to the hospital with you."

He'd been gone before I left for the party. Well, there went that idea. "Did you look in her room?"

"Yeah, why?"

"Was her purse still there? The money she hides in a box under her clothes folded on the top shelf in her closet still safely hidden away? Did it look like she'd taken any clothes with her when she left? I'll bet if you bother to look, the only thing that'll be missing is her nightshirt."

He frowns. "We gave it a once over."

"My, aren't you the top of the class, Officer Dan?" That earns me a glare. "I'm only sixteen and not a cop, and even I know to do more than just peek."

The glare turns even hotter. Not my fault he goofed up.

"All right, smartass, how did you know she was missing?"

Oh, not nice turning the tables there. Sneaky and lippy. "I already told you..."

"Yeah, I know," he cuts me off. "You had a *feeling*." He put a bit of his own sarcasm on the word. "That's not gonna cut it, Mattie. If you want me to help you, you have to be straight with me."

I glare back. "How old are you, anyway? You can't be much older than me."

He laughs. "I'm old enough to be a cop."

"Now who's not being straight with me?"

"I'm twenty," he says, a twinkle back in his eyes. "I'm working as a cop while I get my degree in forensic science at UNC."

"Forensic science, and you didn't give Sally's room more than a look?" I laugh harshly, which earns me yet another look meant to quell me into silence. He so does not know me.

"Look, I'm trying to help you, but I can't if you don't stop being a brat yourself and tell me the truth. If you really want to help Sally, you'll stop acting like a two year old in time-out."

Now *that's* uncalled for, but it does shut me up for a minute.

"Why?" I ask. "She's already been written off, so why do you care?"

"Because I believe you, Mattie." He sits back down. "When we saw you last night, you were scared, more scared than I've ever seen anyone. I don't know why, but I think it has something to do with Sally."

I stay quiet. Officer Dan is going to make a good cop. Terrified out of my mind summed up what I felt last night.

"Look, I get you don't trust anyone. I'm not sure I would either if I grew up in foster care, but you have to trust someone sometime. I want to help you, but you have to give me a little leap of faith here. Tell me why you think she was shot."

"Trust you?" I snort. "You come in here dressed all normal, and what, I'm supposed to just bond with you? Trust is earned, Officer Dan, and I don't know you."

He frowns. "I don't know what to tell you, Mattie, except I'm the only person willing to listen to you, to believe you."

I sigh. He's right, I don't trust people. Why should I? No one ever did me any favors. The earnest light shining out of those big old puppy-dog eyes of his makes me pause. I almost feel like I *can* trust him. The big question is, do I tell him? Will it make him stop believing something's wrong and chalk Sally up to the mass of runaways instead? I don't know.

"You won't believe me," I say at last.

"Why won't I believe you?"

"Because it's crazy." I see dead people…yup,

crazy doesn't even begin to describe what he'll think.

"Why don't you try me and find out? It can't hurt. She's already been reported as a potential runaway. Nothing you say can hurt Sally right now, it can only help her."

Well, he did have a point there. All he'd do is go away thinking I need to be locked up in the nut house.

"Okay, Officer Dan, I'll tell you." I swallow thickly, not sure why I'm telling him anything. My tongue seems to get loose around him, and I don't understand it, but I'm willing to try if it means helping Sally. Like he said, I have to trust somebody sometime, so why not a person in a position to help me? Here goes.

"Do you believe in ghosts?"

Chapter Seven

He stares at me for the longest time. My question seems to erase all that police training of his. I can see the struggle in his eyes. He can't quite figure out if I'm pulling his leg or not. His face shows a mix of surprise and wariness. Now he knows he's dealing with a chick with a few loose screws, or so he thinks. I knew this wasn't a good idea.

"Forget it," I mumble and try to duck my head. I shouldn't have said anything. Why I did is beyond me. It was all that trust talk. For some obscure reason, his eyes make me trust him. The warmth and honesty in them is hazardous for those of us keeping secrets.

"Ghosts?" he asks.

"Never mind."

"Don't get all sullen and pouty."

"I'm not!" I deny. Well, I am, but I'm not 'fessing up to it. "I just changed my mind, is all."

"Yeah, you *are* being pouty," he argues. "Why do you want to know if I believe in ghosts?"

"It doesn't matter."

"Do you have to fight me on every little thing?"

"We're not fighting."

"Really?" He sounds so skeptical, it makes me laugh.

"Trust me, Officer Dan, when we fight, you'll know it."

He sighs. "Mattie, what do ghosts have to do with Sally?"

It's my turn to sigh. "I told you that you wouldn't believe me."

"How can I not believe you when you haven't told me anything?" he almost shouts. His face resembles a small thundercloud. I shouldn't exasperate him. Not that I blame him for his impatience. I have that effect on almost everyone.

"Answer the question, then. Do you believe in ghosts?"

"No," he says. "I don't believe in them, but I'm guessing you do?"

"I wish I didn't." I pick at my breakfast. "I see them."

"You see…ghosts?"

Poor Officer Dan. He's torn between expressions of disbelief and anger. He thinks I'm making all this up. I only wish things could be that simple.

"Yeah, I have since I was little, since my mom…"

"Your mom?"

I shut my mouth before I say anything else. What is it about this guy that makes me say way more than I ever intend to? Now, he's gonna go try to dig through my files. Might as well tell him. He'll find out anyway; he has that same resourcefulness I have. I can tell, because he didn't just write off

Sally. That says a lot, especially to me.

"When I was little, my mom tried to kill me, and then she killed herself. I lived, she died, and when I woke up, I started seeing dead people." I say it all in a rush and then wait for his reaction.

He opens his mouth, and then closes it. I can sympathize; after all, who really knows what to say to that? It's what I expect. There's not much that can be said.

"So…you see ghosts?"

Smart guy. He goes with the dead people instead of a murdering mother. I take a deep breath, only now realizing how shaky I am. It's not every day I open up to people about my ability, let alone to a complete stranger. Will he laugh? If he does, I swear, I'll beat him bloody.

"Yup, dead people." I sit up a little more in the bed and focus on the runny eggs instead of on Officer Dan. It's easier if I don't look at him. I don't know why, but it's important to me that he believes me. Sally needs him to believe, but so do I. It's those danged eyes of his. "Since I was five," I continue. "I woke up after…after everything, and the first thing I saw was an old man. He was shuffling around, looking lost until he saw me and figured out I could see him. I couldn't talk, I had tubes down my throat, but he kept yelling for me to help him. None of the nurses or doctors paid him any attention when he tried to talk to them. Someone else came in, a woman, who told him no one could hear him, that he was dead. Then she took him somewhere."

"You must have been pretty scared," Dan offers.

My eyes shoot up to his. He isn't making fun of me or telling me I'm crazy. Granted, I can't figure out what he's thinking, as his cop face is firmly back in place. Not a lot I can do about that. "Yeah," I whisper, remembering that awful day. Not my finest hour. I was scared, alone, and wanting my mommy. I still wake up like that every day, minus the mommy part.

"I'm sorry," Dan says softly.

"Yeah, well," I shrug and blink back tears. I need to get him out of here fast. He's not good for my defense system. "That's how I got introduced to the world of the spooks."

"So do you see them all the time, or just sometimes?"

"They pop up randomly. Sometimes I bump into them, and sometimes they find me."

"What do they want?"

"I don't know," I answer honestly. "I ignore them. If I do, then they usually go away."

"Why do you ignore them?"

"Do I really look like I want to be Ghost Girl? No one else can see them, and if I talk to them, it looks like I'm talking to myself. I don't *want* to talk to them either. I've ignored them for as far back as I can remember. If it wasn't for Sally, I wouldn't be talking to them now."

"So a ghost told you Sally was shot?"

"No," I sigh. "Sally did."

He frowns. "Are you telling me Sally's ghost told you she was shot?"

"You don't believe me." I slouch as best I can in the bed and yank the blankets up, pouting. I should have known better than to trust him, but those eyes of his tricked me.

"I think *you* believe it," he sighs.

"But you don't."

"Look, Mattie..."

"No," I cut him off. "I shouldn't have told you. Will you leave now?" I sniff. Am I really crying? I haven't cried since I was nine when my foster dad flushed Mr. Goldfish down the toilet because I back-talked him.

There is a knock at the door and Jake pokes his head in. He gives Officer Dan a once over and then frowns.

"Hey," he says. "I dropped by to check on you this morning after you freaked out last night, but Mr. Olson said you were in the hospital. Why didn't you tell me you were sick?"

"Sorry," I mumble. "I just really, really needed to get home. I didn't mean to make you miss the party."

"I don't care about the party, Matts." Then Jake gives me that knee-melty smile. "If you were sick you should have said something and I would've brought you home sooner."

I smile back at him. He is so unlike anyone I've ever dated—like he seems to really care about me. He doesn't push, doesn't ask me to do things I'm not comfortable with, and is genuinely nice. Not the guy I typically attract.

He holds up a bag...oh my gosh...do I smell something good? "I thought you might want something to eat besides hospital food. I grabbed you a cinnamon roll on the way in. I had my appendix out last year in this place. I remember the food was bland and tasted like sandpaper."

I give Officer Dan a meaningful glare that says: See, *Jake* brings me food. Evil Dan, on the other hand, brought food to eat in front of me and never offered to share, the torturer. The smell wafting from the bag Jake sets on my bedside table is making me drool.

"I'm Jake Owens," Jake tells Dan. "You are?"

"I'm Officer Dan Richards," Dan replied. "One of Mattie's foster sisters disappeared last night, and I'm doing a follow up interview with her."

"Oh." Jake looks at me uncertainly.

"Officer Dan was just leaving," I say pointedly. I'm still smarting from him not believing me.

"Mattie," Officer Dan looks directly into my eyes, "it's not that I don't want to believe you, it's just, well…"

I give him the smile I'm known for, the one that says 'Back the hell off and stay the hell away from me.' "Goodbye, Officer Dan."

"If you had some proof, Mattie, it would be different…"

Proof that I can see ghosts? I want to laugh out loud. How can I give him proof when only I can see them? "Well, fudgepops…"

"Fudgepops?" Both Jake and Officer Dan ask in unison, and I feel my face turn scarlet. Why did I say that out loud? I try not to cuss. It's one of the things I picked up in the one-and-only church I've been to in my life. The Sunday school teacher pounded it into our head, and I guess it stuck. Fudgepops is my substitute for a curse word.

Childish, I know, and I'm not sure how it became the substitute word, but there it is.

"Never mind that," I snap at them, embarrassed. I think I know how to give Officer Dan his proof. Mary. The ghost who'd been here before. He could check her out and see I was telling the truth. "My friend Mary was on her way to see her boyfriend Jimmy. She took her bike to his house, but it rained and she had an accident. Talk to her if you want proof."

I hope Officer Dan is smart enough to figure out what I'm trying to tell him. No way am I talking about ghosts in front of Jake. Whoa...now, look how Dan reacted. Uh-uh, not gonna happen in this lifetime.

"Is Mary a g–"

"Good friend! Yes!" I nearly shout, cutting him off before he can say the word. Geez, you'd think he'd know not to blurt out stuff like that. I mean, seriously, he's a cop!

Officer Dan regards me silently for a minute, then understanding dawns on his face and he nods. "I'll do that, Mattie. Jake, nice to meet you. Don't keep her too long. She's tired."

"Jake?" I grouch. "*You're* the one who's been harassing me for the last hour, Officer Dan."

"Get some rest, Mattie." Dan stands and gives Jake a nod before leaving.

"Sounds like you've had quite a night," Jake slides into the chair Officer Dan just vacated.

"Yeah," I nod and yawn. I *am* tired, but glad Jake came by. I was worried last night he'd dump me after my crazy behavior.

"What happened?"

"Sally turned up missing, and I demanded they call the cops." Okay, so I fudge the truth just a little. I don't need Jake thinking I'm crazy too. "I got a really nasty migraine and passed out. Mrs. Olson freaked and brought me to the hospital."

"You're okay, though, right?"

"I guess," I say. "They can't figure out why my head exploded in pain and I blacked out." I'd sure like to know that answer myself. How did the ghost make me bleed? Scares the bejeezus out of me just thinking about it.

My yawn makes Jake laugh. "Get some sleep, Matts. I'll come by later." He stands and gives me a quick kiss.

Once Jake's gone, I settle back and hope Officer Dan can figure out what I tried to tell him. If he doesn't believe me, then I'm stuck dealing with ghosts and trying to figure it out on my own. I *so* don't want to do that.

But what else can I do?

Chapter Eight

Three days after my chat with Officer Dan, the hospital staff still had no idea what caused my massive brain blow-out. So, they let me out with strict instructions I was to come straight back if I had any more symptoms. As if! I hate, hate, hate hospitals! Though to be fair, I'd only seen one real ghost while I was there this time. I still don't know why they all stayed away, but I *did* say a prayer of thanks for the reprieve. My old Sunday school teacher used to say God only gives us what we can bear, and there was no way I could bear another ghost after Mirror Boy. Little miracles I'll take any day of the week.

It's raining. It fits my mood. Mrs. Olson is singing along to Keith Urban on the radio. Her voice isn't half bad, but I can't really concentrate on it. No one will tell me anything about Sally, except that her case is being "investigated." Bah. I even broke down and tried to call Officer Dan. Me, actually call the cops for once? Well, yeah, who knew? I got his voicemail at the police station both times. I stopped calling after the third try. I guess he can't bring himself to believe me. I know I sounded crazy, but I'd hoped Officer Dan would come around. Oh, well. I'll figure it out on my own. I always do. I've never needed anyone before, and I don't need them now. I'm a tough, resourceful cookie.

Well, tough is maybe a stretch, especially at *this* particular moment. We've just pulled into the driveway. All I can think about is Mirror Boy. He can hurt me. My heartbeat accelerates and my breath swooshes out of my lungs. *Calm down*, I tell myself forcefully. *Gotta hold it together or Mrs. Olson will turn around and take you right back to the flippin' hospital.*

The hospital I can't do. I need to move freely to investigate. Mirror Boy will just to have to deal if I see him again. I *will* find Sally, and if that means finding Mirror Boy and disrupting his little reign of terror, so be it. I refuse to be afraid of a stinking ghost. No way am I gonna get bullied by anyone or anything—*especially* ghosts.

"Mattie, you okay?"

Mrs. Olson is eyeballing me with concern. I haven't moved to get out of the car. "All good, Mrs. O." I smile weakly at her. "Just tired." Taking a deep breath, I open the door and force myself out. I am not afraid, I chant over and over.

The other kids are still at school, so the house is pretty empty. Mrs. O had told me earlier we had a new foster kid in the house, but I'm betting he's at school too. She sends me upstairs with the promise to bring me a sandwich and a glass of milk. The doctors said no caffeine for a while, so my favorite drink in the world, Coke, is off limits. At least until I can escape and get to a convenience store. I need it like an addict needs crack.

My room is exactly as I left it, the bed turned down and my clothes thrown into a corner. A simple white dresser and mirror, desk, and a twin bed covered in my worn-out quilt decorate the room. My desk, made of black metal, is the only thing of color in the whole stark-white space. Mr. Olson gave it to me when I'd asked if I could use it for a desk. It's a work table more than a desk. The floor is a dingy gray carpet, nothing special, but the place is clean, to include bare walls. After all, I never stay anywhere too long. There's no point in cluttering them up with posters of bands and the latest teen hotties. I'd only have to pack them again in a few weeks anyway.

My eyes travel to the slightly dark spot on the carpet. They're blood stains—mine. No matter how much she cleans, I don't think Mrs. O will get them out. Not that they are all that obvious; it's just a dark spot on the carpet. Only *I* know what the spot is, but doubt anyone else would. Unfortunately, that means my room doesn't feel like the safe place it once did, and that's not fair. I need my safe haven back. There's only one way to get it back, and that's to figure out where Sally is. That means facing my gift, my curse. I can't run from it anymore.

First order of business, figure out exactly what Mirror Boy did to me. I turn on my laptop and wait for it to boot up, trying to stop myself from looking at the carpet. *Stop that.* It's a reminder of my terror and I've *got* to get past it, but I can't stop my heart from racing. Flippin' ghosts! Maybe I will put a rug or something over it. If I can't see it, maybe I won't obsess. Right.

My laptop sings to me when the logon screen pops up. Last time I turned on my baby, Mirror Boy showed up. His face keeps flashing in front of my eyes, so I close them and slowly count to one hundred. It's a technique I learned in therapy—and the only valuable thing I got out of all those sessions. It actually works to calm me down.

Mrs. O comes in and sets my food on the desk next to my laptop. She tells me to come get her if I feel at all ill and then leaves me to my own devices. My mouth waters at the sight of the food. Ham, cheese, and *bacon*. It's that pre-cooked stuff, but hey, bacon in any shape or form makes everything taste better. Just ask anyone on Top Chef. I can eat my weight in bacon.

I Google "can ghosts hurt people?" and get back over one thousand hits. Ouch, too many to sort through. Let's try it a different way. I type "can ghosts cause physical pain in people?" and see several potentially useful sites on the first page that comes up.

As I eat my heavenly sandwich, I start reading. Some are hogwash, drivel not even worth the amount of cyberspace used to house them. One site *does* catch my attention. It's the site of the famous ghost hunter, Dr. Lawrence Olivet. He has his own TV show, and he does a podcast as well. His site houses a wealth of information about anything you can ever want to know about ghosts. He also lists several other sites to check out for additional information. I bookmark his page and settle in for a long read.

Uh-huh. So ghosts can only hurt you if they are strong enough. Well, okay. The little buggers gain strength from feeding off the energy of the living? Hmm. They drain your energy much like a vampire does blood to survive—oh, that is just wrong on *so* many levels. The people they attach themselves to become tired and lethargic, or if they are feeding from an entire household, the symptoms aren't as obvious, but the household can become argumentative and snippy with each other. This feeds the ghost as well, especially one that has a cause to be angry. Like one who was murdered, maybe? Yeah, Mirror Boy is one angry little ghostie. So…definitely not Casper the Friendly Ghost then.

This doc might have something. I *really* need to chat with Dr. Olivet, so I do what I do best—I lie. The email says I'm an aspiring young adult author who wants to get her facts straight about ghosts, and can he offer some technical advice? Maybe he'll get back to me and maybe he won't. But then again…I *could* have just told him I thought I'd seen a ghost, but I'm betting he gets those emails all the time. Oh, well. Probably he wouldn't get back to me for a good long while, if ever. Fudging the truth, one professional to another, might get me faster results.

My back aches and my neck is stiff from sitting hunched over the computer for so long. I need to get out of this room for a while anyway. It's a bit creepy now. Maybe I'll scour Sally's room for clues. Doubt that I'll find anything, but who knows?

It's worth a shot. The police were pretty much useless when it came to that, so hopefully I can find something. *Or* maybe I'll go for a walk. There's a park just down the street.

I push up and stretch. The hospital stay didn't help much; my muscles are sore. Yes, a walk will do me good, I decide. Grabbing my sketchpad and a charcoal pencil, I turn around and come face to face with a bloody mess.

Oh, no. I scramble back, my legs hitting the bed, and I fall backward, barely containing my screams. "Mary?"

Dear God, it is. Her eyes are still blindfolded, but what I can see of her face tells me a story I don't want to read. Her face is swollen, her lip busted in several places. I can see the shallow cuts of a knife all over her arms and chest. Her shirt has been torn so that whoever did this had access to the soft flesh underneath. They've carved her up. Blood drips down her arms and falls onto the carpet. Bile rises in my throat at the sight. Her hands hang limply at her sides, but I can see the swollen fingers, fingers that are bent at odd angles. Someone has broken them, not just one or two, but all of them on both hands. How is this possible? She's dead, so how is she showing up with new wounds that weren't there before?

"Please, please, help me." She's crying, her voice ragged and rough, like it would be if she'd been screaming for countless hours. *"I just want to go home."*

"I swear, Mary, I'm trying," I whisper. I'd told Officer Dan about her, given him clues. Why didn't he follow up on it? Because he thinks I'm crazy. He's going to have to do something, dang it! If Mary really is still alive, we have to find her. This guy is slowly killing her. Who knows how much longer she can last? Or how long before he gets tired of his game and offs her?

"It hurts so much," she whispers. *"I'm scared. I think...I think he has a gun. I keep hearing a click, click, click that sounds like my Uncle Steve's gun."*

A gun? *Can* it be the same person who killed Sally? Why would he shoot Sally and then turn around and torture Mary? That makes no sense. No, what really makes no sense is the fact that Mary is here and *I* can see her, but I'm pretty sure she's *not* dead.

"Ohgodohgodohgod," she chants, *"I hear him coming back..."*

"Mary, stay here, stay with me!" I jump up. "Can you tell me anything about him? Does he talk to you?"

"He never talks," she says. I can see her jerk at her arms, like she's trying to free herself. I remember her saying she was sitting up, but she couldn't move. Maybe she's tied down to a chair?

"Please stop," she begs. *"Please don't..."* She screams and I cringe. Tears gather in my own eyes as she shrieks. She's terrified. Whatever he's doing to her hurts. *"Please, please, please, no more!"*

"Mary, I swear to God, I'm going to find you."

"No, don't!"

Pain hits hard and fast. I fall, doubling over as my stomach explodes in white-hot agony. Not again, not again. I'd felt what happened to Mirror

Boy and I can't do it again, but it doesn't stop. He's either kicking her or using his fist, but either way, I can feel it. Every blow she takes, I take. I crawl to the bed and manage to drag myself up onto it. All I can do is lie there. I can't stop the pain or block out Mary's screams.

The room gets cold; the lights flicker once, twice, and then go out. My blinds are closed and the curtains pulled, so there is no light at all in the room.

Please, please, please don't be Mirror Boy.

Oh, crap. It's something worse.

"Shhhh…"

Chapter Nine

Hot, rancid breath assaults my nostrils. I panic. I don't remember hearing the door open, but there is someone in my room. His weight settles on the bed, and I try to turn over, but then a sharp pain lances my side. I gasp at the force of the blow to my stomach, and for a second I can't tell if the person on the bed hit me or if it's Mary being hit. A feeling of helplessness overwhelms me. I want to give up, to beg for death in this moment. Mary, it's Mary who wants to give up. She's in so much pain. She's been hurt so badly, she wants to die.

"So pretty," he murmurs, and big beefy hands start to stroke my hair. My own reality leaks back in with the touch of those hands on me. The thought of being raped on my own bed snaps whatever bond I share with Mary. Her pain goes away and my head clears. The helplessness vanishes and my fighting instincts kick in. *Oh, no you don't, you freak!* I roll, pull my legs up and in, then hit him squarely in the chest with both feet, all the while screaming at the top of my lungs. He falls backward and hits the floor. I jump to the other side, so the bed is between us. The only weapon I can grab is the bedside lamp. Not much, but it'll do.

My door bursts open to reveal Officer Dan and Mrs. O.

"Mattie?" Mrs. Olson stares at me, alarmed. Then her eyes fall to my attacker on the floor. "Stevie?"

Stevie?

"Stevie, are you okay?" Mrs. Olson actually bends down and helps him up. What?

"Him?" I shout. "He's the one who attacked me!"

"Attacked you? What are you talking about, Mattie? Stevie wouldn't hurt anyone."

"Really? Then why did he just attack me?"

"Everybody, let's calm down," Officer Dan says. "Mattie, what happened?"

"This...this person came into my room and attacked me!"

"I just wanted to help," Stevie piped in. "You were crying."

"Help me?" I shriek. "You were touching me! *Nobody* touches me!"

"Pretty hair." Stevie smiles at me. That's when I get a good look at him and I understand why Mrs. Olson is not reacting the way *I* am. Stevie has Down syndrome. I calm down, but only slightly.

"Stevie, honey, go on to your room now." When he shuffles out, she turns to me. "Mattie, that boy doesn't have a mean bone in his body. I'm sure he wasn't trying to hurt you. He's special."

"I can see that, Mrs. O. Anyone who looks at him knows that, but it doesn't give him the right to come into my room and *touch* me! He comes near me again, and I swear he won't walk away with hands attached."

"Of course it doesn't, honey," Mrs. Olson soothes. "I'm sure he was only trying to help. Why were you crying?"

"I wasn't," I deny. "I never cry." It had been more whimpering, definitely not crying. I'm a tough girl, crying isn't in my genetic makeup. Usually.

Mrs. Olson sighs heavily and I interrupt before she can try to expound upon the whole tears issues. I turn my attention to Officer Dan.

"Just what are you doing here, Officer Dan?" The sarcasm drips heavily. I'm still pissed at him.

"I know we already did a follow-up interview on Sally, but I wanted to come by to check on you," he says and eyes me nervously. He'd better be nervous, the jerk.

"You have time to come and check on me but not return my calls?"

"Mrs. Olson, may I talk to Mattie for a few minutes alone?" Officer Dan asks and gives her those warm, friendly eyes. She smiles.

"Of course. I'll go make us all some lunch."

"Thanks," he says and closes the door behind her.

I eye the closed door with disbelief. Huh. Does she think just because he's a cop he can be trusted? No way would she let any other guy close the door. Trust me, I've tried. She's like a hawk circling the field watching for the mouse to pop up whenever Jake comes over. Last time I tried closing the door, she lectured me for an hour. Irritating as it had been, it'd still been kind of nice. No one's ever cared enough before to lecture me on my virtue.

Still, just because he has a badge doesn't make him trustworthy. No wonder there's so much police corruption. Everyone thinks they're infallible. They're the police, right? Protect and serve. Hah. Protect and serve themselves. Granted, the bulk of police aren't crooked, but there are more than a few who are, and I've met my fair share of them.

Come to think of it, Officer Dan is the least cop-like cop I've ever met. He doesn't react like one, and he doesn't sound like one either. He has the whole deadpan face down, but I think he more or less mastered that before he became a cop. I can do the same thing. Dealing with social workers taught me to show no emotion when necessary. Sometimes they just shut up when you do that, and you can ride to the new foster home in peace and quiet.

"Look, Mattie, I know you're mad…"

"Mad?" I laugh. Yup, very non-cop-ish. "Question for you, Officer Dan. Just how long have you been a cop?"

He goes from nervous to extremely nervous. "Why does that matter?"

"Just answer the question."

"Technically, eight weeks."

"Technically?"

"Six weeks at the academy and two weeks on the job."

Great, just great. He's a rookie. No wonder he didn't seem like a cop to me the last time I'd met him. I'd trusted him because he'd sounded more like *me* than a real cop. Kids identify with kids, and even though he has the title "adult" attached to him, he's still pretty much a kid at the ripe old age of twenty. It has nothing to do with his eyes, I tell myself. I must have been pretty drugged to imagine his eyes made me trust him. Not that I trust him anymore, mind you; he did blow me off.

"Well, that explains a lot." I put my lamp back and then fall down on the bed.

"Hey, I'm the only one who's listening to you!" he says defensively.

"Really, Officer Dan? I left you like three voice mails, and you never once called me back!"

He runs a hand through his hair and sighs. "Yeah, about that, I'm sorry."

So totally a teenage boy's answer. "It doesn't matter anyway."

"Look, Mattie, it was a lot to take in, okay? It took me a while to believe it, or at least believe *you* believe it."

"So you think I'm crazy now, do you?" I laugh. Sometimes *I* think I'm crazy, so I can't fault him for thinking the same thing. Not that I'll tell him that, of course.

"No, you're not crazy, Mattie. Can I sit?"

"Whatever."

He rolls his eyes at me and then takes a seat on the foot of the bed, tucking his feet under him to mirror me. "Wanna talk about what just happened?"

What I did was a gut reaction. Hit first and ask questions later. It's a rule I learned to live by when I got dumped into the foster care system. I spent years going from one foster home to another, watching my back every second of every day. Years and years of seeing kids who have been traumatized by their parents, left homeless because of deaths, and just plain messed up for no good reason.

I'm sure there are decent places out there, places where people honestly care about the kids they are supposed to be looking after, but I hadn't found one yet. The ones I ended up with only cared about the checks that came from taking us in. My first set of foster parents kept the fridge and the pantry door padlocked to make sure we only ate when we were supposed to. We got a bath twice a week so we wouldn't run up the water bill. We *did* get fed. Grits every morning, a piece of bread and water for lunch, and then dinner was beans and cornbread. We got fed the minimal to keep us alive. Real nice folks.

The Olsons aren't so bad, though. They are by far the best foster parents I've been placed with. They aren't nosy, they feed me, and they make sure I have the stuff I need: a hot bath, clean clothes, and a warm place to sleep every night. I know it doesn't sound like much to most people, but to me, it's the best thing since I discovered Dove chocolate. They don't pester me about where I'm going, and they leave me alone for the most part. They get their check, and I get a decent roof over my head. The other foster kids who live here—six in total—feel the same. It's not a bad place. Doesn't mean it's great either. It has its ups and downs. They can be a little odd sometimes. One minute they are nice as pie, and the next, they can scream at you for not moving fast enough. Just weird.

"Mattie?" Dan prompts when I don't answer

right away.

"I really don't want to discuss it," I tell him.

"That's not a normal reaction, Mattie," he says patiently.

No, I guess a normal person wouldn't react like that, but I'm not normal. I'm a kid who grew up in the system, fighting off one thing or another, including the men I call Mr. Feely Hands. I was six the first time I came across one of them. I was on my third foster home. He came into my room about an hour after all the kids went to bed. There were eight of us, and I was the only one who had my own room. I didn't know what it meant at that age, but I learned fast.

I was almost asleep when I heard the door open, and then he shuffled over to my bed. Before I could ask what he was doing, he clamped his big, beefy hand over my nose and mouth. I can still remember the stench of the liquor on him. He was all sweaty, and his brown eyes were bright. They reminded me of a rat's eyes, small and shiny. He told me to be quiet if I didn't want to get hurt.

Even at the tender age of six, I wasn't stupid. My mom had some pretty seedy boyfriends, and she'd told me exactly what I was supposed to do if any of them ever scared me. Scream my head off. If I couldn't scream, then I was supposed to fight, bite, scratch, and kick until I could scream. That's exactly what I did. He went away bloody, and I was hustled off to the ER. That was the only good thing my Mom ever did for me. She taught me self-preservation.

"Just drop it, Dan, okay?" I sound as tired as I

feel. I don't want to have a heartfelt talk about my past.

He nods and changes the subject. "So, I checked out your story about your friend Mary…"

"*Oh, my god, Mary!*" I shoot straight up, how can I have forgotten Mary? The whole being fondled incident, duh. "She's alive."

"What?" Officer Dan frowns at me. "How do you know? I thought you only saw ghosts."

"I don't know, but she *is* alive. I think. You said you did some digging?"

"Yeah. I found a girl named Mary Cross who went missing about a week ago in Meyer's Park. Her mother said she woke up and Mary was gone. Her bike was missing too."

"Was her boyfriend's name Jimmie?"

"James Mason," he says.

"Still think I'm making it up?"

"I don't know what to believe. It's…slightly insane."

"She's alive, Dan. You have to help me find her."

He gives me one of those deep, probing looks I've only ever read about. It's the kind of look that goes straight through you, like he's trying to see my soul or some such nonsense, but instead of making me nervous, it makes me more resolved than ever. I need him even if he is a jerk and he doesn't believe me. He has access to things I don't. Rookie he might be, but he can use the police resources available to him.

"Can I ask you a question, Mattie?"

"Sure."

"Why did you throw such a fit over finding Sally? From what Mrs. Olson said, the two of you weren't even that close. You barely knew her, but you're talking to…ghosts for her?"

"I'm not sure you'd understand, Dan. You grew up in a good home with parents who love you, right?"

He nods.

"We didn't. Mostly the foster parents are just about the check they get every month. We're a means to an end for them. The only people we have to rely on are each other. If *we* don't take care of each other, then no one else will. Sally and I weren't that close, but we kind of are too."

I take off my shoe and hand it to him. "See the marks there, on the bottom? Each one represents a home we've been in. All of us do it, it's an old tradition. It binds us together, something we can share and always relate to. Sally had five marks. Each of the homes she'd been in had been pretty horrible, until this one. The Olsons aren't bad and actually seem to take an interest, care, even. Sally liked it here. I didn't want anyone thinking she was just another statistic, another runaway. She's more than that. She's family. I don't know if you can understand that or not, Dan."

"More than you know, Mattie. My older brother Cameron and I are adopted. Mom and Dad found him in a home for boys when he was six. They adopted me a year later. I grew up knowing I was adopted and it doesn't bother me. Cam, though, he didn't grow up with loving parents all his life. So, I do understand a little what you're going through.

He doesn't talk much about his life before he came to live with us, but sometimes he gets this look on his face when he watches something on TV or sees something that sparks a memory. He has a family of his own now. He's happy, but he remembers. I think it was hard on him back then, and it's not something he can shake."

How about that? "I don't know if you can ever shake it off," I tell him softly. "Growing up knowing no one loves you or even cares about you is one of the hardest things you can ever imagine."

"I'm sorry, Mattie."

"No worries, Officer Dan. I'm fine. Now, back to Sally. She deserves some justice. Plus, I think she was murdered by a serial killer."

"Serial killer?"

He sounds skeptical. I can't blame him. So I tell him about everything that has happened, starting with the kid in the bathroom and ending with Mary's last episode.

"A ghost put you in the hospital?"

"Hey, don't look at me. I'm just as shocked as you. How was I supposed to know they could hurt me?"

"Because you're the Ghost Girl?"

I snort. "Right. You're talking to the girl who's spent the last ten years pretending they don't exist. I know zilch about ghosts except they are creepy little buggers that have a nasty habit of scaring the bejeezus out of you when you least expect it."

"You're weird."

"Thank you." I give him my best cheeky grin. "It would be so totally boring to be *normal*."

Dan smiles and I realize what a nice smile he has. He's really cute when he grins like that. How did I not see this before? Because I was irritated, that's why. I stare a little harder, but I get no butterflies like I do when I'm with Jake. Huh. Maybe Jake's making more of an impression on my heart than I thought. I can't even appreciate Officer Dan's nice smile. Dang it.

"So, what do you think?" I ask him. "Could they have all been killed by the same person?"

"It's unlikely, Mattie, but the same wound could be a pattern. I wish we had something more to go on."

"How about pictures?"

"Pictures?" He frowns at me.

"While you were trying to figure out if I was insane or not, *I* at least, was productive." I jump up and grab my bag I'd put down beside the door when I came home. I hand Dan my sketchbook. "Will these work?"

Dan leafs through the images. I drew them exactly as I'd seen them, bullet wounds, smashed faces, and even Mirror Boy held a place in my book. I wanted to make sure I didn't forget anything, so I drew them all.

"These are…"

"Weird?" I laugh self-consciously. I don't normally show my work to anyone.

"Brilliant. You have a real gift, Mattie. I might be able to find some of these kids if they were reported missing based on these. They're amazing."

Warmth and pride floods me. He likes them. They are creepy and scary as all get out, but he likes them! I let out a little breath I don't realize I'm holding, and then I frown. Why should I care what he thinks of my stuff anyway? I already admitted I don't like him that way, so why should it matter to me? Dan is like a riddle that has me going round and round in circles. He makes me madder than I've ever been, yet what he thinks of me is important. I don't understand it.

"So you believe me?" I ask softly.

He looks me right in the eyes, and those brown ones of his are full of comfort. Not sympathy or regret, or even hesitation. His eyes make me think of home. I feel at home with him. I've never felt that before, not even when my mom was still alive. She loved me, but never made me feel the warmth and comfort of a real home, but Officer Dan can.

"Mattie. I don't believe in any of that, but I'm willing to take a chance, to believe in *you*."

"Really?"

"Yeah, really, but no one at the station is going to believe this, so I'm going to have to do most of the work by myself when I can. They have me doing a lot of things to get me up to speed. You learn a lot in the academy, but you don't really learn the real stuff until you get out there on the streets, and learn to apply the lessons. It's been a busy couple days or I would have called sooner."

"You were trippin', Officer Dan. Admit it."

He sighs. "Yeah, I was trippin'. It's not every day someone tells me they can see ghosts."

"It's not every day I tell someone I can see ghosts," I whisper. "You're the first person I trusted enough to tell."

"I'm glad you trust me."

"But I don't know why I do. Trust you, I mean. I never wanted to tell you, it just sorta slipped out—well, blurted out."

He gives me another one of those soul searching stares and I fidget. He starts to say something, but then Mrs. Olson opens the door and pops her head in.

"Lunch is ready," she tells us, then sees my sketchpad in Dan's hands. "What's that?"

"Mattie was showing me some of her work," Dan says. "She's really good. I'm going to show them to a few people who might be very interested in them."

"Well, now, that is wonderful," Mrs. Olson says, beaming at Dan. I think she has a crush on him the way she's grinning. I almost giggle, but manage to hold it back. "Did you say thank you, Mattie?"

"Thank you, Officer Dan."

"Mattie Louise!" Mrs. Olson looks mortified at my sarcastic response.

"What?" I ask innocently. "I said thank you."

"It's okay, Mrs. Olson," Dan tells her. "I need to get back to the station and check on a few things. If we hear anything new on Sally, we'll call."

Twenty minutes and two ham sandwiches later, I'm putting my plate in the dishwasher when I hear one of the upstairs doors slam then, *"Mattie Louise!"*

Uh-oh, what did I do now? I leave the kitchen to find Mrs. Olson stomping down the stairs.

"Why is this house so filthy?" she asks me.

"I'm not sure," I say. "I just got home from the

hospital, Mrs. O."

"Is that any excuse for a dirty house?"

"No, ma'am."

"Get it clean, *now*!"

Sighing, I head to the laundry room where the mop and broom are. I swear that woman is bipolar, she runs so hot and cold, but at least it's a decent place here. I can put up with her crazy mood swings for that.

I glare at the broom. Man, I hate cleaning other people's messes. I hope Dan is having better luck than I am.

Chapter Ten

"You okay, Matts? You seem distracted."

I smile at the worry in Jake's voice. Ever since the hospital, he's been treating me like I'm his most prized baseball, card and that's saying something. Jake, his brother, and his dad are huge baseball guys. To say anything against the American pastime is like sacrilege to them.

Distracted. I chuckle. If he only knew. My mind has been spinning for the last two days, trying to find clues in everything that has happened. I'm not the kind of person who can just sit and wait for someone else to do all the work. I'd given Dan my drawings, but I have this need to be out there looking too. I'd joked with Dan maybe I'd be a cop, and he'd told me that wasn't a bad idea. I had good instincts and thought of things even he didn't. So why am I sitting here in a diner sipping on Coke instead of looking for Mary?

Jake Owens.

I have this urge to tell him what's going on, but I'm afraid if I do, I'll lose him. Jake means the world to me. He puts up with my snarkiness, and

I'm not sure why. He's such a good guy, sweet, never a mean word about anyone. I can get so mean sometimes. That why I can't figure out what he sees in me, really. He should be dating Amanda, the shy girl from math class. She's just as sweet as he is. I'm the freak with a warped and twisted sense of morality.

"Jake, why do you like me?" It's a question I've never asked him, but one I've thought of asking a hundred times.

"That's easy, Matts," he laughs. "You're hot."

I laugh as well at the teasing tone in his voice, but I really want to know. "Seriously, Jake, why me and not someone else?"

He picks up my hand, and his thumb starts rubbing slow circles into the back of it. "Mattie, you're not like any other girl I know. All my other girlfriends were boring. All they ever wanted to talk about was what was happening on Gossip Girl or who Kim Kardashian was dating. Like I even know who that is? You're different. You don't care that I'm captain of the football team, you see *me*."

"I don't get it, though. I'm not your type."

"My type? What makes you say that?"

"You're just so…so…so *nice*! I'm not. I'm snarky, sarcastic, and downright mean. Some of the stuff that comes out of my mouth…"

He starts laughing. I glare at him. Here I'm trying to have a serious conversation and he's laughing at me.

"Sorry, Mattie, but I couldn't help it. You sound so confused. Yeah, you're pretty mean sometimes, but I don't think you're totally serious about it, not

77

really. The girl I know cares about people, but she hides behind all that snarkiness. Besides, it's cute. I don't think I've ever met someone brave enough to stand up and call Mr. Clayborne a...how did you put it?"

He's referring to our history teacher. Mr. Clayborne was a college football star with a busted knee. It kept him from going pro. During my first week here, he spent all his time reminiscing about the good old days and boring the class to tears. I'd called him a sad, pathetic, washed-up wannabe who whined instead of moving on. Not my best idea, as it landed me in detention for the first week of school, but *so* worth it.

"That's my point, Jake. You don't seem like the kind of guy who'd put up with that from his girlfriend. Why you haven't dumped me and my mouth yet, I don't know."

He slips an arm around me. "Mattie, you've just had really bad things happen to you. I get that. I know that's why you act like an ass sometimes, but I also see the person you hide. You're a good person, so deal with it. Besides, feel lucky you're dating the hottest guy in school who happens to be a football god."

"Now who sounds conceited?" I laugh. Jake is one of the few guys I've met who has no issues talking about his feelings. Most guys consider it too girly, but that just makes Jake all the more special.

He leans over and kisses me, and I forget about everything for a few minutes. He has that effect on me. He can make me forget myself when he kisses me. I let myself get lost in the emotions, in the butterflies in my stomach and the sensations he evokes. Jake is such a good kisser.

"Get a room, you two," says a familiar voice. Geeze. Can't Tommy come up with anything more original? So lame.

I reluctantly pull away when Tommy, with Meg alongside him, slides into the booth. Meg is grinning like an idiot at *me*. She knows I've been thinking about Jake and sex. We had that conversation the day of the party. Meg's all for me de-virginizing myself. Is that even a word? It should be. I haven't really given any more thought to it with everything else that's been going on, but seeing Meg grin like that makes me remember and start to think about it again.

Sex is not something I've given much thought to outside of making sure I didn't get molested or raped in the foster homes. It gives me hives just thinking about it, honestly. Maybe it's because I associate it with the bad things that happen in some of the homes. After you hear the horror stories from so many kids, it gets to be something dirty and awful. I *know* my idea of sex is warped, but it comes from the environment I grew up in. I'm not sure I can do it without panicking. Look at my episode with Stevie the other day. I *know* he didn't want to do anything. But so help me, I can't get past the feel of his hands and what it might mean. I'm *so* messed up.

Crap. Tommy is staring at my chest again. He is such a slime ball. I cross my arms over my girls. I have decent cleavage—one good thing I inherited from my mom. She'd been gorgeous with a rack most of the girls in my school would sell an appendage for. I'd inherited some of that, but not her model-tall figure. I'm not short, but I'm not tall either. Stuck somewhere in the middle.

"So have you nailed her yet, Jake?" Tommy asks. He's grinning like a leech. What a creep.

"Tommy, shut up," Jake growls, fury in every word.

"What? The way you two were kissing looked like you were trying to crawl inside each other. I just assumed you've banged her."

"Tommy!" Meg yells, face red, looking like she wants to crawl under a rock and hide from the embarrassment.

I'm all for smashing him into goo. "It's none of *your* business who I bang and who I don't," I shoot back.

"This is true, but it *might* be mine," says a new voice.

We turn our heads to see Officer Dan standing not more than a foot away in full uniform. He is glaring at Tommy. Those brown eyes so do not look happy.

"Wait, how is it any of *your* business?" I demand.

He grins and taps his badge. "You're only sixteen, Mattie. Tommy, you and Jake are seniors, right?"

"So?" Jake asks.

"Eighteen?"

"Yeah."

Oh, no. "You wouldn't dare." My mind scrambles for what the legal age of consent is in

North Carolina, but for the life of me I don't remember. Would Dan really go there?

Officer Dan grins wickedly at me. "You bet I would."

"Excuse me for a second." I push out of the booth and grab Officer Dan, pulling him outside the diner.

"Now, look here…"

"No, *you* look here," he interrupts. "I'm trying to help you."

"Help me?" I screech. "Jake is my boyfriend and if I want to…to…well, I will!"

"I'm not worried about Jake. It's Tommy I'm trying to warn off," Dan says, face serious.

"What?"

"Look, there have been several complaints about him, but none of the girls would press charges. I want to make sure he knows someone is looking out for *you*, someone official. I saw the way he was staring at you, and I figured he needed a reminder that you're off limits."

My anger deflates like a popped balloon. "Oh." Wow. Officer Dan is looking out for me? That's really sweet. "Sorry I yelled at you."

"No, you're not," he laughs. "You yell at me all the time."

"True, but you deserve it. Have you found out anything about the kids I told you about?" I switch topics on him, knowing I'll only have a minute or two more before Jake comes looking for me.

"Yeah, a lot, actually. I'm off tomorrow, so I'll pick you up and show you everything I've found out—if that's cool?"

"Yeah, that's great. I need to be home before five, though. It's Saturday, so Jake and I are going to a movie."

"Uh-huh. I'll swing by in the morning around seven then. You can have breakfast with me and my parents."

"Your parents?"

"Yeah. Are you forgetting I'm still in college? Apartments aren't cheap, Mattie. I don't pay rent at home."

I can't stop the laughter from bubbling up. "Oh my gosh, Officer Dan, you still live at home with your parents."

"Shut up," he growls. "It's not funny. It's called being responsible and saving my money."

"If you say so..."

"Mattie, you are such a dork."

That only makes me laugh harder and he stomps away. I'm still chuckling when I go back in and sit down. Jake does not look happy. Ohhhh, is he jealous?

"You know Dan Richards?" Meg all but yells, bouncing in her seat. "He is sooo *hot!*"

"Officer Dan? Yeah, I guess," I say, remembering the horrified look on his face when I'd started laughing at him. "He's more of a pain in the rear than anything else."

"Ass, Mattie," Meg laughs, "He's a pain the ass."

I shrug. "That, too."

"So how do you know him?" Meg asks, but Jake answers.

"He was one of the cops investigating her foster

sister's disappearance." There is a definite bite to his tone. Oh, yeah, my boyfriend is sooo jealous of Officer Dan.

"I forgot about that," Meg frowns. "Do they know what happened?"

I shake my head. "No, they think she ran away, but she didn't."

Meg looks like she wants to say something to me, but isn't sure how. I know that look. I got it from Mrs. Olson and from Nancy. Meg figures she ran away, too. I am not wasting my breath arguing with her.

"Anyway, shouldn't we get going to the game? Coach'll kill you and Tommy if…"

A little old woman I don't know is waving her cane and distracts me from what I start to say. She's standing there in the middle of all the waitresses moving around carrying food to tables, just waving her cane at me. Her hair is a silvery color, with a hint of blue in it. She's wearing old lady clothes, the kind with the floral prints all over them. I blink rapidly. Maybe I'm seeing things, but no, she's still there *and coming toward me*! Another ghost? Great.

"If what?" Jake prompts.

"Huh?"

"You okay, Mattie?"

"Yeah, fine," I say. "Just tired."

The little old woman moves until she is standing behind Tommy. *"I need help,"* she tells me.

"You look like you just saw a ghost," Meg laughs.

"Ghost? No, no ghosts," I deny quickly. Meg, you have no idea what that really means.

83

The woman jabs her cane at me. *"You!"* she says. *"You have to help me. Oliver needs help. He's all by himself in the basement. Someone has to let him out."*

"I think we probably should all head over to the school." Jake stretches. "Coach *will* be mad if we're late."

"Coach?" the woman yells, waving her cane again. It goes right through Tommy's head. He doesn't seem to feel it, but I stare, wide-eyed at the sight of the cane moving back and forth through his head. *"What about Ollie?"* she says.

"Ollie?" I whisper, fascinated as the cane cuts through Tommy's head again and again. How can he not feel that? So cool, and so weird.

"Who's Ollie?" Jake asks, his eyes going from me to Tommy. He can't see the old woman, so he's frowning.

Dang, gotta watch that stuff. "What? No one. Come on, let's go before you two get into serious trouble with Coach." I slide out of the booth then leave the diner, eyes straight ahead, refusing to look at the old woman screeching behind me. Ignore her and she'll go away, ignore her and she'll go away, I mutter to myself. They always do. Right?

Jake takes my hand and leads me to his car. As I buckle the seatbelt, I can see the old woman standing outside the diner, yelling at me, but I can't hear her anymore. She *is* persistent. I have a feeling next time I go back to the diner, she'll still be there waiting for me to help Ollie. None of the ghosts are giving up so easily—now that I've started getting chatty with them. Rats.

"You okay?" Jake asks me while he puts his Jeep into gear.

"I *will* be," I tell him. And I will. As soon as I can figure out what happened to Sally and the others and maybe save Mary. Then I can go back to ignoring the ghosts and maybe they'll go back to ignoring *me*.

God, I hope so.

Part II: Lies

Chapter Eleven

The sound of thunder wakes me. My room is pitch-black and I rub my eyes. The hard sound of rain beating at the walls and the roof drowns out the room's white noise. I can't sleep without some kind of white noise. Never could, not even when I was little. I can hear the wind whipping the trees outside into a frenzy. We live at the end, on a cul-de-sac. Behind the house is a small forest that wraps around the entire neighborhood. I can hear the trees wailing even over the sound of the storm, which is odd.

My eyes roam blearily to the clock. It's 5:47 a.m. Dear God, almost time to get up. Can't believe I agreed to a 7 a.m. meeting of the minds with Dan. It's unheard of to get up this early on a Saturday morning. The alarm is set to go off in exactly thirteen minutes. Do I go ahead and get up, or lie here waiting for the alarm to go off? I'm fond of option two. I got into the habit of it around foster home six. You lie half awake, half asleep, and just watch the clock. It's weird, but I love it. Your thoughts wander, never resting on any one thing.

There is one thought I can't get away from. Why haven't I seen Sally again? Mary seems to find me without problem, but not Sally. I've only seen her the one time at the party, but not since. I don't know if that's good or bad. Sally never was much of a fighter. What if she just gave up? Is that why she isn't trying to find me now? She thinks everyone has given up on her? That bothers me more than anything. What if it were me? What if I thought no one even cared enough to look for me? I'd be pretty depressed, too. Can ghosts even get depressed? I don't think so, but who really knows?

I've been immersing myself in the world of spooks, reading everything I can get my hands on. I even went to the library. Normally, the only time I visit a library is for school projects like a huge research paper. And even that's pretty rare, since I get most information I need online. There's another reason I avoid the library. It's the smell of the old books; it reminds me of my mom. She loved to read and would read aloud to me every night—even when she was high as a kite. I ended up trying to read the book. It was a tradition for her, for us.

My mom has been on my mind a lot the last couple of days. All the ghost activity makes me wonder why I've never seen *her*. I mean, she's dead and all. It stands to reason I should have seen her, at least once. Right? Is she avoiding me? Ashamed of what she did, or just sorry she didn't finish what she started? Some part of me wants to ask her those questions, but another part doesn't. What if I don't like what she'd tell me? Sometimes not knowing is its own kind of hell, but thinking about *knowing* the truth—would it make things worse or better? I think I'll stick with not knowing—for now, anyway.

I glance at the clock and smack the alarm button off. 5:59. I yawn and stretch before hauling myself out of bed and heading to the closet. Where is that old UNC sweatshirt? Then I flip on the light and rummage. I find it and yank, causing a small box to fall down and smack me in the head.

"Ow."

Grumbling, I bend down to pick it up. The contents have spilled out. I freeze as my eyes land on the picture staring up at me. It's the one of me and my mom, the one before she flipped out. Our faces are side by side. I was about two. Strange that we look so normal. I'm all smiles and she's laughing at whoever is taking the picture. I've often wondered if that person was my dad.

She is so beautiful in that picture. I don't look a thing like her. She has blonde hair and brown eyes. I have dark brown hair, almost black, and hazel eyes. Her coloring is a bit darker than mine too. She used to smile so much, before the drugs. In the end her eyes were dull and lifeless. She looked about ten years older than she really was too. It was definitely the drugs. That stuff burns you out, ages you. I won't touch that crap. I've seen what drugs can do. When you see the damage firsthand, you'll never, *ever* even think about trying them yourself.

And I miss my mom. Strange. I miss the woman who wanted me dead. She wasn't always a bad mom. I have some really good memories. Like when I was four, I decided that for my birthday I wanted to go swimming in a pool of chocolate pudding. We were in New Orleans at the time. She went to Wal-Mart, bought one of those little plastic kiddie pools and a humongous amount of pudding and milk. I played in that pool all day, my mom climbing in with me right before she said it was time to get out. She laughed so hard. It's one of the best memories I have of her. That was before she became a junkie. Sad.

So I guess I do want to kind of see her, maybe. Even though I'm terrified of what she might say, I need to see her. She's my mom and I miss her. Either that or I'm just a glutton for punishment. Sighing, I pick my things up and put them back in the box containing what few keepsakes I own. My photo, an old matchbox car from the first foster kid I met—Max. He took care of me while I was with him. I wonder sometimes what happened to him. The ticket from my first movie with Jake. I chuckle softly. I'd put it in my box of treasures even before I knew how much I liked him.

The frame slips from my hand and falls to the carpet, coming apart. Dang it. I scoop everything up and flip it over to fix it. That's when I see the writing on the back of the photo. Curious, I pull it out and read the short message.

For my darling from both of us, Mattie and Claire.

My darling? Who was she referring to? I flip the picture back over and stare at it. The more I stare, the more I can see things I didn't before. There are spots all in the picture, little things you don't normally notice, but it's like sunlight reflecting off the lens of the camera. Wait a second. Could those lights be…ghosts? I remember reading about them showing up in pictures as distorted images or blots of light. Had the ghosts been a part of my life even then?

My mind keeps going back to the "my darling" phrase. She looks so happy in the photo, so maybe it *is* my dad who took the picture. Normally, I don't even think about it, but all this stuff with Mary, Sally, and the other ghost kids are making me very nostalgic for some odd reason. I keep thinking of my mom, who my dad might be, if I have grandparents, aunts, uncles. The things I normally refuse to think about are now haunting me. I never really cared before, but I do now. Maybe it's Officer Dan's influence. Him and his talk of family.

Shaking my head, I put everything away and take a shower. Officer Dan will be here shortly. With my hair pulled back into a ponytail, my UNC sweatshirt over a purple tee and faded jeans, I grab my jacket and bag and head outside to wait for him.

It's cold. That's the first thing I notice when I step outside. Usually October in the Carolinas isn't this cold. We really only ever see cold weather from late December through February. Snow is non-existent down here too. That's one thing I don't miss about Jersey—the snow and the cold. I have every intention of moving to a state that stays warm year round when I am old enough. I've already started researching good colleges in the warm zones.

The rain lashes at the porch and I shrink back. Dan pulls up in a rickety old Chevy truck just as I start to head back inside. I frown—gotta do this, then make a run for it. He has the door open for me. *Good man*, I think, and then jump in. I start to fuss at my wet clothes. He just chuckles and turns on the heat full blast.

"This is not funny," I fume when he continues to chuckle. "I hate getting wet."

"It's just a little rain, Mattie."

"How far is it to your house? Am I going to dry out before I meet your mother?"

"Don't worry. Wet or dry, she'll love you."

"I'm not worried," I deny airily. "Everyone loves me."

"Uh-huh. Sure. That's before they hear your mouth."

"Exactly so."

"Then they'd want to wring your neck." He chuckles and I settle back as he drives.

For some reason, Dan makes me comfortable, complacent almost. It's quite disturbing, this effect. I can't even flirt with the guy. It feels wrong. And when I end up arguing with him, it's not romantic. It's like he's a good buddy, not a boyfriend. And that's weird. But in a good way. I think.

Dan pulls up in front of what I deem is the typical family house. It's in one of those neighborhoods that had been constructed years before the massive housing complexes started cropping up. He actually had a yard and lots of space between his house and the ones around him. The walkway is stone, and there are shrubs in front, with flower beds around the big oak trees shading the property. Gnomes smile at me from within the hidden folds of the garden. The house itself is a two-story brick with shutters, and yes, I kid you not, a white picket fence. It's so homey I could gag if not for the envy tearing through me just then. This was a home—a real home, like Jake's.

"Dan, why did you invite me to your house instead of someplace public like the library or something? I figured you'd be all professional, considering you're a cop and all. So why bring me here?"

"I don't know," he mumbles and ducks his head. "I just did."

I shake my own head and sigh. Nothing ever makes sense when it comes to Dan.

"You sitting here all day, Hathaway?" Dan gives me a crooked grin, recovering from his moment of awkwardness. "We might as well run for it while the rain's let up a bit."

"Ohhhhh." I shake myself. More rain. Why can't it have stopped already? The garage door is going up as I debate sitting here all day just as he asked. At least it's a short sprint this time. Grabbing my bag, I scoot out and sprint. The wind catches my bag and I tuck my head down and push forward into the dry garage.

"You two look like drowned rats."

My head snaps up and over to where a woman is standing in the doorframe. She's tall and willowy. Hair the color of roasted chestnuts is cut short around her face and makes her look younger than she really is, like in her thirties, but I'm guessing she has to be in her forties at least. Her eyes are blue, not brown like Dan's. An apron covers her jeans and her NC State sweatshirt. She sorta does remind me of June Cleaver, just a modern-day version.

"Hey, Ma." Dan hits the button to shut the garage door. "This is Mattie."

She smiles at me a little hesitantly. "Hello, Mattie. Dan said he was bringing a friend by for breakfast. I hope you're hungry. I made a small mountain of pancakes."

Pancakes. Wow. "Yes, ma'am."

"Good, now you two get those shoes off before you come in." She disappears back into the house. I'm not sure she's happy to see me. I get the feeling she thought Dan was bringing by one of his guy friends or maybe a girl he has been dating. Seeing me shocked her a bit. I know the signs, as I've shocked more than my fair share of adults.

"Shoes, Mattie," Dan reminds me. "Mom will make us mop the floor if we get mud on them."

"Me?"

He laughs. "You. Anyone who dares mess up her floors is in for it. She'll make *me* help you, but you won't get out of it."

I think he means it. I kick off my tennis shoes and grip my bag harder. It's not often I go to other people's houses. It makes me nervous. I never know how to act. The few times I've gone to Jake's, we mostly hung out in front of the TV until supper— which was weird for me too. They always eat together, and I was nervous since I don't normally eat in a family setting. I usually grab something and eat in my room.

"Relax, we don't bite, promise," he whispers. I

force my fingers to uncurl from around my bag's strap. I hate it when anyone can tell I'm nervous.

The kitchen is right off the garage. It's bright and airy, done in soft blues and whites. Stainless steel appliances are worked into the beautiful oak cabinets lining two of the walls. A breakfast table done in the same soft honey color as the cabinets is piled high with mountains of pancakes, eggs, and bacon. Orange juice and milk complete the ensemble. She really has gone all out. This much food tells the story of a woman expecting to feed the bottomless pits of two boys' growing stomachs. No one else could eat this much.

"Well, hello."

Dan's dad. It has to be. He's a very tall man, even taller than Dan. Salt and pepper hair, cut short, is standing up on all ends. His wire rimmed glasses are perched on his nose. Eyes as blue as Lake Norman on a clear summer day stare at me with a hint of laughter. It looks like he's just managed to crawl out of bed. He's still in his pajama bottoms and a tee shirt.

"You didn't tell us you were bringing a young lady to breakfast." He turns reproachful eyes on his son. "I'd have gotten dressed." Dan definitely learned some of those guilt and trust stares from this man.

"Sorry, Dad." Dan grins at him. "Want me to go put my pajama pants on so you won't feel completely embarrassed?"

"Don't tempt me." He smiles back. "I'm sorry, let me go change…"

"No worries, Mr. Richards. It's Saturday and you

weren't expecting me. No need to change your routine because of me. I would've been lounging in mine if Dan hadn't hauled me out of the house at an ungodly hour."

"It is at that," Mr. Richards agrees and motions for us all to have a seat at the table. "So what are you two up to at such an early hour?"

"I'm helping Mattie with a project." Dan slides into the seat next to mine and grabs the bacon. His mother promptly gives him a stare that would cause even Mr. Winters, the meanest teacher in the world, to freeze up.

"Would you like to say grace, Mattie?" Mrs. Richards asks me.

"Er…" They pray at breakfast? I have never said grace in all my life and don't even know where to begin. Sure, I had one summer of Sunday school, and I picked up a few things like not cussing, but do I believe in the whole greater power? I still don't know.

Dan sees panic in my eyes and tells his mom he'll do it instead. I'm only half listening, startled at the thoughts of prayers. I hadn't pinned Dan for being the religious type.

"Bless this food we are about to receive and give us the courage to get through the day," Dan mumbles quickly. "Amen."

His dad laughs out loud when Dan and his mom vie for the plate of bacon. Dan wins and grins before handing it back to her. She smiles. It's something they probably do all the time. It has that family feel to it. Something I've never been privy to. This is why I hate going to people's houses. It makes me miss all the things I've never had, gets me sad and feeling a little sorry for myself. Sadness and self-pity, two feelings I hate with a passion. Usually I get really snarky, but I'll *try* to control myself. Maybe. Depends. Only if I let self-pity win today.

"So, Mattie, what grade are you in?"

Dan's dad startles me out of my little mental tirade. "I'm a junior," I tell him and take the plate of bacon Dan passes me.

"And you and Dan are working on a project?" His eyes stray to his son and stay there. Oh, great. I hope they're not getting the wrong idea here.

"Yes, sir," I tell him. "I'm doing an assignment on crime scene investigations for my science project, and Dan is helping me create a mock crime scene and all the boards I'll need for the investigation. I'm doing it from a rookie's point of view, and since Officer Dan here is so new to the force, I thought he might give me the best input."

Dan's eyes widen at the lies that roll off my tongue without hesitation. Yeah. I really *am* a good liar.

"Officer Dan?" His dad grins. "I like that, Mattie, indeed I do."

Dan groans. "Great. Now see what you started, Squirt? He'll never let that name go."

"Squirt?" My eyebrows shoot up into my hairline. "I am not a squirt by any means, Dan Richards."

"Keep calling me Officer Dan and I'll keep calling you Squirt," he counters with a wicked grin.

His dad chuckles. "Now, children…"

This earns him a glare from both of us and he hastily takes a drink of coffee. His dad is definitely smarter than the average bear. I like the guy.

"Dan, be nice," his mother tells him.

"Sure, sure," Dan says and starts breakfast in earnest. "You mind if the guys come over later? We have a Rock Band tournament coming up in a couple days and need to practice."

His mom sighs. "Dan, last time you boys had a practice for one of your tournaments, I ended up cleaning up the most god-awful mess…"

"We'll clean up this time, promise."

I hide a grin. He sounds like a little boy who is promising he'll be good all year if Santa will bring him that one special toy. It's easy to forget he's a cop, easy to forget he isn't just another teenage boy at times like this.

"I suppose…" she says and half-smiles.

"Thanks, Ma."

She shakes her head and turns her attention back to me. "So, Mattie, do we know your parents? I don't remember meeting any Hathaways."

"No, ma'am," I say the same time Dan says, "Mom, don't ask…"

She and his Dad give us both questioning looks and we sigh together.

"Just how did you two meet?" his dad asks at last.

"My foster sister went missing," I say. "Dan was one of the officers who took the initial report."

Surprise flickers across their faces. "You're in foster care?" His mom frowns. Again, I get the feeling she isn't comfortable having me here for some reason.

"Yes." I nod. "My mom died when I was five, and I don't know who my father is, so I grew up in the system."

"I'm sorry, honey," Mr. Richards tells me, and there is an honest sincerity in his voice that is missing from his wife's.

I grin a bit devilishly. "No need to be sorry, Mr. Richards. It's made me into the brat I am."

"Brat is an understatement," Dan mutters.

"Hey!" I shoot him a glare.

"You two crack me up." Mr. Richards laughs. "I swear if I didn't know better, I'd say you've known each other for years."

"She'd have killed me by now, Dad. She's got a mouth on her like you wouldn't believe. Don't let those pretty eyes of hers hide the devil behind them. The girl's got claws."

"Officer Dan…" I start.

"Squirt…" He grins while trying to swallow.

"I'm trying to be nice," I say, eyes narrowed. "Do you know how hard that is right now?"

Dan laughs out loud.

"Finish your breakfast, you two," his dad says, before we start in again. "Mattie, we must have you over more often. I haven't had this lively a morning since Dan's brother lived at home."

"Oh, for heaven's sake, Earl, did you see this?" Mrs. Richards sounds exasperated. "It's Ethel's obituary. They misspelled her last name. R-o-w-b-e-r-t-s instead of Roberts." She passes him the paper, and I glance at the picture accompanying the obituary. My fork freezes halfway to my mouth. It's the old woman from the diner. The one screaming about Ollie.

"Poor Ethel," he sighs. "Fell over into her morning grits at the diner from a heart attack. Terrible way to go," Mr. Richards says, clucking softly.

"Earl!"

"What?" he asks mildly. "Well, would *you* want to die in a bowlful of grits, Ann?"

"Well, of course not," she huffs. "But…"

"But it was funny as he…heck," Dan hastily corrects himself and his dad winks at him. He'd caught the slip-up. "Mattie, you okay?"

I put down the fork and nod. "Yeah, I'm not that hungry. Sorry."

His dad glances at my face and the paper and frowns. "Here we are going on and on about someone dying, and your foster sister is missing. I'm sorry, Mattie. I didn't even think about it."

"No, it's okay…" I mumble.

"Dan, why don't you and Mattie go and start your project?" he suggests. "Your mom and I can handle the dishes."

"Thanks, Dad." He stands and then steps back so I can do the same before leading me up the stairs.

"Leave the door open!" His dad's shout comes from the kitchen. Dan rolls his eyes and I chuckle.

Time to work.

Chapter Twelve

Dan's room is exactly what I expected. The bed is a crumpled mess, posters of his favorite bands line the wall, a desk with clutter over what I think is a laptop, and clothes lay in piles strewn across the floor. The walls are done in a soft, earthy brown, and darker hardwood covers the floor, at least what you can see of it. A flat screen is mounted to one wall with a PS3 on the entertainment stand underneath. A guy's room, all right. It smells just like him too—woodsy and clean.

Well, a guy's room, with one exception. There are whiteboards spread everywhere, with my drawings tacked up beside the actual photo of the missing kids they correspond to. He's got maps with places marked on them with thumbtacks and notes written everywhere on the boards and on Post-Its. The boy's been busier than I gave him credit for. Brownie points to Officer Dan!

"Sorry for the mess," he mumbles and clears off a spot on the bed. "Have a seat."

Instead of sitting, I step over to examine the boards more closely. My sketches had been pretty accurate. It's so strange to see the missing kids smiling out of normal looking pictures, the damage gone and no ugly bullet holes anywhere.

Janey Morris, age twelve, read the first picture. Missing June 2009 from the Rowan County fair. Blonde hair, blue eyes, 5'1".

Emma Johnson, age ten, missing March 2007 from the Rowan County fair. Blonde hair, blue eyes, 4'7".

Michael Sutter, age eight, missing December 2009 from the Hickory Mall. Brown hair, brown eyes, 4'5".

Melissa Jenkins, age seven, missing October 2010 from the Concord Mills Mall. Red hair, blue eyes, 4'3".

Eric Cameron, age seventeen, missing March 2006 after a Statesville high school basketball game. Black hair, blue eyes, 6'1".

Mary Roberts, age sixteen, missing January 2014 from her home in Charlotte. Blonde hair, brown eyes, 5'6".

Sally Myers, age fifteen, missing January 2014 from her home in Charlotte. Blonde hair, gray eyes, 5'6".

There was nothing really connecting them together. It all looked so random. They had been taken from different locations at different times. Busy places, mind you, but still completely random. No distinguishing features, at least not that I can see, make them look similar in any way, except for the bullet holes in my sketches.

"Your drawings helped a lot," Dan says from behind me. "I was able to run them through our database of missing kids and come up with almost perfect matches for most of them. Your Mirror Boy there was the hardest. I could only get an eighty seven percent match. There wasn't a lot to go on."

My eyes stray back to Eric Cameron, a.k.a. Mirror Boy. It might or might not be him. The face is the same shape and the eyes the same color, but aside from that, I just can't tell. His face was pretty mangled last I'd seen it, and that's how I'd drawn him.

He's actually really cute, or he was. His black hair is slightly curly at the bottom and those blue eyes of his are actually quite striking. They are full of laughter too. Quite a difference from the ghost I'd met, but then again, being tortured and murdered might put a damper on anyone's personality. I'd be angry too. I gave myself a mental shake. Mirror Boy was the enemy and a ghost. No need to get all doe-eyed over a ghost.

"At least you know I'm not as crazy as you suspected," I say lightly while reading through his notes. All had been taken in the open. There one minute, gone the next. None of them knew each other. Mary went missing the night before Sally did. So does that mean Sally saw something she shouldn't have? If that's true, then she'd have to have seen it at the house, and we'd already ruled out Mr. Olson. So that left me...nowhere.

"Well, I wouldn't go that far," he says with a grin. "You are one weird chick, Mattie Louise Hathaway."

"Flattery will get you nowhere, Officer Dan." His map has my attention now. It looks like all the kidnappings had taken place in three counties: Rowan, Mecklenburg, and Iredell. It's a fairly small area. Why had no one picked up on this? I ask Dan just that.

"Well, Mattie, until you told me they each had bullets through the head, nothing connected them. They were all random disappearances spread out over several years. There was no reason to think they were related. If I had to guess, I'd say Mecklenburg is the center of the activity."

"Why?"

"Two disappearances in less than forty-eight hours."

"Mary and Sally. That's bugging me." I frown.

"Me too," Dan admits. "It leads me to think Sally saw something she shouldn't have, but how would she have seen anything if she didn't leave the house?"

"Which implies the Olsons."

"We cleared them, though."

"Are you sure?"

Dan rolls his eyes. "I know how to do my job."

"Do you, now?" I smile wickedly. "Weren't you the ones who didn't even search Sally's room? The ones who didn't look to see if she took anything before writing her off as a runaway?"

"You're not going to let me forget that, are you?"

"Not a chance, Officer Dan."

"Well, I *did* do my job here," he insists. "I personally went to the factory where your foster father works and looked at his punch card. I spoke to people who remembered him being there on shift.

He wasn't home when Sally disappeared."

"And I don't buy Mrs. Olson would have done anything to her either," I tell him. "She cares about us. It's hard to find someone who does, and she wouldn't hurt Sally."

"Then where does that leave us?"

"Neighbors, maybe?" I ask.

He nods. "That's one angle we can look at. Can you get me a list? I'll run them and see if anyone has a record and pops up in the system."

"Tell me about Mary."

"I talked to her mom. She had just come home from a long shift and went to bed. When she woke up, Mary was gone. Her bike too, so she thought she was out for a morning ride at first. Two hours later she got worried, started calling friends, and then went out looking for her along the bike trails Mary liked to ride. She called the police around nightfall. We haven't been able to find anything to give us a hint as to her whereabouts."

"It's wet and cold," I tell him softly. "There's standing water somewhere near her."

"How do you know that?"

"I could smell it."

"You really think she might be alive?"

"I don't know," I say and walk over to sit on the bed, suddenly tired. "I usually only see ghosts, but I don't think Mary's dead. Dying maybe, but not dead."

"I think you are the bravest person I've ever met, Mattie."

My head snaps up. He's staring at me in all seriousness. There isn't a hint of laughter in those warm brown eyes of his. Dear Lord, he *believes* me. He really, truly believes me. The truth is there in his eyes.

"Of course I am," I say flippantly.

He shakes his head. "I'm trying to be serious here."

"I know," I tell him. "You make me nervous when you get serious." Why did I tell him that? He so does not need to know he makes me nervous.

"I make you nervous?" he laughs. "I didn't think *anyone* could make the great Mattie Hathaway nervous."

"Yeah, well, don't let it go to your head," I grouch.

"Dan!"

"Yeah, Dad?" he yells back.

"Mike's on the phone for you!"

"Tell him I'll call him back!"

I can't help but to smile at the yelling. We don't do that at the Olsons'. Mrs. O hates loud noise. She doesn't even like the TV on above a whisper. Dan would give her a stroke yelling like that.

"Hang on a sec, let me call Mike and see what he wants." Dan fishes his phone from his pocket. "Why he doesn't call my cell, I don't know."

I don't pay much attention to Dan as he starts to talk. Mirror Boy's picture has caught my attention again. His face calls to me. *He* is the key to this. In that moment, I understand this to be perfectly true. I don't know how I know, but I do. I can feel it. The truth of it rings in me like some kind of gong or bell. How, though? Why is he so important to this? Aside from causing all sorts of nastiness?

"Squirt, Mike needs me to pick him up for practice today. Mind if I drop you off a little early?"

"No, that's fine," I tell him, still staring at Mirror Boy. I needed to do research of my own. I have to find out why *he* is important.

"Do you see something I don't?" Dan asks, brows lifted.

My shoulders lift in a shrug. "I don't know. Let me think about it. Are you ready to go?"

"You want to leave now? We haven't done anything yet."

"Sure do. Besides, I need you to help me with something."

"Help with what?"

"Are you any good at breaking and entering?"

Chapter Thirteen

"This is so *not* a good idea, Mattie Louise Hathaway!" Dan glares at me again. God, he's been harping at me since I told him where we were going. I roll my eyes even though he can't see me. The lock is simple, and I can get it if he'll just shut up for two seconds.

"You didn't have to come," I snarl.

"Did you expect me to let you go by yourself?" he all but shouts, and I wince.

"Keep your voice down." I sigh and keep a weak hold on my temper. "Look, Officer Dan, I have a juvie record already. If I get caught, no big deal. They'll write it off as emotional distress due to Sally having gone missing. My shrink will testify. If *you* get caught, you're a cop. You'll get into a lot of trouble, so…" I spluttered. "You can leave or wait in the car. But *shut up*."

"I'm not gonna wait in the car while you break into somebody's house!"

"Then shut up or we'll both get caught!" That did it. Blessed silence. Thank God. Seriously, I am not taking him along on any more B&E adventures.

He's a pansy. Well, he *is* a cop, so he does have to at least protest, but he does it with such vigor. I swear I can strangle him here and now and die happy. I might feel bad about it later, mind you, but not right now.

I hear the lock click, and I grin. "Haven't lost my touch after all." I pocket my handmade jimmy and stand. Dan glowers at me. No high five? Oh, well. I roll my eyes again, softly open the door, and hurry Dan inside before closing the door behind us. "Kitchen. Ugh." It's so dated; the lime green walls do nothing for the orange-flowered cloth on the breakfast table. The room smells slightly, and that's when I see the flies circling the garbage can. No one has been in to do any kind of cleaning yet. Great.

"Have you ever been in here before?" I ask Dan.

"Why would I?"

"I don't know! Your mom seems to have known her. I thought maybe she'd dragged you over here or something."

"Well, I haven't."

"Are you always this grumpy?"

"Only when I'm forced into criminal acts by high-strung teenage girls."

"You are such a pansy."

"What? I am *not* a pansy just because I'm worried about getting caught and going to jail!"

I shake my head and leave the kitchen. Now I'm in the living room. The furniture here hasn't been updated since the early seventies. The walls are paneled in a deep brown, and the brown carpet has definitely seen better days. There is an ancient brown leather couch and two chairs in the same leather flanking a coffee table. The old floor model TV is off, but I bet if I turn it on, it'll be on the game show channel. Old people, I've discovered, are notorious for watching their shows. You don't stand between them and Wheel of Fortune if you know what's good for you. So says the Voice of Experience.

There is a small door on the right wall; next to it is a montage of pictures. I open the door and find a bathroom. The walls are pink. Seriously. Pink. The woman needed an interior designer in the worst way. Gag. I shut the door on the Pepto-pink horror and look around the living room again. There's a small door on the opposite wall. It blends in so well with the paneling, I hadn't seen it when I first came in. There's a locked deadbolt. Strange. I unlock it and open the door. There are steps going down. Bingo. "The basement." I try the light switch, and a fuzzy yellow light flares to life at the bottom of the steps.

I glance at Dan. "Are you coming?"

He nods, and I start down the steps. It reeks of mildew. I'll bet money the old woman has mold growing down here. It's certainly damp enough. The first thing I see is the washer and dryer. A laundry basket full of towels sits on top of the dryer, ready to be put away. For just a second, I feel bad for the old bat. She hadn't asked to die. She'd planned on coming home and putting away her towels and then probably feeding Oliver.

Speaking of which…"Oliver?"

"Oliver?" Dan whispers. "Who's Oliver?"

"Oh, so now you whisper when no can hear us."

I glare at him.

"Mattie…"

"Jeeze, it's her cat."

"Her cat?"

"Yeah, I saw her at the diner and she was harping at me to let Oliver out of the basement."

"Wait, you saw Mrs. Roberts? When? She's been dead for days…oh."

I chuckle at his strangled voice. "She was at the diner yesterday yelling at me to let Oliver out before he starves. I ignored her, but then remembered when your mom was talking about her at breakfast. I figure what will it hurt me to let her stupid cat out? No reason he has to starve just because she died."

"So we are breaking into a dead woman's house so you can rescue her cat?"

"Pretty much."

"Where did you learn to pick locks?"

I shoot him a wicked grin. "Haven't read my rap sheet yet, huh?"

"Mattie, you're sixteen. What kind of rap sheet can you have?"

"Look it up and then talk to me. Now, where is that danged cat? Here, kitty, kitty."

"You really are an odd girl, Mattie," Dan tells me. "You try so hard to come off as a hard-ass, but you are the biggest softie I have ever met."

"Take that back," I tell him, appalled. "I am not a softie."

"Then why are we here looking for a cat?"

"So the old bat will leave me alone."

"Uh-huh."

"Will you just shut up and look for the cat?" I turn away so he can't see my cheeks flaming. Most people never, ever see past the walls I put up, but this guy can, and it makes me uncomfortable. Jake sees past it a little, but not nearly as much as Dan does. I'm not sure what that means either.

Dan and I explore the entire basement and come up with nada. If that old bat sent me on a wild goose chase, I am so gonna give her a piece of my mind.

"Mattie, are you sure it's a cat?" Dan asks very quietly.

"What else can it be?"

"Big snake?"

"*What?*" I turn around to see Dan slowly backing up away from the furnace. He is inching backward at a snail's pace. I hate snakes with a passion. When I was eight, I got bitten by a black snake and was so sick I thought I was dying. They've freaked me out ever since. When Dan finally reaches me, I peek over his shoulder and my eyes widen. Oh. My. *God.* Uncoiling itself from the furnace is a boa constrictor. Those things are huge. They can get like twenty feet long or something and can swallow you whole. "Holy crap." Um, this one's pretty big. I can see its body start to take shape, and it has to be at least three feet wide and ten feet long. At least.

"Mattie, you need to back up toward the stairs," Dan whispers. "I think it's hungry."

"Duh, it hasn't been fed in days," I whisper back. My feet won't move, though. Snakes really, *really* freak me out, and this one is pretty much the biggest one I've seen.

"Move, Mattie."

"Can't."

"Why not?"

"'Cause I'm scared out of my mind?"

"Right." He curses softly, grabs my hand and takes off at a run, dragging me behind him. I turn mid-yank and try to keep up. My feet work if I'm not looking directly at the mammoth snake. The stairs loom, and I even manage to get up them. Dan slams the door and turns the lock.

Now I understand why there is a deadbolt. We both lean against the door, slightly out of breath.

"Animal control," Dan tells me. "We are calling animal control right now."

"Uh, no we are not." Does he want to get caught? "Are you forgetting that we broke in here? How are you going to explain that one, Officer Dan? Wait until we get out of here, then stop and make an anonymous call at a pay phone."

He stares at me. "You do this a lot, do you?"

I shrug. "I used to."

He frowns.

Whew. That look means I'd better explain. "When I was still in Jersey, I hooked up with some kids who taught me some skills. It was either that or starve. The place I was staying decided we only needed to be fed every couple days. I got stuff for them, and I got fed. I know it wasn't right, that it was stealing, but when you're eleven and hungry…"

"I'm sorry, Squirt."

"Don't be." I give him my best and brightest and falsest grin. "I'm fine."

"You're always fine, aren't you?"

"Yes, I am. Now let's get out of here, before Oliver decides to come through the door."

He laughs softly and follows me to the kitchen, but I stop suddenly. There is something odd. The lime green walls are a little hazy now, almost like they're shimmering. I cock my head and watch. The edges of the walls fade, and I can see what I would call snow. The hazy snow of late winter. It's eating the wall up and I shiver. Things flicker in the snow, shadows of things I can't quite see. I take a step forward, and the snow branches out, creeping to the other wall where the fridge is. I've never seen anything like this before. What is it? The closer I get, the more I want to touch it. By the time I am standing a few inches from the wall, my hand is going up, fingers outstretched.

My fingertips graze the snowy wall. Screaming goes off in my head and I stumble back, falling to my knees. My stomach heaves from the force of the pain. I can hear Dan shouting at me, but the sound is faint; I can barely breathe past the screaming in my head. Then I look up, and all I can see is the snow around me. The world is covered in it. I try to stand and fall forward instead...and keep falling.

I land face down on hard concrete. Ouch. That hurt.

I hear a hissing sound and push myself up.

Oliver.

Chapter Fourteen

Fudgepops, fudgepops, fudgepops.

Oliver is slowly winding his way toward me. I don't know a whole lot about snakes, but the one thing I do know is Oliver can wrap that body of his around me and crush me to death. I remember that from watching Animal Planet.

I push myself up slowly and wince. Yeah, of course, I banged my head pretty hard when I fell. And my ankle is throbbing. Great. There's blood oozing down the side of my face too. Can snakes smell blood? Or is that sharks? Who cares? Panic is setting in full force. I can hear my heart pounding in my ears.

Calm down. You're a tough chickie. You haven't survived the system just to get eaten by a freaking snake. You'll be fine. I scoot backward. I have to get up and run before Oliver can reach me. This is so not good. I'm giving that old woman a piece of my mind when I get out of here! Big time!

My first instinct is to yell for Dan, but if I do that, Oliver there might decide he's especially hungry for one terrified girl. I'm not sure the snake can actually hear me, but it's not a chance I'm willing to take. Instead I look around, remembering the layout of the basement I'd just explored. I'm in the back corner, right under the kitchen. The staircase leading up to the main room is two rooms over. I can make a run for it, but my ankle is throbbing. I might have sprained it in the fall. No way am I gonna sit here and be snake food.

So I slowly scoot back toward the open door. I know the small bathroom is just outside this room. If I can make it there, I can close the door on the snake, and hopefully Dan will figure out where I am. But if he does, he'll have to deal with Oliver too. Double fudgepops. Why, oh why, did I even try to help that old bat? I should have stuck with my policy of ignoring the spooks. My life was a whole lot less complicated before. Stupid ghosts.

Oliver keeps up his slow and steady slithering while I speed up my scooting, afraid to take my eyes off the snake. I might be going in the wrong direction. No help for it, I have to take a peek behind me. Do it quickly. Okay, I'm so close! Only a few more feet.

"Mattie!"

Oh no. Dan is yelling, but the snake doesn't look overly agitated. It's still coming at me, but no faster than before. My hand finally hits what feels like tile instead of the hard concrete of the rest of the floor. Great. I shove myself through the doorway and gratefully slam the door. Safe. I'm safe.

"Mattie!" There is panic in his voice. He sounds closer. The snake. He needs to get back upstairs.

"Dan," I shout through the door. "I'm okay,

don't come down here. The snake is right outside the bathroom door."

"How did you get down there?"

Good question. I have no idea. "No clue!" I yell. "Any idea how to get me out of here?"

"Wait for the snake to wander away and make a run for it."

"Nope, can't. Think I sprained my ankle."

"Just sit tight," he yells at last. "I'll figure something out." I can hear him stomping back up the stairs. I have a feeling snakes terrify him as much as they do me. It almost makes me want to chuckle—almost, if not for the ten-foot, god-only-knows-what pound snake right outside the door, waiting for me to come out.

How *did* I get down here? One minute I was in the kitchen, and the next I was on the basement floor just a few feet from Oliver. It has to have been the snowy stuff. As soon as I touched it, pain exploded and then bam! I was here. But that doesn't make sense. How could *that* have caused me to fall through the floor? The floor would have to have disappeared in order for me to be able to fall through it—and *that* didn't happen. Or did it?

I'm so out of my depth with this spook stuff. All I want is for everything to go back to the way it was. I just want the ghosts to go away, for me to be able to ignore them, and get back to a semi-normal life. I wish I didn't have this cursed gift. It sucks royally.

That thought causes me to think of my mom. Was that why she started to do drugs? Had she seen the ghosts too? Did shooting up keep them away?

Did she try to kill me to protect me from this? These questions I have asked myself for years, and as always, I have no answer. I don't really know why those questions pop up at such random times, but I guess maybe because they're always lurking in the back of my mind.

Sighing, I pull myself up, sit on the toilet, and inspect my ankle. I wince. There's a knot the size of a small baseball already forming, and the skin is starting to bruise. Nasty sprain. I shake my head. How am I going to explain this to Jake? No way can I hop to the movies now. He's already jealous of Dan, and now, when he finds out I spent the morning with him, it could get ugly.

After about twenty minutes of sitting and twiddling my thumbs, I get impatient. No, sitting idly and hoping someone will save me isn't my style. I have always saved myself, and right now isn't any different. Okay...I hop to the door and crack it open. No sign of Oliver. Is it safe to try to hobble to the stairs? It's only one room over. I set my foot down and put weight on it. Pain shoots up my leg into my hip. Uh, no. Crap. I ease off the pressure. Definitely a no-go. Pain I don't do in any way, shape, or form.

I can still hop, though. I cut my foot going out the window in Jersey when I ran away. I had to hop and hobble to the train station and managed just fine. What is one snake compared to a fifteen-mile walk on a foot that ended up with nine stitches? I can do this. Maybe.

The door makes an awful creaking sound when I open it wider. I do a careful search of the

117

surroundings for the snake, but can't see him. Maybe he went back to his furnace. I can only hope so. I take one careful hobble and wait. No hissing. Now that I'm outside the safety of the bathroom, of course, I get nervous. If I fall and can't get up in time, the snake will wrap around me and it'll be game over. I swallow, jump another step, and listen.

Silence.

So far, so good. Another hop, this one bigger than the last. I'm about ten feet from the bathroom door, but at least another ten or fifteen from the door leading into the main room of the basement where the stairs are. Oliver's furnace is the next room over, to my right. He seems to be staying put. Maybe he found a rat or something to munch on.

Four more jumps and I'm at the door to the main room. Yes. I did it.

The hissing starts, and I turn in time to see the snake slinking out from under the stairs. Well, darn it. So much for that. Now can I make a run for it on one leg? That is the question. No. But I can jump. I turn without another look at the snake and start jumping.

It slithers between my foot and the one I have slightly raised and startles me enough to fall flat on my butt. The snake turns before I can get up, but I try anyway. It's on me even before I can stand. Its body starts to wind around my legs. I can feel the pressure of it beginning to tighten as more of it winds up my body.

"*Daaaaaaaaaaaaan!*" The head, where's the head? I look for it, trying not to panic any more than I am. The snake will only respond to panic by increasing pressure. I reach out blindly, trying to find a weapon, but there's nothing. Why couldn't I have just stayed in the stupid bathroom? I can see those little beady eyes drawing closer, its tongue flickering in and out of its mouth. Oliver's mouth opens and I see those awful, sharp teeth.

"Dan, Dan, Dan, Dan, Daaan!"

The door flies open and there are footsteps pounding down the stairs. Men in brown uniforms are there, harnessing the snake's head mere inches from my own. It hisses and only tightens its hold on me, truly crushing me. If they don't get it off soon, I'm going to have broken bones. Then, mercifully, the other one starts to unwind the snake, and then I'm free.

Dan is there, picking me up and carrying me upstairs. Paramedics are there too, and a few police officers. Dan hands me off to one of the paramedics and runs back downstairs.

They check my leg and then tell me I'll need to go the hospital to make sure nothing's broken. Oh, great. It's not often they get calls to check out crushing injuries due to a snake, they say. Well, it's not often I'm near enough to a snake for a crushing injury to occur, so we're even. Plus, they want to make sure I don't have a concussion. The paramedics load me up on the gurney and start hauling me out when I hear the other police officers start to question Dan as to why we were here in the first place. I can't let him get in trouble for helping me.

"Excuse me, Officer?" I make my voice as soft as I can. My face is streaked with tears and I know I have to be white as a ghost, no pun intended. "It's not Dan's fault. It's mine."

"Yours?" The officer who turns to me could be about his mom's age. She looks concerned, but there is a slight frostiness to her eyes. Yup, Officer Dan is in big trouble.

"Yes, ma'am." I nod. I close my eyes and concentrate for a moment, and when I look up, there are tears in my eyes. "Ever since my foster sister went missing, I have been out just walking, hoping if she did run away, I can find her."

The officer's face softens. She can hear the pain in my voice.

"I was walking by here and saw the door open. I thought someone might be trying to rob the place since Mrs. Roberts passed away. Dan was driving by and saw me looking in. He recognized me from the night my sister went missing. He stopped to ask what was going on, and I told him that I thought someone had broken in. He *told* me to stay put, not to go inside, but I didn't listen to him. I went in and saw the basement door open. I wasn't thinking clearly, I guess with Sally's disappearance and all. I thought for a second, maybe it was Sally. Maybe she broke in and just wanted a warm place to stay. I went downstairs, and I heard Dan yelling at me to stop, but by then it was too late. I saw the snake and tripped. I barely made it to the bathroom."

"You poor thing," the officer says soothingly.

"I didn't mean any harm," I sniffle. "I just wanted to find my sister."

"Of course you did."

"Dan told me to stay in the bathroom, that he'd

get me out, but I just freaked out, you know? I couldn't take it another minute. I had to get out. If I had listened to him in the first place none of this would have happened. I'm so sorry. None of this is his fault. It's all mine. He didn't do anything wrong."

"It's okay, honey," she tells me. "Let's get you to the hospital and get you checked out, okay?"

I nod, satisfied that I've managed to thwart the worst of it. Dan is eyeing me with a newfound respect and just a hint of fear. I keep telling him I'm a professional liar. I wink at him as I go by. Now, how am I gonna explain all this to my boyfriend?

Chapter Fifteen

The cold is what wakes me. It's dark, so I don't immediately recognize where I am, but the antiseptic smell reminds me I'm in the hospital. No lights glimmer. It's completely and utterly black. This can't be good.

I try to sit up, but I can't. It feels like there is some terrible weight pressing down on me, and I remember Oliver. I open my mouth to shout for help, but no sounds come out. I struggle but soon wear myself out. Whatever holds me down is too strong. Panic sets in. I feel helpless, and it's not a feeling I'm used to, nor is it one I enjoy.

There's a light. I squint and can just make out the outline of the door. The light is a soft, hazy blue. Instead of feeling relief, I'm scared. There is no brightness in that light. It feels like death, like a dark blanket covering everything, draining the life out the things around it. A dark and depressing weight seems to be in that light and I want to hide from it, pull the covers up over my head and pretend I don't see it. I can't, though. I'm frozen.

The cold intensifies and the glow gets brighter

and stronger the longer it pulses outside my door. It's not going away and I can't move, but I try. I am shouting even though the words don't pass through my lips.

"Be quiet," someone hisses. "It'll see us."

My head whips around, but I can't see anyone. I try to speak again, but I can't. What will see us?

"The reaper."

Reaper? As in the Grim Reaper? The Angel of Death kind of reaper? Wait. I didn't speak aloud. I was thinking. Who could hear my thoughts?

My door slowly opens and that light floods my room. I blink at the harshness of it. When I *can* see I look up. Standing in the doorway to my room is a figure wearing a black hooded robe. It points to me and whispers. I shake my head. I can't understand a single word. Is that the reaper?

The cold creeps toward me, wraps me in its icy clutches. I struggle harder, but my limbs refuse to move. I'm trapped. Good and truly trapped.

Oh, no, it's moving toward me.

Hands shake me, and I slowly claw my way awake, screaming. I can barely breathe and the hands holding me feel like the restraints that held me in that awful place. I fight to get away and distantly hear someone calling my name. The panic is too much. I can't stand it. Something sharp stabs me in the arm and then I am drowning in blackness again.

When I come awake, the soft glow of the light above the bed is on. My eyes hurt a little, but I can see. I remember feeling trapped, unable to move, so I test my limbs almost at once. Good. I'm not strapped down, but still in the hospital, though. My eyes study the room and come to rest on Dan. He's sitting asleep in the chair beside the bed. He looks tired and his clothes are rumpled. Why is he here? Did he stay with me?

The dream…or whatever. I remember it and shiver. I'm so exhausted. No wonder I'm having such awful nightmares. Between ghosts everywhere, worrying about finding Mary before she dies if she's not dead already, and all the crazy stuff I'm seeing, it's a miracle I'm still semi-sane. I should have just left it all alone. Sally was dead, there wasn't anything I could really do anyway, so why? Why subject myself to all this?

Because it's not about *you*, the nagging voice within answers. Because Sally was one of us. I sigh. It always comes back to that. Sally doesn't have anyone else. No matter how much I'm complaining right now, I still wouldn't change anything I've done. Well, maybe the snake. I should have ignored that old lady. That said, if I hadn't talked to the ghosts, I wouldn't have met Dan. I'm glad I met him. He's turning out to be a really good friend. I'm so sure Jake would never have committed a crime for *me*. But Dan was right there with me when I broke into the old lady's house. He complained, but he never ran away. That's important to me. He didn't leave me. I'm so used to having to fend for myself it's unusual to know someone who cares enough to stay.

"Hey, Squirt."

I start, unaware he's awake. "We have to stop meeting like this." He gives me a tired smile and stretches. "I wasn't sure you were ever gonna wake up, you know. All that snoring was getting a little ridiculous."

"I do not snore!"

He grins and reaches out to tweak my nose. "Sure you don't."

"Did you get into a lot of trouble?"

"Not much," he says. "You saved me. Thanks for that."

I shrug. "I know how much being a cop means to you, and it was my fault you were there in the first place, so I owed you."

"Remind me to *never* get on your bad side. You weren't joking when you said you could lie. I almost believed you myself."

"Told you."

He reaches down and pulls a McDonald's bag from somewhere. "I wasn't sure what you liked, so I got you a Big Mac."

My stomach growls, which makes Dan laugh. I glower at him. I haven't eaten anything since breakfast at his house this morning. "What time is it?"

"Almost midnight."

My eyes pop. I've been out for over twelve hours.

"The doctors decided to admit you overnight for observation since you only got out the other day due to unexplained head trauma. They had to sedate you earlier, though," he tells me quietly. "You were screaming your head off. I helped the orderlies hold you down. You're stronger than you look."

I nod, remembering the awful feeling of the

125

reaper coming for me. I shudder at the memory and Dan frowns. My hands shake, but I reach out and take the bag he's still holding. It gives me something to do, maybe take my mind off the nightmare.

"Do you want to talk about it?" Those big brown eyes are staring at me again, inviting me in with their warmth, and I find myself falling prey to the kindness they promise.

"It was a nightmare," I say haltingly. "I couldn't move. I was trapped and then it came for me. I was so scared. I couldn't get away from it and there was no one there to save me."

"What was it?"

"The Grim Reaper," I whisper. "I know how stupid it sounds, but…"

"But you see ghosts, Mattie. It makes sense you'd have nightmares about something associated with death."

"I think it was real, Dan," I say softly. "Or as close to real as anything else, as real as the ghosts I see."

"Can I ask you a question?" He sounds hesitant, unsure.

I nod.

"Back at the house, in the kitchen, what happened? You reached out to the touch a wall, then you started screaming, and then you were just… gone."

"Confused me, too. I don't know what happened either. When we came back upstairs, the kitchen wall was all messed up. It was hazy, like looking at heat reflecting off asphalt. The closer I looked, the more it changed. It was like I was looking at snow, and the snow was eating the surface of the wall. I wanted to touch it, to see if it was real, but the minute I did, my head exploded in pain. It was like the night Mirror Boy got into my head, only worse, a thousand times worse. When I fell, I just kept falling straight through the snow and landed in the basement. I don't know how."

"Has that ever happened before?"

Duh. No! "Never."

He nods, accepting my craziness.

"Can I ask *you* a question?"

"Sure."

"Why are you here? Why did you stay with me?"

"Why not?"

"That's not an answer, Officer Dan."

"Sure it is, Squirt."

I sigh. I probably shouldn't have asked him and put him on the spot.

"Thanks for staying."

"Not a problem. Mrs. Olson was here until around nine or so. She had to go check on the other kids. Said her husband had to work tonight, and she didn't have anyone to watch them, but to tell you she'd back first thing in the morning."

"She was here?" I don't remember her coming in. Maybe it was after my nightmare.

"She got here about the same time I did," he tells me.

"I don't think she killed Sally," I tell him abruptly. "I wish Sally would come back. She might be able to at least show me who killed her."

"You haven't seen her again?"

"No," I grouch. "Not since that first night."

"Bummer."

I burst out laughing. It's such a teen thing to say, it sounds funny coming out Officer Dan's mouth. I constantly forget how young he is. So un-coppish sometimes, and other times so much like a cop, I want to smack him just because.

"What?"

"Nothing." I dig out my cold burger and fries. He hands me a warm bottle of Coke and I'm in heaven for a few minutes. My stomach makes noises of appreciation.

"I saw Jake earlier."

My head snaps back around to him. "I bet he's mad."

"Well, yeah. He didn't appreciate getting the news from me, but he's not mad at you. He's worried."

"He's jealous," I laugh. "It's cute."

"Jealous would be putting it mildly." Dan grins at the memory. "I could have been nice and put his fears to rest, but…"

"But you enjoyed needling him a little too much?"

He just smiles and then looks at the clock.

"Need to go?" I feel almost abandoned at the thought of him leaving.

"Nah," he says. "I'm here all night. I just need to go call my girlfriend. We had a date tonight too, and she's about as mad as your boyfriend at the minute. I'll be back and teach you how to play poker."

He slips out of the room and I finish off my dinner in a better mood than when I woke up. He's not leaving me alone here in this place.

I lean back and close my eyes, sleepy. I really am tired. Dan may end up playing solitaire or some such game. It's been a long day and I'm not only tired, but I'm sore from that danged snake. I could sleep for days.

Then I think I drift off, but when I open my eyes again, the room is cold. Icy cold. I can see the fog of my breath. I look around slowly, but see nothing but the confines of my hospital room. No ghost. That doesn't mean anything, though. The little buggers hide and jump out at you when you least expect it.

There's a thump and I tense.

The thump came from under my bed.

No, no, no, no. I will not look under the bed. I refuse to do it. I am not one of those crazy people in the horror movies who inevitably look outside when they hear a noise. Crazy dead people.

Thump, thump, thump…

I close my eyes. Ignore it and it will go away, ignore it and it will go away…

A whimper escapes from under the bed, followed by more thumping, only it's growing feeble.

I clench my hands, my nails digging into the palms. The thing under the bed sounds afraid. The cold intensifies and I cringe. It feels like the cold from my dream earlier. There's a sense of desperation to the feeble little thumps. I want to cover my ears up until it goes away, but I can't.

Sighing, I force myself up and swing my legs over the bed. I get a little dizzy and my head starts to hurt again. I wait a minute and then slide off and end up falling anyway. I land with my face two inches from a bloody mess. If it wasn't for the blonde hair and the clothes, I wouldn't recognize her.

Mary.

Chapter Sixteen

"Mattie, what are you doing?"

I ignore Dan and concentrate instead on Mary. I realize after a minute that her face isn't shredded like Mirror Boy's. It's just bloody from a head wound. She's bleeding from more places than I can count. She still has a blindfold over her eyes.

"Mary?"

Nothing. I'm not sure she can hear me, but I try again. "Mary, it's Mattie."

She whimpers and thumps her hand against the floor again. I wince at the sound. It's so tired and forlorn.

"Mary, I swear we are trying to find you," I tell her softly. "Please don't give up. I promise I'll find you. I swear it."

"Tired," she whispers at last. *"Just want to sleep."*

"Mattie, who are you talking to?"

"Dan, be quiet. I'm talking to Mary."

"The girl who's missing?" he asks curiously. I hear his feet shuffle and then he's peering under the other side of the bed. He frowns at me. I roll my eyes at him.

"Mary, I know you're tired, but you have to keep trying. Stay with me, please. We're looking for you. Everyone is."

"I hurt."

"I know you do." My voice catches on a sob. She can't die. She can't. "Just hang in there. I will find you."

"Please make it stop hurting," she begs me before giving a last whimper, and she disappears. She's there and then she's just gone. The sheer depth of the pain in her voice is too much even for me, and I can feel the tears start their path down my cheeks. Then Dan is there and picking me up off the floor. He sits on the bed and holds me while I cry. It's been so long since I've cried. Maybe that's why I'm sobbing so hard. I hear the door crack open, and then Dan is saying something and the door closes.

He doesn't say anything, just lets me cry and strokes my hair while I do. I'm not sure how long he sits there with me in his lap and lets me soak his shirt. But it feels like forever when I finally sit up and hiccup. He hands me a tissue he's gotten from the little nightstand beside the bed. I blow my nose loudly and sneeze, and then scoot off his lap and settle back in the bed.

"Tell me what you know. Everything you've discovered about the cases."

"It's not much. I was able to get the jackets only on Sally and Mary's disappearance since they are both CPD cases. The disappearances are in a three county wide radius. All the victims were taken from busy public places. There is no connection between the victims except your bullet holes. It's not a lot to go on, Mattie."

"Mirror Boy. He is the key to all this. If we find out what happened to him, then we can find out what happened to all of them."

"How do you know that, Mattie?"

"I don't know how, but I know it's true, Dan. I just do."

I can feel the sigh go right through him. It's hard for Dan to believe me, but he is trying, which is more than I ever expected from anyone.

"Okay," he says at last. "I'll try to get the case file from the Statesville PD tomorrow and then we'll go through it."

"We?"

"Yeah, we." He grins down at me. "You're pretty good at this stuff, Mattie."

"Do you think we can find her before she dies?"

"We will."

"Dan?"

"Yeah?"

"Thanks."

"You're welcome, Squirt."

"Didn't you promise to show me how to play poker?" I ask.

"Yeah, but why do I feel like I'm about to be fleeced?"

"Would *I* do that?"

"Yup, I bet you would."

He helps me settle back into the mountain of pillows. I know most hospital beds only come equipped with one, so I'm betting Dan had managed to swing a few extra for me. I need lots of pillows, lots and lots of them to get comfortable.

Dan grabs his jacket off the chair and fishes out a deck of cards. He jumps back onto the foot of the bed and sits cross legged, Indian style, before opening the cards. He gives me a rundown on the rules and starts explaining different types of pairs to me, using the cards to show me what they look like.

"So what do you do for fun Dan? Besides helping the psycho ghost girl?"

He shrugs. "The usual stuff. I hang out with my friends, play a little Rock Band."

"And the girlfriend," I remind him. "Don't forget her."

"Yeah, and the girlfriend." He laughs and starts shuffling the cards. "My mom doesn't like her, though."

"Really?" I ask.

"She says I can do better."

"Can you?"

He shrugs. "I like her."

"That's all that counts, I guess." I pick up the cards he's given me and do my best not to cringe. I *do* know how to play poker, and I've been dealt a losing hand. Dang it.

"What about you, Squirt? What do you do for fun?"

"I draw," I say, "but you already know that. I have a secret love of Star Trek too, but only the newer ones. Captain Picard is awesome."

"You're a closet Treky?" He laughs and arranges his cards. "You do not look like a Treky. I'm going to have to take you to Vegas to one of the conventions so I can see you all dressed up in full

134

Klingon costume."

"And how, pray tell, do you know those are held in Vegas?"

"Because my dad is a Treky. I grew up watching Deep Space Nine and Voyager. I guess that makes me one by default too."

"Your parents are nice," I tell him, changing the subject.

"Yeah, my dad is great. Mom's usually a lot friendlier. I don't know what was up with her."

"She wasn't expecting you to show up with a teenage girl in tow," I say. "Unless you bring home jailbait every day?"

"No, I don't bring girls home very often. I think I've only ever had two of my girlfriends over before."

Curious. Most guys tended to bring their girlfriends home. Jake had practically dragged me home after three dates.

"Can I ask you a personal question?"

"Sure, Squirt."

"Have you ever thought about finding your parents? Your birth parents, that is?"

He sighs heavily. "Yeah. I did. I used to think about it a lot. I always wondered why, ya know? Was it because my mom was poor and couldn't afford to keep me, or was she forced to give me up? Or was it something worse? The more I thought about it, the more I realized it didn't matter. I had two people who loved me, who raised me, and who would give up everything for me. That's really what life is about. The people who love you. It's all I needed. So I didn't go looking for my birth parents

135

even though I could have. Mom and Dad would have supported me and helped me any way they could, but I didn't need to find what I already had."

I nod. "I think about trying to find my dad."

"Your dad?"

"I don't know his name. Mom never told me, but I don't think he's dead. I wonder about him all the time."

"If you want to find him, Mattie, then we'll find him."

My head snaps up. "You would help me find my father?"

"I'm all in, Mattie."

And he is. I can see it. But why? "Why?"

"Hell if I know, Squirt," he grins at me. "I don't know why you matter to me. I mean, I barely know you, but I need to know you're safe, that you're happy, and that you have everything you need. You're important to me. That's about all I've figured out right now, at least until you get a little older. You really *are* jailbait until you turn eighteen."

My mouth falls open. Did Officer Dan just admit he *likes* me?

"Close your mouth, Squirt." He smiles at me and his brown eyes are full of warm chocolate gooeyness. "Pick up those cards and let's play. I want to win at least a few hands."

Well, he did win a few, but he threw me for a loop there with that admission. I mean come on! This puts a whole new perspective on things for me. Am I ready to think about Dan like that? *Can* I think about him like that? Danged if I know.

Instead, I turn my concentration back to the game and take him for every dime in his wallet.

Chapter Seventeen

I growl in frustration. This is supposed to be easy, but it's not. I stare down at the pans in hopelessness. Jake is coming over, and I told him I'd make him breakfast. Well, it is almost eleven, but breakfast sounded easier than lunch. I figured eggs and bacon would be a piece of cake to make. Not so much. The bacon is shriveled little black things in the blackened pan, and the eggs…well, the eggs don't need to be discussed.

After all, I want to do something nice for Jake since he's put up with so much from me over the last little bit. I'd buried myself in research on Mirror Boy while I was in the hospital, thanks to Mrs. O bringing me my laptop and the hospital's free Wi-Fi. There was no real information about him, though, other than what Dan had already told me. I know he's the key to this, but I just don't know how. I think I'm gonna have to be brave and try to contact him again—even though he scares the bejeezus out of me.

"Do I smell burnt bacon?"

I turn to see Jake leaning against the doorframe

to the kitchen and sigh. Well, I never said I could actually cook, only that I would. "Sorry," I say with just a hint of disgust as I start scraping food into the sink so I can put it down the disposal.

Jake laughs and strolls over to inspect the mess. "It's the thought that counts, Matts."

"I wanted to do something nice..."

He shushes me with his lips and I melt as always. He sure does know how to kiss, I'll give the boy that.

"Let's get this cleaned up and then we'll go down to the diner for some food." He picks up the pan I'd dropped and shakes his head. "This needs to soak." He runs a sink full of hot water, cleans the egg pan and then drops the burned bacon pan into the water.

I watch him, bemused. Most guys I know would never pick up a dish and wash it. They'd think it was beneath them, but not Jake. He just jumped in and started helping with the clean-up. I take the dishrag from him and clean the counters and the stove. He amazes me, really. Sometimes I wonder how long I can keep him. He deserves better than me. He deserves someone as nice as he is. I'm a lot of things, but nice is not one of them.

Then I throw the rag in the sink and grab my coat. It's gotten a lot colder this week. Usually we never drop down below thirty degrees in Charlotte in the winter, but it's barely twenty-two degrees outside. The wind tastes like snow too. I absolutely hate the snow. It's one of the things I don't miss about Jersey. We always had snow in the winter, but not so much here in the Queen City. We only get the occasional ice storm. Snow is rare.

The ride to the diner is quick, and as soon as we are in the door I realize why Jake was so quick to suggest it. The Rock Band tournament is today. I'd forgotten all about it, but it's been advertised for like the last month or so. I remember Jake telling me he wanted to enter the drum solo competition. The place is packed with people. A huge fifty-inch screen TV has been placed on the far wall and the tables moved away to make room for the mock stage, which is really just the drum set and three big red X's where the singer and the two guitarists are supposed to stand. It's not fancy by any means, not like the big tournaments they hold in downtown Charlotte, but it looks like everyone is having a blast. People I've never seen before are milling around, and I assume they go to some of the other schools and colleges in the area.

I hear my name and turn to see Meg waving at me from a booth just a few feet from the stage. How early did she arrive to get that table? Jake and I weave in and out of the mass of people and slide in one side.

"Isn't it so exciting?" Meg asks right away. "Tommy is signing up for the guitar solo competition."

"I guess," I murmur. It seems like a bunch of nonsense to me. I know Jake loves the game, though. "Jake, didn't you say you wanted to do the drum thing?"

"Yeah," he says. "I need to sign up. Give me a sec." With that he's gone and I look around for the crazy old woman who'd sent me to rescue her snake from starvation. I am so gonna let her have it, even if I have to go into the bathroom and lock the door. She is conspicuously absent, though. Hiding. No wonder. She'd almost gotten me and Dan killed.

"Infinity, you are up for your practice round in five minutes." I look up to see Steve Giles at the microphone. He's the local DJ and renowned amongst the high schools as *the* DJ to have for parties. I'd seen him around here and there. He does some good work.

"Well, what do you want me to do about it? I can't help that Jim's appendix ruptured. If we can't find a drummer like right this second, we have to forfeit."

That's a voice I would know anywhere. Officer Dan. He is standing with another guy and some blonde chick. They are all dressed in black jeans and jean jackets. His band, I presume.

"Yeah, well, we are gonna lose anyway. It'd be better to forfeit than get embarrassed." The other guy sounds disgusted. He is about Dan's height with chocolate hair and gray eyes. Very cute.

The blonde speaks up. Her voice is high and whiny. "What do you mean, we are gonna lose? Dan is awesome, you play pretty good, and so does Jim."

Cute Guy stares at her pointedly.

She lets out an outraged squeal. "Are you saying we are gonna lose because of *me*?"

"Yup, sure am."

Kudos to the cute guy for standing up to the bimbo.

She rounds on Dan. "Are you going to just stand

there and let him insult your girlfriend?"

Girlfriend? Jeez. I thought Dan had more taste than that.

"Jennifer…"

She gasps. "You think I sing bad too?"

He winces. I laugh. I can't help it. He looks torn between lying and just telling her to shut up. He hears me, though, and looks around. I don't know how Dan can pick out my laugh in the mix of voices in this din, but he does and smiles at me. The blonde chick frowns and looks to see what he's smiling at. Her eyes narrow when she sees me and Meg. I bet she's trying to figure out which one of us he's smiling at. Meg and I are both hot girls. We know it and we do tend to flaunt it given the chance.

Dan comes over to the table and takes a seat.

"Problems, Officer Dan?" I ask him.

He sighs. "We've been practicing for the last month and my drummer's in the hospital. If I can't find a replacement, we can't play. You don't know how to play, by chance?"

"Me?" I scoff. "Foster kid here. Game systems were not in my vocabulary growing up. I've never played before." I see Jake frowning at Dan and making a beeline for the table. His jealousy is so adorable. Then I have an idea. "But Jake can play. He signed up for the drum solo thingy."

"Jake?" Dan perks up and then almost grins at the glower on Jake's face, but barely manages to control himself. "Hey. Mattie says you know how to play the drums. I need a drummer. Wanna sit in? We can't play unless I find a replacement."

"I don't know the songs you guys practiced," he

142

says and sits beside Meg since Dan took his seat next to me.

Dan gives him the lineup of songs and Jake is nodding. They're ones he's played before. They get into a discussion on difficulty levels and I zone them both out. Games are not my thing. Meg is ogling Dan, and I grin at her. She looks around sheepishly for Tommy when she sees me grinning, then shrugs. I think she might actually be getting tired of him and I am *so* glad.

Next thing I know the blonde is huffing over to our table, cute boy in tow. Dan introduces them as Jennifer and Greg and then tells them Jake will be playing the drums.

"Infinity, you're up!" DJ Steve yells into the mic, and the guys move to the stage to take their positions. They actually sound pretty good, at least until Jennifer starts to sing. I wince and want to cover my ears.

She's belting out the lyrics and completely ignoring the people around her openly laughing or booing. I feel bad for everyone else on stage.

"She's not singing, that's caterwauling," Meg tells me with a wrinkled nose. "No way can they win with *that* awful voice."

I nod. The first song finishes and the scores pop up. The guys all come in at 95 and up, but Jennifer has barely managed to pull out a 55. Meg's right. They are so not gonna win.

"How's the ankle?" Meg asks while we try to stop laughing at the awful sounds coming out of Jennifer.

"It's a little sore. If I hadn't torn a couple

muscles it wouldn't have hurt as much as it did."

"So what's up with you and Dan?"

"Huh?" I pull my eyes away from the stage and focus on Meg. She's grinning like the Cheshire cat from Alice in Wonderland. "What do you mean?"

"Well, you two are hanging out a lot lately. Even Jake mentioned it to me the other day. He thinks you might be crushing on him."

"Dan just a good friend, that's all."

"Uh-huh. You have to admit it's weird he seems to be there every time you get hurt. That implies you and he are spending a lot of time together."

I roll my eyes at her. "Honest, that's all it is."

"So if I asked him out, you wouldn't try to bitch-slap me?"

"No."

Well, that isn't exactly true. A part of me did want to hold on to Dan and yell 'Mine!', but if it's from jealousy or something else, I can't tell. It's not like when I think about other girls dating Jake, this goes a little deeper than that. It's almost an innate response to hold onto him.

"Good. I've heard stories about you from some of the other high schools. You're pretty scary, Mattie."

I let out a long, low chuckle. Yeah, I *did* have a bit of a reputation, since more than once I beat down some chick because she got in my face. Nice to know my reputation precedes me.

"So I take it you and Tommy aren't getting along anymore?"

She grimaces. "I don't know what's up with him. He's been pretty distant lately. I think he might be seeing someone else."

I try to look shocked, but honestly, I already figured that out. He leers way too much at other girls, including me. "Have you said anything to him?"

"No," she sighs. "I almost don't want to. I love him."

"But if he's cheating on you…"

"It's none of your business," Tommy snarls at me. Meg and I both look around, startled. Neither of us had heard Tommy sneak up.

"It is *so*," I snarl back. "Meg is my friend. That makes *her* my business."

"You have no idea who you are messing with, little girl." He leans down and gets right in my face. I can smell his breath. He's been drinking. "I can hurt you in ways you've never even thought of."

"Really?" My right fist connects firmly with his nose. I hear a nasty pop, and blood flows. I twist so my legs are free of the booth and place a well-aimed kick at his kneecaps. He goes down hard. I'm up out of the booth before he can even catch his breath, and I get in a kick to his stomach.

"Better people than *you* have tried to hurt me," I tell him softly. "I learned a long time ago how to take care of myself. You come near me again and I promise you, I'll hurt you in ways *you* never thought of."

"Bitch," Tommy snarls.

"I know *you* are, but what am I?" I smirk.

"Mattie, you okay?" Dan and Jake have scrambled off the stage and rush to my side.

"I'm fine," I say. "He might need some ice for

that nose. I broke it."

Dan hauls him up. "You wanna press charges?"

"Yeah, I sure the hell *do*!" Tommy spits out. "She attacked me."

"I wasn't talking to *you*, shit-for-brains." Dan glowers at him. "Mattie?"

I shake my head. "Nah, he's not worth the paperwork you'd have to fill out. Just get him away from me."

"*That* I can do," he says and forces Tommy away from the table and toward the door. I know I over-reacted. Probably shouldn't have hit him, but it's a built in defense most foster kids have. Hit first, hurt them before they hurt you. We learn it early, and it's a lesson that stays with us forever.

Jake is looking at me strangely as I sit back down. It's a look I know. Most guys who get to know me eventually give me that look. It says, 'Who are you and what did you do with my girlfriend?' I knew it wasn't gonna last, but I'd hoped I could keep him a little longer. After today, though, that might not be an option. My chest hurts. The thought of losing Jake is making me sick to my stomach and my heart actually hurts. He's the first guy who's ever seen past my walls. I glance at Meg, and she is staring at me, too.

"Damn, Mattie, remind me to never, ever get on your bad side," she whispers. "Where did you learn to fight like that?"

My mind drifts back. "David Green." I half-smile. "He and I got put into the same foster home together when I was ten and he was sixteen. He said I needed to be able to protect myself, and he spent almost six months teaching me how to fight."

"You guys must have been pretty close," she says.

"Not really." I shrug. "Foster kids just take care of each other. He used to get picked on a lot, and Eric taught him how to fight, and he was just paying it forward."

Wow. It's been years since I thought about David. He'd been as close to a big brother as I'd ever had. I might shrug it off to Meg, but we had been close. He'd taken care of me and took most of the beatings our foster dad dished out. He said if it hadn't been for Eric he'd have never survived. Eric had saved him and he'd saved me.

Wait.

Eric Cameron.

No… it couldn't be.

Oh. My. God.

"Mattie?"

That was why Eric was so familiar to me. I know his freaking name.

Mirror Boy had been a foster kid.

Chapter Eighteen

It's all I can do to sit still while the bands play. I can't believe Mirror Boy was in the system. I don't know if he was when he died or not. He could've been adopted or something, but now I have a starting point. I have to start researching *this* angle. I want to do it now! Nancy will be my best chance, but how am I going to get answers out of her without twenty questions? Now, *that's* going to be the tricky part, but I'm a sneaky girl by nature. I'll figure it out.

My phone starts buzzing. I frown and pull it out of my back pocket. It had better not be Mrs. O. She's been freaking out recently over the smallest things. Just yesterday, she yelled at all the little kids for playing too loud. I mean seriously, they're kids. It's what they do. They like to laugh and squeal. The woman needs to chill and cut them a little slack.

I have a text from an unknown number. I almost delete it like I do any text from people I don't know, but I find myself curious. I'm not sure why, but I open it and nearly have a heart attack sitting there in the booth.

I'm giving a lecture at UNC in Charlotte tonight at 4pm. I left you 2 passes at the door. Meet me after - Olivet

My mouth drops open in shock. Holy crap. He actually responded! My ghost expert responded. I never expected him to get in touch. Whoa. It was just an off the wall shot in the dark. This is my chance to get some answers. I text Dan to ask him if he can take me. Jake and Meg are out of the question. Neither of them know my dirty little secret. Plus, I'm not too sure if Jake and I are kosher right now. I can't get that look of his out of my mind.

Jake slides into the seat opposite me. Not a good sign. Dan takes the spot beside me. Jake does look up at that and glares. Dan completely ignores him. He looks downright depressed.

"You should have forfeited," I told him snidely.

He sighs and nods. It really was that bad. "Yeah, but you did a great job, Jake. Thanks, man."

"Whatever."

Dan finally looks up at him and frowns. He looks ready to say something when Jennifer comes over. Greg is behind her and looks ready to commit a serious act of bodily harm. My kind of guy.

At that moment, Dan digs his phone out of a pocket and scans his messages. He glances at me once, so I know he's read my text. The next question is given how Jake is obviously feeling, do I want him to know I asked Dan to take me somewhere and not him? Not a chance.

"Jake, can we leave now? I'm tired and my ankle hurts."

"They haven't even started the solo challenges yet," he says. "Can you wait just a little longer?"

"That's okay, Jake," Dan tells him. "I can take her home. I was gonna leave since I'm not signed up for any of the solo stuff and we stand zero chance of winning anyway."

"But *I'm* not ready to go!" Jennifer complains. I can see Dan wince and I just barely stop myself from grinning. She *really* is not who I pictured him dating.

"Greg…"

"Hell, no!" Greg almost shouts.

"Then stay as long as you want, Jen. I'll swing by later and pick you up."

Her eyes narrow into slits and center on me. I can see the calculations there and can't suppress a smile. That really sets her off. Dan rolls his eyes and slides out of the seat.

"You are actually going to leave me here and take some little kid home?"

Little kid? She so did not say that. Meg and Jake both wince. They know me.

"Yeah, he's taking this *little kid* home." I let the sarcasm drip. "At least I won't whine like a spoiled brat, unlike *you*, you bleach-blonde brainless moron. Really, *Officer Dan*, I am sooooo disappointed in you. This is your girlfriend? Really? I thought you had better taste than *this*."

Poor Dan looks a little uncomfortable, but honestly, even *he* has to know what an idiot she is.

He obviously isn't dating her for the stimulating conversation.

"Looks like," he says at last, and Jennifer's expression turns murderous. He stands up so I can get out.

"Jake, call me when you make up your mind." I push myself up and out of the booth. Jake nods, and I realize I'm right. He *is* rethinking our relationship. I feel tears try to well up. I don't cry. I am not a person who cries. I take a hasty step forward, and pain shoots up my leg from my ankle. White-hot pain. The little show with Tommy earlier had done more damage than I thought.

Dan catches me before I fall. "Can you walk, Mattie?"

"Yeah, it's fine," I wave him off and take a tentative step forward. He has to catch me again. Dang it. Before I can say anything, he swings me up in his arms and asks Greg to get the door. Jake is standing, looking like he wants to hit Dan, but I see Meg catch him and pull him back.

Once we are in Dan's truck and headed for the interstate, I stare pointedly out the window, trying to ignore the tears that are streaming wet paths down my cheeks. I guess maybe I thought Jake really could look past everything, but deep down, he's like every other guy I've ever known.

"Do you want to talk about it?" Dan asks quietly after a while.

I shake my head, refusing to look at him. I hate the fact that he's seeing me like this.

"He's a jerk," Dan says. "I can still press charges if you want."

"What?" I turn startled eyes on him.

"Tommy. If you're this upset, I'll turn around right now and go arrest him."

He thinks I'm upset over Tommy? I almost laugh out loud. If that was all it was. I may have just lost my boyfriend. Crap. Being me crushes the best things that ever happen in my life. At the rate I'm going, Mrs. O. might ship me off any day.

Get ahold of yourself, Mattie. This place, these people have gotten past my walls, and this is not a good thing. I need to distance myself from everything. It's these danged ghosts. I'm feeling more emotions because of them. I feel what *they* feel. When I used to ignore them, I didn't leave myself open to all these emotions. I *knew* letting them in was a bad idea, but I did it for Sally. Where has it gotten me? Nowhere. I'm sitting here crying and feeling worthless and not an inch closer to finding her killer, not really.

"I couldn't care less about Tommy," I whisper and turn away from him. I don't want him to see me cry. I need to stop these tears. This is not me. I am fearless and I will not let myself get hurt like this, not ever again.

"What's wrong, Mattie?"

"You are such a guy," I say at last. "I think Jake finally figured out that I'm exactly who everyone says I am, the reject foster kid with a chip on her shoulder. He put up with a lot from me, but when he saw me actually get in a fight, I think that was it. It was just too much for him."

I hear Dan exhale slowly, and then he pulls the truck over on the shoulder of the interstate. He turns off the radio before reaching over to unbuckle my seatbelt. He hauls me over and lets me cry all over his shirt.

"Mattie, you were defending yourself against a creep. If Jake doesn't realize that, then he's an idiot." His hand is patting my back and I hiccup. "You are not a reject. You are wonderful, and special, and yes, you are a little weird, but it's a good weird. Don't ever let anyone make you feel bad about the person you are. You are *not* worthless. You are you, and I for one wouldn't trade you for all the mundane girls in the world. I like you just the way you are, a fighter, a hellion, and a person I care a great deal about."

"You don't understand, Dan." I pull away from him and stare into his eyes, flashing with anger. "I've never met a guy before who looked past all the walls I put up and saw me, who liked me for me. Jake was that guy. He saw *me*. I kept thinking to myself, this is too good to be true, eventually he'll get sick of my crap like everyone else and leave. I think today was his day to leave."

"Why? Because you hit a guy who got in your face and threatened you? Any girl would have…"

"No," I stopped him. "They *wouldn't* have. Most girls would have cowered or waited for their boyfriend to take care of it."

"You're not most girls, Mattie Louise."

"I *know*!" I yell. "That's my point, Dan. I'm screwed up and it eventually costs me everyone who means anything to me. My first reaction is to hit before I get hit, to hurt them before I get hurt."

I burst into tears again and I see the sadness in

Dan's eyes. I can't take his pity and try to move away from him, but he won't let me. "Shh," he soothes and pulls me back into his arms. "It's all right, Mattie. I'll make you a promise, okay? I promise no matter what you do, I will always be here for you. I will never leave you and I will never let you drive me away, no matter how hard you try. You're stuck with me, kid."

There is a wealth of emotion in his voice, and I know if I look up, I'll see his face full of determination. I know he means it. Officer Dan is the only person who has ever managed to make me feel like anything except the poor little foster girl. Jake is great and I know he likes me, but sometimes I think he only asked me out in the beginning because he felt sorry for me. I was the new girl, the foster kid who had no friends. That's the kind of person he is. It's why I knew he and I would never last. I just didn't think it'd be over this soon.

Dan is different. I know he cares, that he means exactly what he says. I've never in my life connected with someone like I have with him. It scares me more than I can say, but I won't give it up either. I need Dan in my life. He makes me feel safe.

"So," he says when I pull myself together, "why are we heading to UNC?"

"Dr. Olivet." I wipe my face with the napkin Dan pulls out of an old McDonald's bag. It smells like fries, but I know my face is a mess. Dan's truck is old so it doesn't have mirrors in the visors and I'm grateful that I'd put on very little makeup today, only a bit of lipstick.

"Who?" he asks, and pulls back onto the interstate.

"He's a parapsychologist," I tell him and try to finger-comb my hair. "I found him on the internet."

Dan's sigh is loud enough to make me wince. "Mattie, tell me you didn't go trolling the internet looking for ghost hunters?"

"What?" I ask defensively. "I need a little help here, Dan. I may have been able to see ghosts my entire life, but I don't know anything about them, not really. I certainly didn't know one could hurt me. I have to be able to protect myself. This guy has a lot of press, he seems to know what he's talking about."

"All it means, Mattie, is he is good at BS and a Twitter fanatic. I bet he has thousands of followers on Twitter, doesn't he?"

I refuse to acknowledge this is true. He has over three million followers.

"Mattie, ghost hunters are just there to take advantage of people and fuel their nonsense beliefs. They find reasons to take a situation that has a perfectly rational explanation and make it into the haunting of the century. I can't believe you of all people would fall for that. I gave you way more credit."

"So you think what I believe is nonsense? You don't believe I can see ghosts?"

He sighs. "Mattie, I firmly believe *you* think you can see ghosts, and yes, I've seen some pretty weird stuff around you, but to say I believe in ghosts? I'm still not there yet."

"You think I'm crazy? Then how did I know all

that stuff about Mary? Huh? Think I imagined that?" I'm yelling, I know I'm yelling, but I can't help it. Dan was the one person who I thought believed me. Now he's saying he doesn't.

"No, you're not crazy. If I thought that, I'd not be helping you try to find a killer no one else thinks exists. Yeah, you do know a lot of stuff you shouldn't, stuff that wasn't released to the general public, especially about Mary. That's why I'm here. I will go as far as to say you might be a little psychic, but ghosts? I'm just not sure, Mattie. I told you I'd keep an open mind, and I am. Just give me some time, okay?"

I nod, but turn to stare out the window again. I am shocked he doesn't believe me. I thought for sure he did, that finally I'd found someone I could confess my secrets to and not have them scoff in my face. He's not scoffing, but he doesn't believe me, not really. He is rationalizing why I know so much. He's a cop, I remind myself. Cops never believe you, no matter what they say. They never trust you are telling the truth. Especially people like me with not only a record, but a foster kid to boot. I should have expected this. I just didn't see it coming. It hurt. Even more than possibly losing Jake. The tears won't come, though. Some things hurt too deep for tears to touch, and this is one of them.

How had I let this happen? How did Officer Dan Richards come to mean more to me than anyone I've ever met? It makes no sense to me, but it is what it is.

The rest of the ride is silent. We then spend a lot of time looking for parking. After twenty minutes, we finally crawl out of the car. I end up alternating between hopping and limping. Dan tries to help me, but I push him off. I am not in the mood. Gotta put my walls back up. I am tired of getting hurt. I am *not* that girl. I *won't* be that girl, not even for Dan Richards.

We stop at the first building we come to and Dan asks where we can find the lecture hall Dr. Olivet is in. Oh. He's not in a lecture hall. He's in the theater.

The theater? Really?

Dan rolls his eyes as if to say 'I told you so,' but I ignore him. I know this is the right thing to do, that Dr. Olivet will have the answers I need. I just do.

Chapter Nineteen

The theater is housed in Robinson Hall, where the College of Performing Arts plays the bulk of their performances. There are two separate facilities, the black-box Lab Theater, small and intimate, and the main one, the Anne R. Belk Theater. Dr. Olivet's lecture is in the main one, allowing for a seating of three hundred and forty. We arrive early and find seats fairly easily.

Dan complains about my choosing the middle. If we are in the back, we'll miss things, and if we are in the front, we'll miss things because we're too close. The middle is perfect. It puts you just above the heads of everyone below you, and plus you get a full view of the stage. My reasoning doesn't improve Dan's mood, though. I think he's being grumpy because he thinks it's a waste of time. Maybe it is, but I have to try.

It is a beautiful theater. The orchestra-like box seating around the stage gives off a very intimate feel, black seats gleaming amongst the white pillars holding up the theater boxes that go up three levels. It looks very old and elegant. It's a place I would love to sit in and sketch. The orchestra pit was filling up with the orchestra as well. Now what was this? It's not a concert. Were we attending a lecture or a show? The stage curtains are still tightly drawn, but I hear a lot of movement behind them.

After about twenty minutes, the place starts to really fill up. At first, I'd thought there wouldn't be that big of an audience. There were only about twenty or so people here when we arrived, but now, there's hardly a seat to be found. That could be a good sign, right? I mean, why would so many people show up if he didn't know what he was talking about?

"Richards?"

Dan and I glance up to see a guy heading our way. Dan has an empty seat beside him and he groans. I almost laugh at the martyred look on his face. I'm still mad at him, so I refuse to give in to the urge. The guy falls into the seat next to him. I don't mean sits heavily, he literally falls into it with no thought to the poor seat. My kind of fella. His blond hair and blue eyes are a stark contrast to Dan's darker looks. He looks at me with very curious eyes.

"Hey, Mason," Dan greets him. "What are you doing here?"

"Bored. Nothing else to do, so I figured I'd come see the spook doctor's performance."

Then Dan snorts. I glare at him.

The guy leans forward so he can see around Dan. "I'm Mason Jones, by the way."

"Mattie." I smile at him. He's really, really cute. I may be hung up on my maybe-still-boyfriend, but even *I* can appreciate a cute guy. How can a girl not? It's not the looking part that counts anyway. It's the touching. My theory is you can look at all the eye candy you want and still appreciate what you have at home. Though at the moment, I'm not sure I do have anything at home.

"She's too young for *you*," Dan growls.

Mason's eyebrows fly up at Dan's tone. So do mine.

"Ignore Officer Dan," I say. "He's being a jerk today."

"*That* I can believe." Mason laughs. The sound is rich and deep. "He can be a little uptight sometimes. I'm surprised he's here at all, given his opinions on anything…supernatural."

"Opinions?"

"Yeah, he's a firm believer that there is a rational explanation for everything, and anything with a supernatural element is just a fabrication."

"Oh, really?" I ask, glancing up at Dan's face. It's a tight mask. He is so trying not to say anything that might get him in even more trouble with me.

"Really." Mason is openly laughing at Dan's expression, and it makes me a little angry that he is making fun of Dan's beliefs.

"Well, he let me drag him here," I tell Mason, suddenly feeling like I should defend Officer Dan. "He gets brownie points for that."

"And just who are you, Jailbait?" Mason grins at me.

"She's a friend of mine, Mason," Dan tells him. "Leave off."

I sigh and roll my eyes. Good Lord, he's as bad

as Jake. "I'm sixteen so he feels it necessary to make sure anyone over the age of seventeen doesn't hit on me."

Mason laughs outright. "Well, I guess he's gonna have to deal. I plan on hitting on you all night, Jailbait."

Dan growls, literally growls, but Mason only laughs harder. He is such a cutie. I feel guilty because I like him, given that Jake and I might or might not still be together, but I'm vain enough to enjoy the attention.

The lights go down about the time Dan opens his mouth to tell Mason what he thinks of that, and I shush them both.

Whispered excitement runs through the crowd, and then a hush falls over the audience as the curtains open. The orchestra begins to play, the melody dark and low. It reminds me of those times during the middle of the night when you wake up in the dark and shiver for no reason, like there's someone watching you when you know there isn't. The haunting music inspires that feeling in not just me, but in several other people nearby. Even Dan shifts a bit uncomfortably. We all have that inner fear of the dark, no matter how old we get. It's an ingrained instinct to fear the velvety blackness of the night, of things you can't quite see, but know deep down in your bones are there, waiting.

The stage is dark at first, then a light starts to glow softly. A man sits before a fireplace. I would place his clothes around the turn of the twentieth century. He looks to be in his early thirties or so. His head is bent forward, reading some book. The soft glow of the light expands to see a woman sitting on a small couch, a settee. Her dress, a warm, rich burgundy, sweeps the ground even though she's sitting. The light is focused more on her hands than her face, which is why I notice she's knitting. The back and forth of the needles is almost hypnotic.

She looks up and stares intently into the flickering flames of the fireplace. Her hands keep moving in that back and forth motion, and I find myself leaning forward. She stands abruptly and walks over the fireplace, head bowed. The man is seated only a foot from her. He is not paying her any attention at all, his focus entirely on the book.

It's then I catch the glint of metal in her hands. She still has the knitting needles firmly grasped in each hand. She has her fists clenched around them, the yarn trailing. She turns to face the audience, her face a mask of determination. Then she takes a few steps and brings the needles down hard into the man's back, before yanking them out of his flesh. He stands up with a roar, but she doesn't give him time to fight back. She rushes him, needles stabbing and slashing until he stumbles and falls. She goes down with him and the needles strike him again and again, sending blood everywhere.

At last she stands, adjusts her skirt, and sits back on the settee. She begins to knit again, the back forth movements still as hypnotic as before, but her hands are covered in the blood of the man lying motionless on the floor.

The curtains close.

Silence fills the hall. No one expected that. Even

Dan looks a little shocked.

The music then shifts, changes to something a little softer, a little less frightening, and the curtains open again. This time a man is standing at a podium a little to the left of the center stage. He reminds me of Eric McCormack from *Will and Grace*. He's a lot younger than I expected him to be, maybe thirty-five or forty. I was thinking an older man in his sixties. His hair is the color of chestnuts and he's smiling at our reactions.

When he speaks, his voice is warm and a little lulling.

"What you just witnessed was the first in a series of brutal murders that took place in Savannah, Georgia, starting in July of 1917 at the Steel Water Plantation, and ended just five years ago with the death of an entire family. Mrs. Emily Goody, wife of Robert Goody, simply decided one night to stab her husband of ten years to death. She told authorities a ghost made her do it. Over the next century, four more families inhabited the plantation and more deaths occurred. Each time, the perpetrator simply said a ghost made me do it."

He pauses to let that sink in before continuing.

"Is it a coincidence that the stories never wavered? Was it simply that someone read about the original murder and wanted to use a unique defense to try to get away with a nefarious deed? Mental conditions? No one can really say. What they *can* agree on is that all four people were considered normal, pillars of the community, even. This is what draws parapsychologists to the scene. Can a ghost make you hurt someone, or is it just the evil that lives in us all coming out to play?"

He steps away from the podium and comes closer to the end of the stage. "My name is Dr. Lawrence Olivet, and I want to thank everyone for coming out tonight to listen to me ramble on and on about the spooky things that go bump in the night. Now, let's have a show of hands. Who came to hear the spook doctor because they were bored?"

Chuckles break out and a smattering of hands go up, including Mason's. He smiles in response. "Now, how many of you were dragged here by a friend or significant other?"

Most of the hall fits into this category, including Dan, who refuses to raise his hand. I grab it and push it up for him. Mason laughs outright at Dan's disgust right before he jerks his hand from mine. I giggle at the glower he sends my way, which makes Mason laugh all the harder.

"Well, that's okay. I wouldn't want to come to a ghost lecture either," Dr. Olivet tells us conspiratorially. "So, let's not have a lecture then. Let's have some fun with it."

I can see why he's so popular. First, he looks absolutely nothing like what I figured a professor would look like, nor does he look like one of those grungy ghost hunters you see on TV all the time. He looks normal and, well, cute for an old guy. Like Detective Stabler-cute on SVU. This man has that same something going for him. He's not boring either. He's made almost everyone laugh or at least chuckle. Charismatic. That is the word I'm looking for. Charming and charismatic.

"So I guess the first place to start is why do I

spend time looking for ghosts? The truth? I spend my time trying to debunk the so called haunting. Most people out there want to see ghosts in things they can't explain. It's easier to believe and more romantic than the pipes being rusty or the house creaking because it's a hundred years old. I've disproved more hauntings than seen anything truly supernatural."

Dan grunts beside me. I don't think he'd expected that. He was all up for the guy going on and on about how ghosts are real and everything that can't be explained is a ghost waiting to jump out at you.

"Most of us here grew up with parents or grandparents that taught us there is a higher power out there in the universe, whether you call it God, Allah, Buddha, or whatever your religion dictates. Most people believe there is a force out there, even if we don't pay too much attention to it unless we need to. You'd be amazed at how many self-proclaimed atheists will start to pray right before they die. So, why am I going on and on about religion, you're thinking. Isn't this supposed to be about ghosts?"

There's a general murmur of assent.

"My point is death, ladies and gentlemen. No one wants to believe that when we die, that's it. Everything we are, that we were, will just cease to exist when we die. We need to believe there is something more out there. If there isn't, what's the point of all this? That is why deep down, we all believe in that higher power. We have to believe that when we die, we go on, that something is out there besides an empty void, or that the energy that makes us unique will simply extinguish. It's an instinct ingrained in every human alive. Now, that said, if you believe in that higher power, in the fact that we go on after death, why are ghosts so hard to believe in? Why can't the energy that once made up a human be trapped here on this plane of existence for reasons we can't even begin to understand?"

He moves, and the dark background begins to shimmer with colors, streams of blues and reds and greens start drifting around on the back wall of the stage. It has to be some kind of screen and projector, but the effect is totally cool.

"We can all agree that energy in one form or another powers everything. You need energy to move an inanimate object like a bike. Your feet push the pedals which cause the bike to move. Your body uses energy to help you do this. All living things are made up of energy. When we die, that energy goes somewhere. Is there a bright light waiting for us at the end of a tunnel with our loved ones beckoning us? I don't know. I've read and listened to many of the same stories you have about people who have died and seen this mysterious light at the end of a long tunnel. I've sat with dying people and listened to them talk to loved ones who have been dead for years. Could it just be their minds trying to find some sort of comfort in a situation where they are terrified of death? Most likely that is the truth, but what if there's more to it than our rational mind wants to accept? What if when a person dies, especially in a violent manner, their energy, the essence that makes them unique, is trapped by their own fears? What if they can't pass to that next plain of existence out of fear?"

The energy of the light show starts to morph together, to coalesce into cohesive humanoid shapes. They dart back and forth, the orchestra's melody changing to a tune to inspire confusion and fear. The darkness of the theater compounds the effect and it's almost impossible not to think of all those times when you are alone, in the dark, and you shiver for no reason.

"I was fifteen when I had my first experience with what we commonly call ghosts today. It was at a funeral for a kid at our school who had died in a car crash. He was well liked, popular, had everything a high school kid could ask for. So why would he have just driven his car off a cliff? The police deemed it a suicide because they could find no sign of anything wrong with the car or any signs of foul play to suggest he'd been run off the road or that there was some sort of accident. He'd simply driven in a straight line right off the edge.

"I remember the church was full and the minister was preaching about how life is short and we need to seize every opportunity. It was hot and stuffy, and I kept wishing he'd hurry up so we could get outside and be on our way. I did not want to be there, but my parents made me go out of respect to the boy and his family. The wallpaper was peeling in spots and I kept counting all the little pieces hanging down. That's when I noticed the odd light. It was hovering around the casket. I could only see it when I turned my head to the right, when I looked out of the corner of my eye, but I saw it. At first, I tried to tell myself it was just a reflection of light from the sun, but the drapes had been pulled for the service. It couldn't be that. When the boy's mother stood up to speak and started to cry as she talked about her son, the temperature in the room dropped drastically. It turned almost freezing, and the vase of flowers sitting on the table beside her crashed to the floor. Everyone thought she'd done it, but she hadn't. I'd seen that light moving frantically back and forth around her, around the vase.

"I firmly believe it was the ghost of the boy there, trying to tell his mother that he was still here, that he was right there beside her, but she couldn't see him, couldn't hear him. It had to be so frustrating, and I think it was that frustration that allowed the ghost to harness enough raw energy to make the vase wobble enough to crash to the floor. No one else saw the lights or felt the cold, either. I was the only one. I can tell you it scared the hell out of me."

There is a little rumble of chatter that goes through the audience, but mostly they are hushed, listening as the professor weaves his tale. He's really good at storytelling. He has his audience enthralled.

"That's when I started to pick up a few books on the supernatural, ghosts in particular. Back then, the library was still the main source of information. The internet hadn't exploded yet, so I was stuck digging through old books." He gives us all a pained look at that statement, causing many to laugh along with him. "Can you imagine not being able to Google your question? Research is much easier these days."

I think back to my own research. I Googled everything I'd wanted to search for. If I'd had to go to the library and do the same kind of research looking for answers, I'd have screamed and thrown in the towel. No way do I ever want to try to do anything without my trusty Google search.

"So there I was, full of questions and ideas. I looked up a fairly local branch of ghost hunters. They agreed to let me "intern" with them, and so I did what any fifteen year old would do. I got my best friend to tell my parents I was going fishing with him and his uncle while I was really over in rural Virginia at a supposed haunted house. I was so excited, my first time out with real ghost hunters. Biggest disappointment ever."

Dan is frowning and leaning forward now, listening with interest. I shake my head. Mr. Disbeliever over here sure is interested all of a sudden.

"What I found was a bunch of people 'looking' for ghosts where there were none. Every creak was a ghost trying to communicate. Every draft in a drafty house evidence of a ghost's presence. Their equipment was something out of a really bad sci-fi novel. I just shook my head in disbelief. Suffice to say, I gave up on ghost hunting for a while after that. I figured maybe I was trying to see something where there had been nothing too. I finished high school and then went to college. It was while I was in college I got interested in ghost hunting again. I was hanging out in an old dorm that had been closed years ago with some friends. We were just goofing off and making out with our girlfriends. My girlfriend, who shall be known as Jane from here on out, and I wandered into one of the empty rooms on the third floor. We had a flashlight with us and nothing more. Lights would have had campus security on us in a heartbeat. It was close to the end of the year, and summer was coming upon us. I went to school in Miami, though, so it's always hot there. With no electricity or central air, the dorm was blazing hot, which is what the guys and I were counting on."

There were a lot of laughs at this point and several good natured shoves from girlfriends.

"So there Jane and I are, doing things I will leave to your imagination, when I start to feel a little chill creep up my back. I don't notice it at first, but when Jane remarks on how cold it is, I look around. It *had* gotten cold. I grabbed the flashlight and gave the room a quick look. As my flashlight passed the partially opened closet, Jane let out a little shriek. I figured it was a rat or something, but she swore she saw someone standing there. I rolled my eyes at her. You know how skittish girls can be." He pauses and winks. "But, ladies, we love you that way. Gives you an excuse to clutch us during horror movies."

Mason and Dan, as well as most of the guys around us burst out laughing. I glare at them both. Skittish? Me? So very *not* me.

"So, me being the big man and all, I go over to check it out. Jane is right behind me, refusing to stay by herself on the floor. I have my trusty flashlight pointed at the closet and there's nothing I can see. I push open the sliding door and look inside. Nothing but empty space. I turn around and give the room a once-over again. Even *I* notice how cold it's gotten by now. I can see my breath in front of me in the light of the flashlight. I'm a little freaked, but I'm playing it cool. Can't have Jane thinking I'm a wuss. I turn around to tell her it was nothing and suggest we head back downstairs, but I stop and stare. I don't see anything, but Jane's hair is floating. Not like in the movies where the hair sort of gently wafts in the air from a fan, but like someone is picking pieces of it up and holding them up for inspection. She doesn't feel a thing. I'm debating about telling her when the closet door slams shut, trapping her hair with it. This she feels because it pulled her backward and her head pretty much slammed into the mirrors on the closet doors. She starts screaming and I frantically try to get the door open, but it's locked tight."

The quiet in the room is palpable. This guy can tell a story. The girls look horrified, the guys intrigued.

"She's freaking out, and I hear the guys shouting from below. I'm struggling with the door, when suddenly I can feel something cold and damp touch my face. I'll be honest and admit, I screamed like a girl. I was so freaked, I almost ran away, but I didn't. The dorm room door flew open and our friends piled in. Jane hadn't stopped screaming, so we were easy to find. As soon as they burst in, the temperature in the room shoots up and the door I've been yanking on slides easily open. Because of how hard I'm pulling on it, I go flying backward with the force I was using to try to pry it open. Jane runs and the girls go after her. I just shrug it off and tell my friends it was dark and she got her hair caught on the door somehow and then the door got stuck. Did you guys really think I was going to tell them it was a ghost? Even *I'm* not that much of a glutton for punishment. I never would have heard the end of it. Now, as soon as I get back to my dorm room, I power up the old archaic computer and do a search on the dorm we were in to see if anything strange had happened there. Guess what?"

"It was haunted," someone shouts out.

"No reports of hauntings," he shakes his head, "but there *was* a girl who died there, on the third floor in the very room we were in. She overdosed. It was about a month after that they closed the dorm down. They'd just built a brand new co-ed one and moved the students over to it. Did Jane and I really experience a ghost, or was it the imaginations of two very hormonal teens? I think it was a ghost, but there are those I'm sure who don't. I'm not here to make you believe in ghosts, only introduce you to the possibility that there is something else out there, something you can't explain away or make fit perfectly into the puzzle that is our reality.

"I started to look more closely at websites having to deal with ghosts, and eventually I was able to figure out one thing. About ninety-nine point nine percent of all those websites are garbage. I did, however, find one site that got my attention. It was a guy who was trying to debunk all the ghost stories. I sent him an e-mail and he and I started talking. And before you ask, no, I will not reveal his name as he asked me not to. He and I became friends and eventually he showed me some of his work, his equipment. Now here was a real ghost hunter. He actually had equipment that worked. The guy taught me how to work them all and why each one was in important in proving or disproving the whole ghost theory.

"I went with him on several hunts. Almost every single one we went on was just a wild goose chase. I started to get discouraged, but then we hit the mother lode. It was an old plantation house in Georgia."

A murmur went through the crowd. The scene at the beginning of the lecture.

"We spent only one night in that house, and I can tell you this: I will *never* set foot in that house again. All that equipment I was starting to think was useless came alive. We picked up recordings of voices, thermal sensors picked up readings where I know for a fact there was no one. It was only the two of us, and we decided almost as soon as we stepped in the house, we wouldn't split up. That's why we know the sensors worked. I didn't sleep that night. I could stand here for days and tell you about what went on there, but I'm not going to. Suffice to say, it scared the hell out of me. I was a believer after that night.

"I started a website about my own experiences and a blog soon after that. I picked up a lot of readers, and when Twitter exploded onto the scene, the site only got bigger. Do you guys know why my tours are so popular?" He waits a moment and then says, "I don't lie to people. I don't claim to know everything, I just tell you all about my experiences and hopefully entertain as much as educate you on the other realm of existence."

"Now, I'm going to open the floor to questions. Ask me anything you want."

People start asking stupid questions and I am about to raise my own hand to ask a question when all the gizmos and gadgets he has sitting on a table start to light up and make noises. That's when I see him. Sitting on the edge of the stage, close to the curtains on the right side, is a boy. He is staring at me with a fierce determination. His face is pale and pasty, his eyes sunken and dark. His head is bent at an odd angle and he doesn't look happy. No, he looks downright furious.

He jumps off the stage and heads straight for me.

Chapter Twenty

"Would you look at that?" Mason points to the stage. The table beside the podium, which bore a variety of different machines, is now lit up like a Christmas tree. Even the professor pauses and looks at it. His eyes go out and sweep the audience, coming to rest on me. I know my face is a frozen mask of horror.

"Dan," I whisper. He's not listening. He's too busy watching the equipment. I poke him in the ribs. "Dan."

"What?" He turns his attention to me and a look of concern crosses his face.

"Get me out of here," I tell him, my eyes never leaving the ghost walking with purpose straight to me.

"Mattie, we can't just leave in the middle…"

"Now, Dan." My fingernails dig into his hand and he winces. My voice takes on a note of desperation. "Please, I need to leave right now."

He nods and stands up. I try to get up, but my ankle is not working properly. Dan pretty much picks me up by the waist. My feet are hanging suspended off the ground. He carries me out of the row and toward the entrance, all the while apologizing to anyone he's stepping on.

I can barely breathe by the time we hit the hallway. I feel hands closing around my throat and squeezing. The harder I try to breathe, the more difficult it becomes. The invisible hands just grip my throat tighter. Tears spring to my eyes and I'm clawing at my own throat, but there are no hands there. Dan is shouting at me, but I can't hear him. Black spots appear before my eyes and I know I'm going to pass out soon.

Black eyes swim up in front of my face. They are gleeful and enjoying my pain. The boy from the stage. He's doing this to me, but why? What did I do to him? My vision blurs, the light narrowing down to just pinpricks, and my lungs burn from lack of air. He's killing me.

That's when I get mad. No one, especially not some freaking ghost, is going to murder me. Been there, done that, and I won't do it again. *Okay, concentrate, Mattie.* I'm desperate, but force my mind to calm down enough to think. I focus on the hands around my throat and I shove with all my mental might. The ghost grips my throat harder and I snarl at him. With the last little bit of energy I have, I put every thought into making him back off.

A white flash of light flares between us and I can breathe. I gulp air as fast I can into my oxygen-deprived lungs. I slowly become of aware of voices, muted at first, but then realize they are shouting. I blink and look around. Dan and Mason are yelling at each other, not more than a few inches from where I am lying.

"What did you do to her?"

"I didn't do anything to Mattie!"

"Then how the hell did she get all those red marks around her throat? It looks like someone tried to strangle her!"

"D..D..a…" Even though it's a whisper, he hears me and is instantly there, helping me to sit up.

"Shh, don't try to speak yet, Squirt." He glances at Mason. "Go find her a bottle of water or something."

Mason gives me a worried look and then heads toward the left hallway.

"Are you okay?" Dan sounds just like a worried mother. "You scared the hell out of me, Mattie."

"Me…too," I whisper. My hands go up to my throat. I can still feel those fingers gripping my neck, squeezing. I close my eyes and all I can see are those crazed eyes. Who was that boy and why was he so angry? *No, Mattie. You will not start asking questions like that. It will lead you nowhere good. Just stop it.*

"Here." Mason shoves a water bottle at us. Dan takes it and removes the cap before handing it to me. My hands shake as I sip at the water. When did ghosts develop the ability to hurt a person? First Mirror Boy, and now this guy. I so don't wanna spend the rest of my life getting attacked by angry ghosts.

"Is someone gonna tell me what the hell is going on?" Mason demands.

"No," Dan tells him. "Why don't you go back inside? I'm taking Mattie home."

"*No!*" My shout is more a strangled whisper than anything else. But at least my voice is coming back, if slowly.

"Mattie…"

I shake my head. I came all this way to talk to the spook specialist. One lousy ghost isn't going to scare me away. "I…have…to…talk…to…him."

Dan is frowning and I glare at him.

"Look, why don't we all go over to the coffee shop across the way?" Mason suggests. "Mattie sounds like she needs some hot tea with honey."

I nod vigorously while Dan shakes his head. "Don't make me hurt you," I whisper.

Mason laughs at this. I send *him* a glare.

"It's no joke, Mase," Dan tells him. "The girl's got some skills."

Mason scoffs. "She's too tiny to do much."

"Yeah? I just watched her bring a guy three times her size to his knees."

Mason sizes me up and then grins. "I like a girl who can handle herself."

This guy Mason amazes me. He is either insane or one of the coolest guys I've ever met.

"Give me your phone." Mason holds out his hand.

"Why?"

"I'm putting my number in it so you can call me, duh!"

I hand him my phone with a hoarse laugh. I'm not sure what to think of Mason. Dan isn't glowering at him, he just looks resigned. Not that it'd matter anyway. I'll do what I want.

While Mason is busy, Dan helps me up. I'm

limping, but at least I'm up and walking. Mason hands me my phone back and gives me his. "Your turn."

"You *do* remember I'm only sixteen, right?"

"I'm only eighteen."

I frown. Eighteen?

"How do you two know each other?" I ask, curious as I program Mason's phone with my number. I like Mason. I feel a little guilty, too, especially since I'm not sure what is going on with me and Jake, but there is something about this guy standing here grinning at me like a goof that I can't shake off. I like him. It's an instantaneous feeling, like what happened with Dan, only different.

"I know him from around." Dan is looking anywhere but at me when he says that. Mason laughs out loud and then says, "I'm his Chemistry tutor."

I smile at them both. Dan is embarrassed and Mason is enjoying being the cause of that embarrassment.

"Mattie, are you ready to go?" Dan grouches.

"Coffee shop," I remind him. I need to talk to Dr. Olivet.

He sighs and nods. "Can you walk or do you need help?"

"I can walk. Mason, I'll call you later, okay?"

"Sure you will, Jailbait, but that's why I have *your* number." He pats his phone. "Promise to tell me what the hell happened out here when I call?"

Absolutely freaking no way. Mason will run faster than Forest Gump if I tell him I almost got strangled by a ghost. I'm still shaking, but Mason made it all a little less scary with his insane chatter. Dan makes me feel safe and Mason just makes everything seem less frightening. Odd.

"Maybe," I lie.

"She has no intention of telling me, does she?" Mason asks Dan.

"I wouldn't hold my breath," Dan tells him. "Go back inside, Mason. I'll take care of Mattie."

Mason eyes narrow ever so slightly. He gives me a wink, though, and then saunters away into the hall. Dan looks like he is ready to start arguing again, so I turn and walk out of the theater, leaving him to follow and head to the café I can see from here.

Dan is not going to let me get away from explaining things, and I need something to fortify myself. Tea would be great right about now. I start hobbling toward the street.

Chapter Twenty-One

Thirty minutes later, Dan is sipping his double something or other frappe latte. His order nearly made me cross my eyes trying to keep up with all the extra stuff he added. I still don't get what everyone sees in all those overpriced flavored coffees. Don't get me wrong—I *love* my caramel macchiato from Starbucks, but even I can't see paying five dollars every couple of hours for coffee. You'd spend an entire paycheck in less than a few days on the stuff.

The place is nice, though. There are over-stuffed chairs and couches scattered around small, cozy tables. Several students are sipping coffee and studying while others are just hanging out and having fun. It's very relaxing, especially after the whole strangulation thing a few minutes ago. I'd texted Dr. Olivet to let him know where we were and what table to find. I hope he gets here.

"Explain."

I wince at Dan's clipped words. I can see the worry on his face, so I can ignore the steel in his voice. He's upset, but then again, so am I. He wasn't the one who nearly had the life literally choked from him. Why should I try to explain? He pretty much just admitted on the way over he didn't believe me. Oh, wait, he believed I believed it. Did that mean I had some kind of mental break and choked myself? Mattie the orphan who thinks she sees dead people. Nutcase he feels sorry for.

"Why should I?" I snarl back. "It's not like you're going to believe me anyway."

He sighs. "Mattie…"

"No," I whisper. "I trusted you, thought you believed me, but you don't. So don't sit there and pretend you do now."

He rubs his forehead tiredly. "I'm trying, okay? It's hard to believe, but I'm trying to keep an open mind here. So please, tell me what happened in there."

It's my turn to sigh. I sip my tea and debate if I should tell him a ghost tried to strangle me or not. It'll only make the crazy girl look even crazier. Do I really want to open myself up to that kind of ridicule? Though to be fair, Dan has never once made me feel like a freak when I told him about my ghost girl abilities. He just blinks and nods. Usually.

"There was a ghost on the stage. He wasn't there in the beginning. He sorta just appeared."

"Was that when all the equipment on stage started to go crazy?"

I nod cautiously. At least the ghost gear gave me a little credibility here. "He was angry, and no, I don't know why. He jumped off the stage and headed right for *me*. I knew something bad was gonna happen and I had to get out of there. He didn't say a word, just started to strangle me even before we got out. I couldn't breathe. The more I fought, the more he squeezed."

My hands creep back up to my neck. I had zipped my jacket all the way up earlier to hide the marks, but I can still feel them there. "I got mad. No way was I gonna let another freaking ghost hurt me. I remember thinking really hard that I wanted his hands to move and…"

"There was a light," Dan whispers. "I saw it. If I'd blinked, I wouldn't have seen it, but it sorta flared up around you and then you were breathing again. Mason came out and distracted me about the same time."

"So maybe I'm not so crazy then, Officer Dan?"

His eyes are wide, but he's not shaking his head in denial at least. That's something. I know I have marks on my throat. Mason had been yelling about them. Even Dan can't explain those away. Maybe my getting hurt today actually helped my case with him. He's a cop. He believes in what he sees with his own two eyes, and the strangulation marks on my neck are real.

Time to switch topics. His not believing me feels too much like a betrayal.

"I figured out why Mirror Boys was so familiar to me."

He blinks. "Mirror Boy?"

"Bloody face in the mirror? Remember him?"

He nods. "Yeah?"

"He was in foster care."

"How do you know that?"

"I recognized his name," I tell him. "There was a

boy who taught me how to protect myself, and he told me Eric Cameron had taught him to take care of himself. He was in the system."

"You can't be sure it's the same person," Dan argues, already going through a whole list of possibilities in his head.

"Even *you* have to admit it's a pretty big coincidence." I take another sip of my tea. It is doing a fabulous job of soothing my throat. I'm not usually a tea drinker, but I've never tried it with honey either.

"It's an angle we can look at," he says at last. "I checked out that list of neighbors you gave me, too. Everyone on your street is your average middle class family-types. Well, most are borderline poor, but you get my point."

Well, there went *that* angle.

"So I did an expanded search," he continues. "There are eleven sex offenders within ten miles of your house, two just a couple blocks over from you."

"Really?" Now *that* is just creepy.

"Yeah," he nods. "I am checking into it. I'll find out where they work tomorrow, and before you ask, I just got this information today."

"Did you check out the Olsons?" I hate to think they had anything to do with it, though. Mrs. O is probably the best foster mother I've ever had.

"I did. Clean as a whistle except for a couple traffic tickets over the years." He frowns. "They are the most likely candidates, but there's no evidence to suggest they're anything but what they appear to be. Decent folks trying to help people."

"We have to figure this out, Dan. Mary didn't look good the last time I saw her. I don't think she has much time left."

"Have you seen her since the other night?" he asks hesitantly. I can see how hard it is for him to even ask that question, but he did. Brownie points to Officer Dan.

"No," I tell him. "I don't know how much longer she can last. If she's even still alive. I see dead people, not ones who are still breathing, but I don't know, she didn't feel dead to me."

"I'm doing the best I can, Mattie."

"I know."

And I did know. Whether he bought the whole ghost business or not, he's put a lot of time and effort into everything I gave him. He'd found names for the drawings of the dead kids, found out information about them, mapped out where they were taken, and above all else, he treated this like it was real, like they were important and they had been killed in the way I'd described. He's a good guy and I need to remember that instead of getting all hurt and huffy over him not believing I can see ghosts.

It just feels like we aren't getting anywhere and that frustrates me. I'm the kind of person who goes out and gets things done, but instead I'm trusting Dan to use his connections to find out stuff it'd take me a long time or possibly never to find. It's funny, really. Me, trusting a cop.

"I promise you, Mattie, we *will* figure this out."

"I can't believe I trust you," I growl at him. It rankles that I trust him and he doesn't trust me back. If he did, he'd believe I could see ghosts, no questions asked.

"You sound furious that you do," he laughs.

"I am," I tell him in all seriousness. "I've never, ever trusted anyone since my mom, not even Nancy, not really. I'm mad because I trust you and you don't trust me. Do you know how hard it is for me to trust a cop?"

"I trust you, Squirt."

I laugh bitterly. "No, Dan, you don't. If you trusted me, you'd believe me no matter how insane it sounds, and you don't."

He stares at me, his warm brown eyes all full of gooey liquid gold. I hate it when he uses that look on me. It makes me want to tell him things I normally wouldn't. I have to keep a lid on my runaway lips from now on. I need to distance myself from Officer Dan.

"Mattie, it's not that I don't want to believe you, it's just hard to believe ghosts are real."

"And that is the crux of the whole thing, isn't it? No one wants to believe ghosts exist because then they'd have to re-examine everything they believed to be true."

We both turn to see Dr. Olivet standing a few feet from us. Neither of us saw him come in or walk to our table. I'm not one to let people sneak up on me. Maybe I need to just leave this freaking town altogether, get away from Dan, Meg, Jake, Mason, Mrs. O. The whole lot of them. They're getting way too close.

"Ready to talk about ghosts, Mattie?" Dr. Olivet asks, distracting me from my internal tirade.

I smile at him. I'm more than ready to talk about ghosts. The faster I can learn to protect myself from them, the faster I can get out of this place and get my life back.

Part III: Truths

Chapter Twenty-Two

Dr. Olivet takes his time getting a coffee with more bells and whistles than Dan's did. I'd rolled my eyes when Dan had given the barista his order. Why do people doctor the flavor of their coffee so heavily or drown it in whip cream? It ends up tasting nothing like it should.

Once he's settled and sipping his coffee, he smiles. "So, ghosts?"

Now, there's a loaded question if there ever was one. There's so much I want to ask him, but at the same time, I don't want to tell him the truth and have him laugh at me either. Where to start? How do I ask the questions I need to ask without sounding like I'm nuts? Dan kicks me under the table and I turn and glare at him. I know I'm gawking, but it's not every day I meet someone who has potential answers about my curse.

Dr. Olivet starts the conversation for me. "You said in your email you were working on a novel?"

I want to smack myself. I'd forgotten I'd told

him I was writing a novel and wanted some information to make the story more believable. This is perfect! I'm so brilliant I amaze even myself sometimes.

I nod. "Yeah. My main character can see ghosts. I don't mean see the outlines of ghosts out the corner of her eye, but actually *see* them. They are as clear to her as you are to me."

It's Dr. Olivet's turn to nod. "There are several cultures who believe in that, actually. It's a rare gift, but not unheard of, certainly."

"Really?" There were others who could do what I can? I'm so gonna have to go look up some more stuff. "I didn't think that was possible."

"You'd be amazed at what is possible in the world of the supernatural," he says. "The very fact that you even thought of it tells me you've either done a lot of research or you're more open to the supernatural than most."

"I Googled some stuff on ghosts, but what I can...what my character can do, well, I didn't find anything about that on the internet." Crap. I got so excited there for a second I almost slipped. Too much stuff to handle today.

"There's not a whole lot of information about that particular skill on the internet. I read about it in actual books." He grins at my involuntary cringe before continuing. "There are many theories about why people can see ghosts that range from sheer nonsense to very scientific explanations."

"So you believe people can see ghosts?" I ask him.

"Of course," he replies immediately. "The

degree to which we can see them is debatable, though. I've never actually met someone who could see them as an almost physical entity, but I've met enough people who see enough to prove to me they're the real deal."

"So it wouldn't be believable if my character could not only see them but talk to them too?"

"Ghosts can communicate with us." He takes another drink of his coffee, a calculating look in his eyes. "Everything in the universe is made up of energy, and in order for things to interact with other things, energy is needed and used. The same can be said of ghosts. They can communicate from the energy they've stored up. Once that energy is depleted, they need to recharge. I've seen things move, I've heard whispers in my ear, and I've recorded anomalies on camera. It's all just degrees of energy, so yes, it would make sense that your... character could sense when a ghost is trying to communicate with her."

"Okay, let's say that my character has a special gift that defies those laws. She can see ghosts clearly, have conversations with them, and they can physically touch her and cause her harm."

He stops sipping his coffee and just stares at me. It makes me extremely nervous. Dan inches closer, somehow sensing I need the support. He knows me so well, and I can't figure out how he does. Dr. Olivet sets his cup down and leans back, those eyes never leaving my face. They have gone past calculating to something very unusual. He looks like a kid who just got a brand new PS Vita for his birthday.

"Then I would say you are an extraordinary person, Mattie."

My mouth goes a little dry. There is no way he could... "Look, Dr. Olivet, this is all for my novel. I can't see ghosts."

Dr. Olivet smiles kindly at me. "Mattie, the first time I contacted my mentor, I didn't tell him I'd seen ghosts or felt them or anything like that. I simply told him I wanted some research for a psych paper I was working on. Your e-mail reminded me of the letter I sent to him. It was direct, to the point, and said nothing about your having experienced any of this yourself. *That* is why I contacted you. I suspected you were one of those people sensitive to the energies spirits give off. I'm not here to ridicule you, and if you are not comfortable talking about your gift, I understand. I want you to be able to ask me anything and I promise I will do my best to answer your questions."

Dan's hand grips mine and gives it a gentle squeeze. I latch on with a death grip. Dare I admit to this stranger that I can see ghosts? He doesn't look like he is mocking me. He seems sincere. Dan doesn't believe, me and I so very badly need someone to believe me. I didn't even realize that before this moment. Can I trust him, though?

"I understand this is hard for you, Mattie," Dr. Olivet tells me softly. "Do you want to tell me what happened in the auditorium? All my equipment lit up and then I saw your friend drag you out. What did you see?"

My fingers touch the throat again and I shrink back from the memory of those hands strangling

191

me. This man might be able to help me learn to protect myself from the random ghost attacks. He could also be a load of bumpkus just like Dan said. Is it worth the risk? The bruises on my neck say yes.

"There was a boy on the stage," I say hesitantly. "He came right at me and I made Dan get me out. We barely cleared the doors before he started choking me."

"You could feel his hands?"

"It was a little bit more than feel, Doc." I unzip my jacket and show him the fresh bruises on my neck. His eyes widen and he shifts closer.

"These weren't here before?"

"No," Dan tells him. "I've been with her for the past several hours, and I can say for a fact they weren't there before."

I glare at him. He sounds furious that he has to admit that.

"Don't be angry with him, little one," Dr. Olivet chuckles. "Facing the truth of ghosts can sometimes be more than most of us can handle."

"I'm not sure I buy that." Dan shakes his head.

"Then how did I get them, Officer Dan?" My voice has gone whisper soft, not a good sign. I know myself and I am nearing the point of hitting my friend.

"You were clutching your throat pretty tightly, Mattie. I couldn't pry your hands loose."

"So you think I did this to myself?"

Before Dan can answer, Dr. Olivet holds up his hand to interrupt. "Mattie, can you place your hands on your throat for me?"

"Why?" I frown.

"Please?"

Sighing, I do as he asks and that's when Dan swears softly. "What?" I ask.

"There is no way you could have made those marks," Dr. Olivet explains. "The finger impressions are twice as big as your own. Only a man could have done that to you."

Ah…the proverbial light bulb goes off and I smile, feeling vindicated. Dan only looks angrier. Maybe it really is too hard for him to believe, I realize, and my smile fades. He will never believe me. That hurts more than it should. After this is finished, Officer Dan and I are finished too. I can't let anyone get this close, not ever again. I don't do pain of any kind, especially the kind that lingers when it comes to emotions.

This is going to get us nowhere, and I came here for answers, not to convince Dan of anything he doesn't want to accept as truth. "Dr. Olivet, you said there different versions of how people can do what I can. Which one do you think is true?"

His brow arches at my change of subject, but he doesn't push. Smart man. Instead he answers me.

"I honestly think it comes down to what you believe, Mattie. Are you religious?"

"I don't go to church every Sunday, but I believe in God, if that's what you mean."

"Good, this will be much easier for you then." He smiles at me and takes another sip of his coffee. "A few years ago, I was helping out a friend in Scotland. He had the ruins of an abandoned monastery on his land. There were reports of ghosts haunting the property and he asked me to come take a look. He didn't mind the ghosts. He hoped they were there so he could use it as a lure to get more people to his small bed and breakfast."

"Were there any ghosts?" I ask, curious.

"Not a single one I could find," he laughs. "I still remember how upset old Pete was over the loss of his ghosts. I did find something, though. There was a small underground chamber that housed a library of just a few books. They were old, almost brittle, and it terrified me to pick them up. Pete let me have the books to study. I handed them over to the university in Wales and they translated the works for me. One volume in particular told a very interesting story."

Dan leans forward, his coffee forgotten. The doc is a great storyteller. He makes the most mundane statements sound interesting. I see why he's so popular. He's just that charismatic. Dan is evidence of this. He doesn't believe in ghosts, but even he can't dredge up his normal sarcasm. Instead he's hooked on the sound of the guy's voice as much as I am, and I'm sure everyone else who's ever heard him speak.

"We all know that according to scripture there is a day that is appointed for us to be born and a day appointed for us to die." He sets his cup down and leans back. "When we die we move on to the next plane of existence, or to Heaven, if you will. We've all heard people say that when we die, we see our loved ones. Maybe we do, maybe we don't, but according to the text, death comes to collect you. Not Death as in the Four Horsemen Death, but a reaper. He or she is there when you die so they can help ease your confusion and take you to the next plane."

"Kind of like the ferryman in mythology?" Dan asks, his curiosity getting the better of him.

"Every culture has some sort of reference to the reaper. This particular text I had translated talks about how reapers came to be. They are not angels, not in the sense we think of angels. They were in life ordinary people with an extraordinary gift. The gift activates when they die and are brought back to this plane of existence. They have the ability to see lost souls and help them move on to the next plane. Souls get trapped on earth for one reason or another and these special people help them to see that they are dead and need to move on."

Help the little buggers? They scare the crap out of me, and I'm supposed to help them? Not in this lifetime. No way am I opening myself up to that nonsense twenty-four seven. No freaking way. Hold up—did he say die?

"I've never died before," I tell him.

"Are you sure, Mattie? What about when you were little? Were you ever in an accident where your heart might have stopped even for a few seconds?"

Dan and I look at each other, both unwilling to say what we are thinking. I might have died when my mom tried to kill me. "I don't know, Doc," I tell him. "I don't remember a lot about my childhood."

"Okay." He nods. "Let me finish my story and then we can get back to that." The doc takes a long drink of his coffee and sets the cup down again before continuing.

"The book tells the story of a young woman, probably thirteen or fourteen. Her parents brought her to the abbey because she was talking to people who weren't there. They were afraid she was possessed and wanted to free her soul. Back then most of those poor people were put through treatments to cure them of their possession. They endured unspeakable horrors because of their gifts. This particular girl's name was Cathleen. She refused to admit she was possessed. She told the monks over and over that she was only trying to help someone. Brother Aien tried to stop the other monks from their torture. He believed the girl, but the others did not. She died at their hands. According to the journal I found of Brother Aien, Cathleen came to him in a dream bathed in the most beautiful white light. She thanked him for trying to stop her torture and told him not to worry, that he had helped her. She could now do in death what she was unable to do in life, to help the souls that came to her."

"What did she mean?" I ask.

"The people who are born with your gift, Mattie, become reapers when they die."

"What?" I gasp, startled. "I don't want to be a reaper." I can't help but remember the dream I had of that ugly thing in black coming for me while I was in the hospital. My first thought had been the Grim Reaper. I so am not becoming that thing.

Dr. Olivet laughs softly. "It's not what you're thinking, Mattie. You are imagining some dark creature, when in fact a reaper only comes to help people move on. They might even be able to take on the shape of a loved one to make it easier. It's nothing to be afraid of."

"No, you don't understand," I tell him, a little frantic. "I've seen a reaper, one almost attacked me in the hospital."

That gets his attention. "Tell me."

I tell him about the thing that had haunted me there. It may have been a dream, but it had felt real and I still can't shake it.

He is quiet for a long while before speaking again. He sounds a bit shaky. That is so not good.

"That wasn't a reaper, Mattie. That was a shade, or wraith as some people call them. Ghosts who have gone mad and hunt other souls. They are very, very dangerous, especially to people like you. They can feed off you as well since you are essentially made up of ghost energy."

"Come again?"

"That is how you can see them, talk to them, and interact with them. Your aura gives off a homing beacon for them. You are their comfort in a sea of confusion. You have the ability to calm them, to take away that confusion, and make them understand this is not where they belong. They need to move on. You can open the gateway to the next plane for them because of who you will one day be."

Flippin' fantastic! Not only do I have to deal with ghosts, I have to worry about shades who can eat me or something. How much weirder can I get? Wait, did he say gateway? The kitchen at the old lady's house had become a gateway, maybe?

"There's something else," I say hesitantly. "You

said I can open a gateway? I think I may have done that already accidentally." I tell him about what had happened in the kitchen, about the white fuzz bleeding over everything and about falling through the floor.

He swallows several times and reaches for his coffee, only to find it empty. He is staring at me like I've just sprouted horns and said I could fly. This can't be good to spook the spook doctor. Even Dan is staring at him askance.

"Mattie, you shouldn't be able to do that for years, if ever. You are seeing what is referred to as 'The Between.'"

"The Between?"

"It's a dark place where it's said the Shades reside. It's the space between this world and the next. Reapers guide souls through The Between safely to the other side. We must all pass through it to get to where we need to be."

Dan and I are both frowning now. That sounds beyond ridiculous. We've crept into some weird science fiction novel territory here.

"You've heard people who have had near-death experiences say they were in a tunnel and there was a bright light at the end of the tunnel? Some even said they saw loved ones waiting for them there. That bright light is The Between. The loved one is their reaper waiting to help them navigate the dangers of that place."

Well, that actually makes a little bit of sense. Everyone always talked about the white light, but no one had ever actually made it there before they were pulled back. Who's to say it isn't some dark, scary place?

"Mattie fell through the floor." Dan frowns. "Literally disappeared and then ended up in the basement."

"She shouldn't be able to even see it." Dr. Olivet frowns at us both. "Your gifts are highly advanced, which makes them dangerous. If you can travel The Between, it makes sense that ghosts can touch you. You have to be able to hold on to them as you both travel. This is very disturbing. I am going to make a few calls and see what I can find out. Mattie, if you see that again, I want you to run. Turn and run in the opposite direction as fast and as far as you can. There are things in there that make your deepest, darkest fears seem like a child's playroom."

His stare is intense and I can read the fear in his eyes. I had just scared him. I'm already scared to begin with, so he doesn't have to tell me twice. See the white snow, run. Check.

Dr. Olivet looks at his watch and frowns. "Mattie, I have to go. I've got a few things I need to do and appointments I can't blow off." He pulls out his card and writes something on the back. "Here, my home phone and cell are on the back. Call me anytime, day or night, if you need me. I'm here to help you, I promise you that."

"You really believe me?" I whisper as I take the card.

He smiles. "Of course. You're a very special young woman, Mattie. I will do everything I can to help you."

Dan and I follow him out of the coffee shop. We both need to get home. Dan looks thoughtful on the drive home and I don't push him. As much as I tell myself I am going to push him away, the very thought makes me cringe. What am I going to do about Officer Dan?

Chapter Twenty-Three

Dan lets me off at my house and I drag myself inside. My ankle is killing me and I have a headache. Dr. Olivet gave me a ton of things to think about and to scare me more than I already am. Like I need that?

It was an extremely uncomfortable ride home, to say the least. The silence bothered me. Usually I can count on Dan to be chatty, but I guess he got a few facts shoved in his face he couldn't ignore. He'll either accept them and me or not. I shouldn't care. I should call him and break things off with him right now. Break things off? I laugh out loud. It sounds like we're dating, but we are not. I'm not sure what we are doing, honestly. Another reason to push him away. He's dangerous to my heart.

No one is home. There is a note from Mrs. O on the fridge. She's out with the little kids and to find myself something to eat. She's probably pissed. I was supposed to be home hours ago to watch the little kids so she could go shopping today. It's Friday, so she probably took them with her. I know she promised to let them see that new 3D cartoon in the theaters, so they probably ended up there. I'm gonna get yelled at when she gets home, though.

I grab a cold Coke from the fridge and confiscate last night's leftover baked chicken and rice before heading upstairs to my room. Setting the plate on my bed, I grab my laptop off the desk and then settle back against my pillows. My foot is throbbing, but I forgot to get the Motrin downstairs. I don't feel like walking all the way back down there and making my ankle hurt worse. I'll just wait and see if it gets better.

My phone buzzes and I look to see a text from Mason telling me to call him or he's gonna keep text stalking me till I do. I shake my head. That boy. I've only just met him, but I really, really like him. I feel guilty for it too. Technically, Jake and I haven't broken up, but it *feels* like we broke up. The urge to cry is gone, at least, which bothers me too. I thought Jake might be the perfect guy for me. He saw me and didn't judge, or didn't until he saw my classic Mattie moves. Hit first and ask questions later. I don't think I'll ever be able to break that habit. You learn it early enough and it stays with you. I learned it at the age of five, so…that's just a part of me. Period.

One thing's certain; I'm completely screwed up emotionally and mentally. Maybe Dan's right and I only convinced myself I can see ghosts. I've had a pretty messed-up life. The shrinks all agreed it wouldn't be unusual for me to make up scenarios that are beyond belief to help my mind make sense of what's happened to me growing up. Not that I ever told them I could see ghosts, mind you, but it was something they always talked to me about. I drew some pretty creepy stuff as a kid. They told me it was my way of manifesting my fears. Maybe my seeing dead people is just an outlet for me. Maybe they aren't real. Maybe it's just me being crazy.

My hand comes up to my throat. The bruises are real, though. Even Dan admitted that, but he also said he had a hard time getting my hands away from my throat. Could I have done that to myself? Maybe I'd shifted my hands around enough to make the impressions bigger or something?

I can't do this to myself. *I* know ghosts are real and I'm letting Dan make me rethink everything. No. I refuse to change who I am just for him. I don't think he'll ever accept that I do see ghosts, and *that* means he'll never be able to accept me. Okay, fine. I'll figure out what happened to Sally *and* I'll help Mary, I'll just do it *my* way. I've never needed anyone before, and I don't need anyone now. I don't.

I call Dan's number and it goes straight to voicemail. Figures. "Hey, it's me. I've been thinking. I don't think we should hang out anymore, Dan. You can't believe in me, and I know it's not your fault, but I need someone who does. I trusted you enough to tell you my secret, and I don't trust anyone. That's why I need you to believe me. If you can't, I understand, but I just wanted to call and say thanks and to tell you good-bye."

He said he'd never leave me. He promised me. I guess I'll see if he lets me push him away. Part of me hopes he shows up and tells me I can't get rid of him, and the other part that is attuned to survival says good riddance to the pain he's caused me. He doesn't care as much as he says he does or he'd believe me, no questions asked. He should believe me. Tears well up and my chest hurts. It feels like I can't breathe and I choke back a sob. I hate feeling like this.

I grab my sketch book from where I'd let it fall on the floor and start to draw. I lose myself in the images that come to mind as I put them down on paper. Pain, grief, anger, frustration, they all come out onto the pages. I look up a little later and am surprised to see it's almost ten o'clock. I'd been drawing for hours. Then I check my phone. No texts or voicemails from Officer Dan. I had several from Mason, but not the one person I needed one from. I sigh and rub my eyes. They are bleary from crying and from staring at my sketchpad for so long.

Now that I'm not concentrating on my drawing, I realize my foot is still throbbing. Time to buck up and head downstairs to find the Motrin. Hopefully Mrs. O has already gone to bed and I don't have to hear her yell until in the morning. Not that I don't deserve it, but I'd rather it waited until in the morning when I'll have enough time to get my walls back up. I feel a little too raw right now to deal with anything.

I wince and mutter all the way down the stairs. Mrs. O keeps all the meds not in the medicine cabinet in the bathroom, but in a small kitchen cabinet over the fridge. You have to climb on a chair to reach it. She said it was so the little kids couldn't get into it. Makes sense, but it just irritates me at the moment because I have to drag a chair over and hop up. The phone starts to ring while I dig through the cabinet and I ignore it. The machine will pick it up. The bottle is all the way in the back. Figures. Nothing is easy today.

There it is. I pop the top and count out three pills. I know you're only supposed to take two at a time, but between the nasty headache I'd gotten over the last hour and my ankle, I need more than two. It's been a really long day.

I hear the beep as I jump down and then sort-of listen to the message until I actually hear what it's saying. My mouth drops open and I almost fall flat on my face. No way. I run over to the machine and hit 'play.'

Before I can skip all the old messages, I see something I'd given up hope of seeing again.

Sally.

She's standing in the doorway, directly to my left, wearing the same old ratty night shirt I'd seen her in before, hands tied behind her back and gagged. The bullet hole in her head glares at me. I thought maybe she'd gone on to…well, to wherever ghosts go, but she didn't. Instead, she's staring at me in confusion. I don't think she knows she's dead. Sometimes ghosts don't realize they died. I can't count the times they've screamed at the people around them to look at them. It's kind of sad, but freaky.

I approach slowly, not wanting to scare her, and stop about a foot away. She's always been skittish, so I figure ghost-Sally still is. Her eyes dart everywhere. They are wide with shock and horror. I can so relate right now.

"Sally?" I whisper. "Can you hear me?"

She focuses on me and nods. She tries to yank her hands loose, but it's no use. Whoever did this used duct tape and that is not something she could break when she was alive, let alone dead.

"Do you remember what happened to you?" I ask her softly.

Her eyes close, and when she opens them, they are swimming with tears. Ghosts can cry. Most people don't realize they can, but hey, why not? Like the doc said, it's all about energy and perception, so if Sally wants to cry, she can. She *does* know what happened to her, even if she doesn't know she's dead.

"Where are you, Sally? Can you tell me where you are so I can find you?"

She frowns at me. Ghosts can also be easily confused. This I know from experience. They are always mumbling and ranting about how they were just at one place and somehow ended up in another.

The air around us drops to freezing and I shiver. Sally looks around, her fear starting to overwhelm her. I can see ice start to form on the windows over the sink. Nails on a chalkboard start to screech in my head. Mirror Boy! Oh, no you don't. Not this time. You will not stop me from helping Sally and those kids!

"Think, Sally," I tell her urgently. "Where did you get hurt?"

Her eyes are wild and crazy. Mirror Boy must scare her pretty badly too. "Show me," I say. "Please, Sally, help me find you."

She nods and disappears, only to reappear at the kitchen door and then she goes through it. I blink back tears as the screeching in my head gets worse, and I run for the door, ignoring the pain in my ankle as I run after Sally. She's standing in the driveway. As soon as I get near her, she moves again, reappearing further up the road. The farther from the house I get, the less pain I feel in my head. Thank God for small miracles. I limp for maybe half a mile or so, darting through a small park as I follow Sally.

We end up in the one place I never even thought of.

Hartford House.

It had shut its doors about three years ago. It used to be a state group home until it was closed due to some pretty nasty things that were happening to the kids there. The building itself was three stories, and the ramshackle look made it look like a haunted house straight out of a Stephen King novel. The windows are boarded up; shutters hang off their hinges and the paint has grayed and is peeling. Spookville. I *so* do not want to go back in there, but Sally is patiently waiting at the steps for me. I've come this far. I can't let her down now.

Instead of going into the house, Sally moves from the steps and starts for the side. Where is she going? I dodge around to the back and see Sally roam over to an old shed. Her body's stashed in a shed? It's not locked so I pull it open, muttering because I don't have a flashlight. There's enough moonlight to see by, though. I swallow hard at the sight that greets me.

It's Mary's canary yellow bike.

My fingers run over it gently and I reach for my phone in the back pocket. I have to call Dan. He needs to get here right now. I frown as I search my pockets then slap myself. It's still on the bed. I hadn't put it back in my pocket after calling Dan the first time. Flipping fantastic.

"Great, Mattie," I mutter. "Now you're going to have to go back to the house and call Officer Dan."

"I don't think so." I hear the soft whispered words right before I feel the whack to my head and then it goes dark.

Chapter Twenty-Four

Pain explodes in my head the second I become aware again. The back of my skull throbs like nobody's business. It feels like someone took a hammer and hit me as hard as they could and then decided it was not enough to hit me once, but continued to do so over and over. I groan and reach up to rub the agonizing pulse point.

But my arms won't move.

I pull at them, hard, but they are frozen in place. Well, not exactly. I can move my fingers. I stretch them and then mold them to the surface they are lying on. Wood. It feels like the arms of a chair. I glance down to see and realize that I can't open my eyes. Panic creeps in and I take a deep breath to calm myself, but find it doesn't work when I can't move my legs or stand up.

Panicking is not good, Mattie, I tell myself and try to remember what happened. Had I been in an accident? Am I lying in a hospital bed right now hooked up to tubes and wires stuck in coma-land? That would be just my luck, especially since I found Sally…oh holy crap!

Sally. She'd shown me Mary's bike and then... then... I'd heard someone whisper and...*they hit me!* Holy crap!

No, no, no, no, no. This can't be happening. Had the killer nabbed *me*? Please not that. Not *me*. I try again to move, but can't. I rotate my arms a little and feel the abrasive texture of a thick rope around my wrists. I'm literally helpless.

Don't panic, Mattie, I tell myself. *Calm down, focus. You will get out of this.*

But how? A bitter laugh bubbles up. I try taking a few deep breaths and gag. The smell of mildew and stagnant water invades my mouth. Don't throw up! For just a moment I am back in that New Orleans apartment with my Mom, fending off water and the occasional rat that floated in. I hated that place. *You're not there*, I reassure myself and shove that memory to the back of my mind. I have worse things to concentrate on right now.

"Hello?" I call out, grateful my mouth hasn't been taped shut. I am not sure why, but then the killer hadn't taped up Mary's mouth either. It was only Sally I saw with tape over her mouth now that I think about it. He hadn't taped up any of the other kids' mouths. Strange.

Silence greets me. I expect that anyway. Psycho killers tend to play with their victims. At least they do in the TV shows I love to watch. I listen instead, but the only thing I hear is the sound of my own breathing. There's a slight shuffling off to the right of me and I flinch. It's a sound I know well.

Rats. I hate rats. When I was seven, my foster family decided I needed to learn to do as I was told.

They locked me in the basement for two days with no shoes or socks. It was dark, cold, and infested with those little beady-eyed monsters. For two days, I fought them off, felt them make a meal of me, crawl all over me. I'd had nightmares for years, still do sometimes. The scars on my feet are a constant reminder of them, and it's a fear I've never been able to shake. I can hear them now, scuttling back and forth. I can't fight them this time if they decide I'm supper. I'm tied down to a chair and no one knows I'm here. I have never felt so helpless in my entire life.

No. You are not helpless, Mathilda Louise Hathaway. You are stronger than this. I tell myself this over and over, making myself breathe in and out slowly. I calm down and take stock of my situation. Okay, my hands and legs are tied to the chair. I lean forward, and much to my amazement, find that I *can* lean forward. While I might have my appendages tied up, my attacker didn't see fit to strap a rope around my upper chest. This could be good. He'd tied a rope around my chest right at elbow level only to keep my hands and arms from moving. I lean forward as far as possible. Almost! I can almost reach the ropes around my wrists. If I can get to them, I can pull at the ropes around my wrists hard enough with my teeth to loosen them— *and* pull one of my hands loose.

I'm mere inches away from the ropes when I hear the footsteps. They are heavy and loud, coming toward me. I sit up, not wanting him to realize what I'm up to. A door creaks open somewhere near my left and he's in the room moving about, not saying anything, and then he stops. The utter silence is deafening. I can't even hear him breathing. Where is he? I strain my ears, trying to pick up any sound, but there is nothing. Why did he stop moving? Is he behind me? In front of me? I can't see and I can't hear anything. It's driving me a little mad the longer I sit here trying to hear any sort of sound.

A thump sounds directly to my right and I jump, trying to shift in that direction. The ropes prevent me from moving very much, but I try. The silence is driving me insane. It's the not knowing. *That's* what's terrifying me. I can't see him or hear him. I don't know what he's doing, or what he's planning. Why isn't he talking to me? Shouldn't he be laughing or taunting me? This isn't like the shows I watch on TV. This is scary and he's not behaving like the psychotics on those shows I watch. He's silent and this is a torture all its own, not knowing what he is going to do or when he's going to do it.

"Mr. Olson?"

Maybe if I talk to him, he'll talk to me. Anything is better than this silence.

"I know it's you, Mr. Olson. I heard…I heard the message your friend left you on the answering machine."

I can hear the message playing over and over in my head…

"Hey, Henry, it's me. I need you to do me a favor. Clock in for me tomorrow like I did for you a couple weeks back. Lynn wants to meet up and the wife can't know. Thanks, buddy."

I hadn't been able to get that message out of my head the entire time I followed Sally. I still can't quite believe it. Sure, Mr. Olson is quiet, and has a temper sometimes when the kids don't pick up their toys, but this? A cold-blooded killer? I never suspected. Then again, it's *always* the quiet ones you have to worry about.

I hear something scrape across the floor behind me. What is he doing?

"Mr. Olson? Please talk to me. You're really scaring me."

I strain my ears and that is when I hear it. It's so soft I would have missed it had I not been listening so hard. Just behind me and to my left, I hear a soft whimper. Mary? Could she still be alive? I hear a heavy thud, and the soft whimper turns into a low muted scream. Her voice is hoarse and barely above a whisper, but I can hear it. Dear God, what is he doing to her? Footsteps walk away from the whimpers and then I can hear him rifling through metal. I know its metal because I can hear the clanging. He has to be looking through his torture tools. They always have torture tools. Remembering all the dead kids who came to me the last few weeks and their mangled states, I don't want to think about it, but I can't stop thinking about it. Images of broken, bloody body parts keep flashing through my mind. Mirror Boy's mangled, unrecognizable face has a starring role. Is he doing that to Mary? Is he going to do that to *me*?

I have to get out of here. I pull futilely at the restraints holding me. They are tied very tight. He knows how to tie a knot.

More screams assault my ears and I cringe. I yank harder, but to no avail. I can't take the screams anymore. She won't stop. What is he doing to her?

"Stop it!" I yell. "Leave her alone!"

But it doesn't stop. I can't block it out. All I want to do is put my hands over my ears and cry. Her screaming is hoarse, low, and barely recognizable, but I can hear it. My ears are picking up the smallest sounds now that my eyes can't see. I can smell the tinny fragrance of blood as well. How much more can she take? I scream in sheer rage. There is nothing I can do and it makes me furious.

"You are nothing but a coward!" I shout, anger and bitterness dripping from my voice. "Why don't you hurt someone who can hurt you back?"

Silence. Dead silence. It's as if all the sound has been sucked out and I'm left in a vacuum. Even Mary's whimpers have ceased. Guess he didn't like hearing the truth. Then he moves, his footsteps carrying him behind me. I can hear the metal clanking of tools being sorted through. My throat tightens. I think I made him really, really mad. At least he stopped hurting Mary.

I feel it then, the icy cold that accompanies a ghost, only this time it's magnified, the cold so deep it seeps into my bones, filing me up. I can feel them around me, whispering softly, but I can't make it out. The temperature in the room has to have dropped a good twenty degrees or more. It's freezing. I wonder if Mr. Olson can feel it, or if it's just me. I hope to God he can feel it and he knows it's the ghosts of everyone he's murdered.

He's moving again, coming closer to me.

I tense and the cold intensifies. They can see what he's doing, and I can't. It's almost like they are trying to help me, to comfort me. Oh, God, what is he going to do to me?

He stops next to me and I cringe. Why can't I learn to keep my mouth shut? I smell the bitter scent of his sweat mingled with Mary's blood. It makes me nauseated, and I try to control my gag reflex. He runs a gloved finger down my arm and I flinch. The leather is warm against my cold flesh. The finger retraces its path back up my arm, my neck, and finally coming to rest against my lips. I move my head away, but he grabs my hair and yanks it hard, holding my head still. I can't turn away from the exploration of his fingers against my face.

"Don't touch me you filthy, nasty pedophile!" I scream. I can hear the fear in my voice. I can't stop him and I hate it.

"Shut up," I hear the whisper. *"Don't make it worse."*

Mirror Boy? He's here? "Eric?" I whisper.

Mr. Olson's hands still at my whisper. His hand in my hair tightens, his grip beyond brutal.

"Hush, Mattie. Just stay still and it'll be over soon, I promise."

"I don't want to die, Eric."

"We're here with you." That's Emma, the little girl from the bathroom. I recognize her voice.

"You're not alone." A dozen or more voices whisper that over and over...*you're not alone.*

I spent my life pretending they didn't exist, and now, in my moment of need, they're here for me. Guilt floods me. I ran from them, and they are trying to comfort *me.*

"I'm sorry," I say. "I'm sorry I didn't help you."

The first hit comes in response to my words. It's just a slap really, but a hard one. I taste blood. Part of the blow landed on my lip, and it split. Another blow lands, this time his fist. Then another and another. He never moves his hand from my hair, keeping my face upturned and immobile. He's breathing hard now. This excites him. I feel sick knowing my pain is how he gets his kicks.

"It's almost over," Eric whispers in my ear at the same time Mr. Olson releases me. Pain explodes in first one hand and then the other. He's hit my hands with something big like a sledgehammer. The pain radiates up my arms. I can't move my fingers. I think he broke them. I just want it to stop, please make it stop. There are small sounds coming out of my mouth, sounds I didn't even know I could make. The pain is unbearable. His hands wrap around both of mine and squeeze. The pain overwhelms me and then the darkness claims me.

Chapter Twenty-Five

The cool cloth feels good against my aching face. I sigh in appreciation before I remember why my face hurts. Oh God, oh God, oh God…

"Shh, it's okay, Mattie. I'm right here, honey."

Mrs. O? I try to move, and pain vibrates throughout my entire body. I then suck in a breath to keep from screaming at the agony that tears through my hands.

"Be still, Mattie," she fusses. "I'm trying to clean you up, honey." Another swipe of the wet cloth goes over my face directly under the blindfold.

"Mrs. O?" I shake my head, trying to clear the last of the fuzziness from my mind. "What…"

"I tried so hard to keep you safe, but you just wouldn't listen to me," she interrupts. "If you'd only left it alone, Mattie, you wouldn't be here. He's wanted you in this chair from the moment he saw you, and *I* protected you. Why couldn't you leave it be?"

It takes a minute for me to sort through what she's just said, but when I do, my mouth drops

217

open. Mrs. O knew about Mr. Olson? They were in it together? The headache from earlier bursts behind my eyes with a vengeance as I try to understand that the person I have grown to depend on is one of the reasons I'm in this chair, broken and bleeding.

"Why?" I ask her, barely able to force the words out of my swollen lips. "I thought you cared about me." She betrayed me just like everyone else I've ever cared about. "You were supposed to take care of me."

She slaps me hard. "I *have* taken care of you! All I've done since you walked in my door is take care of you. I made sure you were fed, had clean clothes, a hot meal, and that you had a decent place to sleep every night. I sat with you in the hospital praying you were okay. I care, Mattie, about all my kids. Don't you dare accuse me of not caring about you! I've worked hard to protect you, but even I can't stop it now. It's too late."

I feel a pinprick in my upper arm and then a rush of fluid. What did she give me?

"You'll feel better in a few minutes, honey. It'll help with the pain. Don't tell him I gave it to you. He likes you alert, but I can't let you suffer like the rest. I won't."

If I could open my eyes, I know the room would be spinning. I *feel* dizzy. The pain is dulling already. Whatever she gave me works fast, but I'm sleepy. I can't pass out, not yet, not until I talk to her.

"Please, Mrs. O, I'm sorry. I promise I'll be good. Please, please just get me out of here." I can hear the tears in my voice. "I'll do whatever you want me to, just please don't leave me here."

She sighs, and when she speaks, there are tears in her own voice and my heart sinks. "I can't, Mattie. If I let you go now, then you'll go straight to that police officer you are friends with. I can't let you hurt him. He means everything to me. I'm sorry."

Her warmth fades and I know she's stepped away from me. Desperation claws at me. "Please, Mrs. Olson! Please don't leave me here!"

"I'm sorry. I have to go now, Mattie."

After the door opens and closes, I give in to a fit of tears. I'm going to die down here. The soft scurrying of tiny little feet catches my attention again. Rats. They must smell the blood. I don't know if Mary is on the ground or if she's even alive anymore, but the thought of the vermin munching on her makes me shudder.

The slightest movement of my fingers brings about another round of agony. I breathe in and out slowly to get through the pain. The injection Mrs. O. gave me is helping, but it still hurts like the devil. What am I going to do? All the hopelessness I'd felt earlier swamps me again. No one knows where I am. The Olsons will say they came home to find me missing and that I'd run away. I let out a bitter laugh. I have a track record of running away, so it won't be a stretch to believe it. I'd even called Dan to say we shouldn't see each other anymore, like I was saying good-bye.

How stupid can I be? I let my insecurities rule me once again and it might have cost me my life this time. Classic Mattie move. I groan in sheer frustration. Mrs. O? I still can't wrap my head around it. I honestly never suspected her. She seemed to care about us too much. I thought she cared about me. I don't know, maybe she *does* in her own sick, twisted way, but that doesn't mean I am not going to do some serious harm to her when I get out of this—*if* I get out of this, I remind myself.

My head is getting fuzzier by the minute. There's no way I can loosen the ropes if I fall asleep, but I can't just sit here and do nothing, either. Where are the ghosts when you need them?

Maybe if I call for them?

"Eric? Emma?" My voice is little more than a whisper. One of the blows had caught me in the throat. I'm guessing it's swollen and that's part of why it's so hard to speak. I noticed the tenderness earlier when I'd been talking to Mrs. O, but it seems to be getting worse now. The talking probably aggravated it.

"Please," I try again. "Are you here?" A cough escapes me. The more I speak, the worse it gets.

The cold slams into me, seeps into my bones. The suddenness of it leaves me breathless. I'm so cold it hurts. My mind goes fuzzier and I know I'm so close to passing out it's not even funny. I don't know if it's because I'm in that place between sleep and awareness or something else, but I can feel them. It's not just Eric and Emma. There are more here, so many more that I can feel the ache settle in my bones and stay there. My teeth start to hurt from the sheer cold that is bleeding into my body. I can separate them in my head. There has to be over a dozen ghosts here. Dear God, how many people have they killed?

"Eric?"

"Hush," he whispers. *"They're not gone. Don't make them come back and hurt you again."*

"Eric, you have to help me," I say, desperation clear in my voice. For once, I don't care how pathetic I sound. I need him to help me.

He sighs. I feel it against my ear. *"I don't know how."*

"You have to get help," I say. My throat burns.

"How?" he asks. *"No one can see me but you. How can I help you?"* He sounds as miserable as I feel.

"You're a ghost, Eric. Ghosts are made up of energy. All you have to do is focus that energy to make someone see. Find Officer Dan. Use the computer, something to tell him where we are. Tell him we are at the Hartford House."

The door opens. I can hear the thud of boots. He's back. "Please, Eric!"

The cold intensifies and I understand why. They are afraid of Mr. Olson too. They are manifesting their fear as the cold.

He comes to stand beside me. His hands lift up my face. He's wearing gloves. Heavy work gloves made of that scratchy material I hate. His fingers brush lightly over my swollen face, admiring his handiwork. I spit at him.

"Don't," I hear the ghosts wail in unison. Too late. He hits me again and then caresses the spot, almost apologizing with his touch. One hand trails down my face, my neck, and then to my arm. The arm that has a needle mark on it. He pauses and I can feel the anger radiating off of him. He's figured

out Mrs. O. gave me something.

He moves away, going behind me. His torture rack must be back there. It's where he'd gone earlier to find his tools. There's no noise, though. He's not rummaging around. Maybe he's looking at them, trying to make up his mind about what to use? I wish I could see. At least then I'd know what was coming. I shake my head, trying to clear it. I'm so sleepy, but *must* stay awake. I don't know what he'll do to me while I'm passed out. *Please, God*, I pray, *please don't let me pass out*.

The thud of his boots move again, only away from me. They are heading toward where Mary is. At least where I *think* Mary is. What is he going to do to her? I hear the sound of sawing, but nothing else. She's dead. My heart sinks. If she is alive, she'd be making some kind of noise. It isn't fair. I tried so hard to find her, to save her, and I couldn't.

I hear a loud thump. I want to gag. It's the sound of a body falling. He's just throwing her away, like she's yesterday's garbage. I hear the sound of running water—no, wait...It's spraying like the water hose we have outside does when Mrs. O. waters her flowers. He's cleaning something. Maybe whatever he had Mary tied down to? Why would he be cleaning it? The answer pops into my mind as soon as I ask the question. He's cleaning it for me.

The water shuts off and then I hear the sound of a knife being sharpened. I recognize it because I'd seen Mr. Olson sharpening the kitchen knives last week. He's going to cut me. I know this, I try to prepare myself for this, but I can't. I'm terrified of knives. Ever since my mom, I can't bring myself to even pick one up for longer than a few seconds. Fear coils in my stomach, knotting it up. Not a knife. Anything but a knife.

He walks toward me; the steps are slow. My breathing is ragged, labored from the intense terror the thought of the knife is causing. He cuts through the bonds on my hands and then moves to my feet. I try to kick out, to hit him, but I can't. My body is stiff and sore, my muscles refusing to work. I'm not sure how long I've been tired up or if the shot Mrs. O gave me is helping to keep me docile, but there's nothing I can do as he hauls me up and drags me by the hair over the floor. I'm hoisted up onto a table. It's cold like steel. He grabs my wrists and wraps rope around them both, tying them tightly. I scream at the pain. He pulls my hands above my head and then secures them to something I can't see, but when he's done, they are pulled so tight I can't even move them. The pain is agonizing.

My feet are next. He ties them spread-eagle to the table. Is he going to rape me now? My mind shudders away from that, but then I feel the tip of the knife. It's pressing against my throat. He skims it up my face, traces my lips with it. I can't move, I can't breathe. Panic is choking me. The knife blade moves down, the edge catching on my t-shirt, slicing it open. I feel the cold air against my skin. The blade presses down, making a shallow cut right above my left breast where it peeks out of the top of my bra. I scream. I can't help it. I'm terrified. I haven't been this afraid since I saw my mom swinging a knife at me. *Please pass out, please pass*

223

out, please pass out, I chant.

The blade continues down my abdomen, making shallow cuts as he goes. I'm crying now, begging him to stop, to please stop. He ignores me, the knife continuing its exploration of my body. He stops to inflict a deeper cut above my right knee. His fingers probe the cut, pushing deep so it bleeds more. I twist, trying to buck him off, but there's little I can do. He's tied my hands and feet so I can barely move. He seems to know it's driving me past the point of fear into cliff-jumping terror.

Then he stops. I hear him step away. What is he doing? Where did he go? Music fills the room. It's dark and somber. I'm not prepared for the jet of cold water that hits me square on the belly. I jump, causing more agony to tear through my hands as I pull at them. The water pressure is on full force and it hurts as it makes contact with my skin. It stops then another blast hits me on my thighs and then another on my chest. He continues until I'm soaked, shaking from cold, bleeding from over a dozen shallow cuts, and crying.

I rear up as far as I can when his hands clutch mine and squeeze. The pain is intense, more intense than my body can handle, and for once I welcome the darkness that swallows me.

Chapter Twenty-Six

I'm groggy, but the steady drip, drip, drip wakes me. It must be either a sink or the water hose. I hurt everywhere. I try to move, but I'm tied down too tight. I listen for Mr. Olson, but I can't hear anything. He might be gone, but then again he might be waiting. The ghost chill is still here, so I know I'm not alone, at least. I still can't believe they are here for me, trying to comfort me after the way I've treated them all these years. They actually give me strength.

The knife had reduced me to a blubbering fool. I can still feel it against my skin, slicing here and there. As much as I hate admitting the weakness, I can't stop the shudder from running through me. I have to get out of here before he uses that knife again. I need help, though.

I try to speak, but can't. My throat is too swollen. I can barely draw in a breath. So not good. *Think, Mattie.* Dr. Olivet said I was connected to them, that my energy was a beacon for them. Thoughts are a form of energy. Maybe I don't have to speak for them to hear me. Ridiculous, but who knows?

"Emma, Eric, can you hear me?" my mind sends.

Silence. I try again. *"Can any of you hear me? I can't speak, but know you're here. I can feel you. Please say you can hear me."*

The cold presses closer. I can feel it start to crystalize on me. Maybe they can hear me after all. *"I know you're scared. I'm scared. Will you talk to me? Please?"*

"We tried to warn you, to stop you." was the answer.

Yes! They can hear me. I don't recognize the voice, though. It's no one I've talked to before. *"What's your name?"*

"I'm Tina." She sounds older.

"Tina, I need you to help me get out of here," I begin.

"How?" is her tentative question.

I have nothing to lose. Just tell her. *"I need to get the ropes loosened enough so that I can work my hands free. Can you do that? I know it's hard, that it requires a lot of energy to make things move, but together, can you do it?"* If I could get enough breath, I'd be holding it, waiting for the answer.

"I have tried, but I can't. We all have tried so many times for so many others. We can't."

I groan—very softly, since my throat hurts. So, they're ghosts. I can't expect much from them because they're confused and scared. Asking them to move something would be hard, let alone trying to untie me. It would probably require more energy than they all had put together. Okay, so there went plan A. On to plan B. What *is* plan B? I don't have a clue.

"Do you see us? Emma said you could." It's a little boy this time, but I don't know how old he is. *"She said you saw the scary place, the white place."*

Right. The Between? I saw it once. Where is the kid going with this? Dr. Olivet told me to run from it if I ever saw it again, that there were things in it that were not so nice. Then again, I'm trapped in a place that's not so nice at the moment too. I think back to when I'd seen it. I'd fallen from the upstairs down to the basement. Literally went through the floor. Could I do that again? Could I move from one place to another by going into all that white fuzz? It might get me out of the bonds holding me too. Then again, I might get trapped in the dirt. I'd fallen before and am pretty sure I'm in the basement. Crap. There's nowhere else *to* fall.

"No, Bobby, she'll get hurt," That was Tina. *"There are things there, things that will hurt us. Eric said so."*

Oh, really? Mirror Boy told them not to go there? They have to go there to cross over to the other side. Who does he think he is, denying them their right to cross over? I'll tell them.

"Bobby, Tina, the white place is scary, but someone is there to help you, to guide you," I tell them, remembering what I'd learned from Dr. Olivet. *"Did you see someone waiting for you?"*

"I thought I saw my grandma," Bobby says, *"but Eric said it was a trick. He said the bad things wanted to eat us."*

I couldn't argue with Bobby there. The bad

things might want to eat us, but his guide would have protected him. At least if I believe the doc's theory. Maybe I do. All I want is to get these kids to cross over, to give them some peace. Well, I want that after *I* get out of here. Next question.

"Bobby, how do I find the scary place?"

"Don't tell her anything," Tina hisses. *"Eric will be mad."*

Oh, yeah? Good. *"Where is Eric?"* I ask them.

"He went to find your friend, the one who's a cop." I catalogue the new voice. It's a guy, in his late teens, maybe. His voice is deeper than some of the other kids. He also sounds like he has an attitude.

"Who are you?" I ask, hoping I have some attitude left.

"Ricky," he tells me. *"Tina's right. You need to stay out of the Between. Bad stuff in there."*

And bad stuff isn't *here*? *"I'll take my chances, Ricky. I just need to be there long enough to take a couple steps and move away from the table."*

"No, no. You got no idea what's in there, chica. A few seconds is all it takes for them to eat your soul. That's what they want, you know. Your soul. I tried to go in once, to leave this place, but those... things... they almost got me. Eric saved me. He saved us all. You need to listen to Tina."

"Noted," I tell him. *"I am still going to try it. Can you tell me how to find it?"*

Silence. No one wants to tell me. Maybe if I can make them remember what happened *here*, they'll start talking.

"You guys are scared of Mr. Olson, right?" I

feel the cold burn my skin, it intensifies so fast. *"You remember sitting in that chair, being tied to this table? You remember not being able to see what he was doing, waiting to feel what new horror he'd think of? You remember what he did to you while you were tied up and helpless? Do you? What if someone gave you a choice of escaping, even if it meant you might find something just as deadly waiting for you? Would you choose to fight or just sit here and wait to die? I don't want to die. Please, please help me."*

A chorus of voices starts hammering away at me. My head hurts and it makes it harder to filter them. I think they're arguing, but I can't tell. I can feel their terror. I made them think about things they didn't want to, and it hurts to remember those things. I hate that I did that to them, but I need to get out of here.

"Be quiet!" The awful screeching of nails on chalkboards assaults us all.

Oh, goody, Mirror Boy is back. My head hurts enough without his particular brand of torture. It scatters my thoughts and the pain is almost as unbearable as the pain in my hands.

Silence settles once more and the nails stop raking hot coals across my battered mind. Finally, I can think again. *"Eric, did you find Dan?"*

"Yes, but I don't know if it helped. I did everything I could, Mattie. He doesn't believe in us like you do." Eric did not sound happy.

I sigh, knowing it had been a long shot to begin with. Dan would refuse to see anything supernatural if it hit him in the face with a big neon sign that said *ghost.* Back to plan B where I save myself with a little ghostly help. Here goes. *"How do I get to the Between?"*

"Mattie..." The screeching edges into Eric's voice.

"No," I cut off Mirror Boy. *"I am not just going to lie here and die if I can do something about it. I know the risks, I know what's in there, and I'm willing to take that chance, Eric. I need to find it."*

"Okay. It's the cold," he says at last. *"Concentrate on the cold, on looking for where it comes from and it will find you. You have to want to see it."*

I think back to my one encounter with it. I hadn't been feeling cold at all. What is Eric talking about? Well, fudgepops! I know for a fact I hadn't felt any ghost cold when I'd seen it. What had I felt? We'd been talking about my extra-curricular criminal activities. I remember Dan had felt sorry for me and it brought back a lot of memories too. I'd been scared and alone, trying to survive. I'd lived in a cold harsh world then...cold. Eric's not talking about ghost cold. He's talking about emotions. Ghosts manifest emotions with the cold. Eric said I had to really want it. I want it. So I force myself to think back to my time as a thief. I remember how I'd gone to bed hungry almost every night until I started stealing. I'd hated doing it, but it had been me or them back then. Shame also floods through me. What I'd done wasn't right, still isn't. I haven't ever done it since, but the guilt is something I can't shake.

"It's working," Eric hisses. *"I see it coming.*

Everyone get out of here now!"

The ghost cold dissipates, all except for one. *"Eric?"*

"I'm here," he whispers. *"I won't leave you, Mattie. It's at your feet. Can you feel it?"*

I concentrate, trying to sense anything but Eric and my own fear. There. The pain I remember is starting to eat its way up my body, like a live flame is burning me from my toes up. It hurts so much, but I welcome it this time; I don't try to fight it. I can't breathe when it reaches my face, it's burning me alive. The pain goes up my arms and then I hear the door open. No…

The feeling of the snow goes away and I groan in frustration. Eric does the same. So close, we were so close.

The door closes with a bang and my body focuses on that one sound. Fear pushes every other thought out of my mind.

He's back.

Chapter Twenty-Seven

The movements I hear are lighter, softer. It has to be Mrs. O. I hear the water turn on and then she's moving all around the room. She's muttering as she works, which only confirms my suspicions about who it is. She sounds frustrated. If I can get loose and distract her, then maybe I can get away. Maybe we don't need to try the scary snow after all.

"Mrs. O?" My words come out slow and slurred. My face feels like it's ballooned up and my throat continues to swell. It might cut off my windpipe soon. I remember the feel of being choked to death earlier today by the ghost at UNC. This feeling is remarkably similar, just less obvious.

"Just a minute, Mattie. Let me get the things I need to clean you up."

"Bathroom?" I choke out. It's a long shot, but I'm hoping some of that motherly love she claims she feels for us will help me out. I need to be untied if I hold any hope of getting out of here before her husband comes back.

"I don't think that's a good idea, Mattie," she says after a long minute.

"Please?" I try again.

"Don't do anything stupid at first, Mattie," I hear Eric whisper. *"Use the bathroom. Have her help you so she thinks you are helpless. Then on the way back, we'll strike."*

I had a thought. *"Can you and maybe some of the other ghosts make it cold enough so she feels it, or is it only me that it works on?"*

"No, it works on everyone," Eric says. *"Why?"*

"Does she know who you are?" I ask.

"Yes."

The feelings behind that simple word make me want to cry. There is *so* much pain and anguish that I feel it to the depths of my soul. I will help Eric cross over no matter what. *"She knows your name?"*

"Yesss..."

I flinch, knowing the memories I'm stirring up must be beyond painful for him, but I need every advantage I can get. I swallow painfully. I need to talk, and I need Eric to back me up with his ghostly abilities.

Mrs. Olson moves to me, untying my restraints with gentle care. She helps me to sit up, giving me a minute to orient myself. My head swims and if I could see, I'd be puking. Strange that I can feel the room spinning even if I can't see it. I must have a heck of a concussion going on.

My feet are unsteady and I lean on Mrs. Olson as she helps me to the bathroom. I really do need to pee. I try to fumble with my jeans, but can't stop the harsh cry that slips out when pain lances up both arms. My hands are useless. I'm pretty sure they're both broken in multiple places.

Mrs. Olson makes a *tsking* sound and helps me get my jeans down and seated on the toilet. Relief is instant. As much as I should be embarrassed, I'm not. I haven't been to the bathroom in Lord knows how many hours. I *need* to pee.

I am so focused on my acute relief, I forget Eric. I feel my face explode in rush of heat and scarlet fire. I can hear him chuckling. He is enjoying my embarrassment. As much as I have come to rely on Mirror Boy, no way do I want him seeing me sitting on the toilet. Not only is it embarrassing for so many reasons, it's downright rude.

"Focus, Mattie." Eric's laughter reverberates through my head, making me wince. The slightest noise is starting to bother me. I'm not sure if it's the head wound or if it's from prolonged ghost conversation.

"Mrs. O?"

"Hmm?" she murmurs, turning on the water, presumably so I can wash my hands.

"Do you know how I knew Sally didn't run away?"

She pauses. I can't see her, but I feel it in the lack of movement. My other senses work much better since I can't see. I'm actually grateful for it.

"I saw her."

"Wh…what?"

I nod and fight back the pain it causes me. "I saw her that night. It's why I came home early and wanted you to call the police." My throat is on fire and it hurts to breathe. I take a few slow breaths and try to force the pain to the back of my mind. I have to rattle her or this won't work. "Can you help me up, please?"

She pulls me up and helps me fasten my jeans. Her movements are jerky, hurried. I take a step toward the running water. *"Eric?"*

The cold starts to creep in and I know it's more than Eric. I can feel them, like I did earlier. There are more this time, almost two dozen different souls pressing in on me. I'm not afraid, not at all. It's their way of comforting me, letting me know I'm not alone. I welcome the ache that settles in my bones.

I can hear the ice forming on the mirror and Mrs. Olson's gasp of shock. The water is icy as it splashes over my hands. It doesn't register, not really. I can't feel the cold of the water past a sensory perception of it. I know that when I breathe in and out fog will be swirling in front of my face.

"You are going to have to push her, Mattie. If you turn to your right and shove with all your might, she'll fall over," Eric went on. *"I don't know if she'll be down long, but you need to run. Turn around and run straight. The door is directly across from this one. Run fast."*

"Don't you want to know how I saw Sally?"

"You couldn't have seen her," Mrs. Olson denies.

"I did," I tell her softly, the words coming slowly. "She was wearing her favorite night shirt. There was masking tape on her mouth and she had a bullet hole in her head."

"No…you couldn't have seen…"

"To quote an old movie, Mrs. O, I see dead

people, ghosts if you will. I saw her ghost."

She flinches away from me and I blink back tears of sheer pain. Be strong, I tell myself. You only have one shot at getting away. Forget the pain, focus on escape. "Can't you feel them all, Mrs. O? They are here with us right now. Emma, Tina, Bobby, Ricky. They're all here."

"How do you know those names?" I can hear fear in her voice. Good. Fear is good.

"They told me their names. I saw them, what Mr. Olson did to them. I know what happened to them."

The room plunges to freezing. I wouldn't be surprised if the sink water started to form into an icicle. Wow. I've never felt anything so cold in my life.

The sound of nails being sawed through by a chainsaw starts to creep into the room. "There's Eric," I sigh wistfully. Mrs. Olson moves closer, her body pressing into mine. I can feel her fear, feel her shiver.

"Eric?" she whispers.

"You remember Eric, what Mr. Olson did to his face?"

She gasps in horror. I struck a nerve. "His face is so bloody and mangled you can't really even make out what he looks like."

I lean on the sink and brace my feet. "He's standing right here next to us, Mrs. O. Can't you feel it, the cold? The cold is all the ghosts you've helped kill. That scraping sound, that's Eric."

"No, no, no, no, no…" she wails.

"Now, Mattie, do it now!" Eric orders.

I push away from the sink and shove my body

into hers as hard as I can. She stumbles and falls hard. I don't wait, I run.

Chapter Twenty-Eight

The door is an obstacle. My head is fuzzy and I blink rapidly as I skid to a halt in front of it. I yank off the blindfold with the palms of my hands and then grasp the knob and attempt to open it. Pain nearly knocks me to my knees. My fingers are useless, but I have to get the door open!

"Hurry, Mattie," Emma says. *"She's getting up!"*

Closing my eyes, I take a deep breath and then turn the knob as hard as I can. It pulls open and I say a short prayer to the Man Above. Definitely owe Him at least a month of Sundays for this.

"Run!" That was everybody.

I don't have to be told twice, so I dodge out the door and turn left. Definitely, I'm in the basement and I take a second to orient myself. I've been here before. This was one of my foster homes before they closed it. There's only one entrance to the basement level.

Heavy sounds, thumping, heavy breathing. Yep, I can hear Mrs. O in the room behind me. I duck into the first room I see, leaving the door open and stuffing myself behind it. If I close the thing, she'll know. Maybe this will buy me a few minutes.

"Mathilda Louise Hathaway, you get back here right now!"

I flinch at the fury in her voice, but try to be quiet. She's running, but in the opposite direction, which tells me she's heading for the stairs. I turned wrong, dang it! Now she's upstairs. And I have to try to get up and past her. Right. I need a weapon, but what can I use that doesn't need my hands? Nothing comes to mind and I groan.

Nope. I'm not done. I made it this far, I can make it out.

"She's upstairs looking for you," someone said.

I let out a strangled shout and jump at the sound of Eric's voice. He nearly scared me to death! I turn to glare at him and then stop. My mouth falls open just a bit before I catch myself. Whoa. He looks normal, not mangled. I'd forgotten what he looked like. I don't know how, considering I'd stared at his picture for hours on end. I haven't been able to really shake his image since Dan showed me the picture. It's his eyes. The vibrant blue is the darkest, but clearest color I've ever seen.

"I have the kids looking so when she goes up to the second floor we'll get you out of here," he tells me.

The head wound must be doing some serious things to me if I can stop and ogle a ghost right in the middle of my escape plan. So not good. I sigh. At least he's here and didn't leave me.

"Are you okay?" The concern in Eric's voice is…odd.

"Yes," I answer him silently. *"Just really, really tired."*

"Mattie, I will get you out of here, I promise."

I smile and try to believe him. He sounds fierce like a warrior, but as sincere as my old Sunday school teacher. I wouldn't have gotten away without him. Mrs. Olson got a little terrified when I said his name. I frown. Why? There's something to that. I remember thinking Eric was the key to all this, and I think that is why she's afraid of him.

"Eric, why is Mrs. Olson afraid of you?"

He sighs just as heavily as I had. *"I got away once and tried to find help. It was before they moved us to this place. I'm the reason they had to move their playhouse. They found me before I could get help. But that is when I learned their secret."*

"Their secret?" My heart thumps wildly.

"Yes..."

"She's upstairs!" Ricky screams in my ear and I jump. I push away from the wall and hobble down the hall as fast as I can. My ankle is on fire and only gets worse with each step. I've probably done a lot more damage to it. The stairs loom ahead of me and I press my shoulder to the wall for support as I drag my legs up them one at a time. I come out into the hallway right off the kitchen. There is a kitchen door and all I have to do is get there.

I hear the shouts and cries of fear and dismay all at once. Two dozen voices hammer at me and I nearly scream at the white-hot agony that rips through my aching head. Something has changed, something scared them all. Eric hisses and his cold seeps into me, like he's trying to hold me and can't.

This is so not good, so very, very not good.

The archway leading into the kitchen is blocked. A man is standing there watching me. He's wearing a dark hoodie and I can't see his face, but I don't need to. There's only one person it can be—Mr. Olson. There's only one place to go. The back stairs go to the second floor. I grit my teeth and run.

He's whistling as he follows me. He's not running, just walking steadily and whistling. How weird. Why run, though? Not like I have anywhere to go now, is there? Just upstairs to where Mrs. Olson's lurking, waiting to find me and put me back in that chair. Not if *I* can help it.

The second floor has about nine bedrooms and the third floor about six, and three bathrooms. I bypass the second and head for the third. All the rooms are locked except the bathrooms and none of them have windows big enough for me to get out of. The attic stairs are at the end of the hallway. I can't go back down. He's searching and I don't trust my ability to slip past him on the stairs, either.

"He's on the second floor checking bedrooms," Emma whispers and I nod.

The attic door is slightly ajar and I hesitate. Is Mrs. Olson up there?

"She's not," Emma tells me and I go in, pushing the door shut, but it springs back open as I knew it would.

The attic is huge, but not dark. I can still see daylight streaming into the windows. How long have I been here? I look around quickly and don't go for the corners. They'll look there first. Instead I look at the middle of the room. There is junk everywhere from broken toys to office furniture. The desk draws my attention. There are two trunks sitting in front of it. If I can duck under it…

"Don't you watch horror movies?" The sarcasm in Eric's voice is heavy. *"It's always the idiot girls who get killed first! Putting yourself in a place you can't run from is the stupidest thing I've heard in a long time."*

"Yeah, well, you got any better ideas?" I snarl at him and limp toward the middle of the room, my eyes searching frantically. I need a place to hide.

"Over by the door," Eric tells me. *"Hide behind those boxes stacked up. When one of them comes in, you run out the door and downstairs as fast as you can. We'll do our best to help you."*

Like that's any better than my desk idea? I roll my eyes at him, but hobble over to my new hiding place. It's not like I have a lot of options. My head feels like it's gonna explode, my hands are on fire, and my ankle is past the point of pain. God knows what kind of damage I've done to it on top the sprain.

How did I get myself into this situation? Dan's right. I've gone soft. I ignored my own rules about ghosts. When I saw Sally, I should have just ignored her like I did every other ghost. I should have…I sigh.

I need to get a handle on this situation. Should've, could've, would've…none of that will get me out of this. I take a slow, deep breath and take stock of my situation. Okay, I'm hurt. I have two psychos trying to kill me, and, oh yeah—I'm surrounded by ghosts. I want to laugh. It's either laugh or cry. Mathilda Louise Hathaway doesn't cry.

Footsteps on the stairs interrupt my tirade. I tense. Each heavy thud brings him closer and closer. I have to be ready. The cold closes in around me. I don't see them, but I can feel their terror. It only magnifies mine. I've seen what Mr. Olson has done to them, what he plans to do to me. What he's already done to me with his knife. My body starts to shake. No, no. No more of that! Don't obsess about the knife.

"Calm down, Mattie," Eric whispers. *"I'm right here. Just calm down."*

"Easy for you to say," I grouch in answer. *"He can't hurt you anymore."*

"What?"

"You're already dead, Eric," I say. *"He can't do anything else to you."*

"But I can feel him hurt me every day," Tina whispers brokenly. *"I'm back in that chair every minute of every day."*

Oh, God, like I have time for a Dr. Phil session? But if I can make them understand that he can't cause them any more pain then maybe they will fight harder. I frantically search my memory for all the things I've read on why ghosts linger.

"No, he can't hurt you," I tell them softly. *"You died a horrible death and that is your last memory. It's the clearest memory you have and that is what you focus on. You relive it every day, but that's all it is, a memory. He can't see you, can't touch you, can't talk to you. He can't hurt you anymore. I promise."*

I turn to look at Eric, one ear to the door, listening. Mr. Olson is almost up the stairs. *"But, he can hurt me! I need all of you to help me. Please don't let him hurt me."*

I see the shadow fall across the floor.

He has the knife.

Chapter Twenty-Nine

I take a deep breath. My first and only thought is escape. He just needs to get far enough into the room so I can slip by him and back down the stairs. Mrs. Olson is down there, but I'll take her over the knife in his hand any day.

He stops in the doorway and looks around. His head moves slightly from side to side, the face still buried in the shadow of the hoodie. He takes a step inside and I freeze, doing my best to be quiet. I can hear my heartbeat pound away.

Come on, just come in already, I think to myself. Why doesn't he move faster? I need him to walk around so I can sneak out.

My wish comes true in the next second, but he closes and locks the door behind him.

Fudgepops, fudgepops, fudgepops. How am I going to get out now? My hands can't unlock and open the door in enough time to run from him even if he walks all the way to the end of the room. I'll bet good money that's what he's banking on. He knows how badly I'm hurt since he was the one who caused the injuries.

"You can't get the door open." Eric's whispered words are full of defeat.

"Well, duh," I say in my mind, knowing he and the other ghosts can hear. *"We just have to figure out something else."*

"What?" He sounds almost desperate. *"You can't hold a weapon even if we could find you one."*

I frown. He has me there. I can't hold anything that would do damage.

Mr. Olson starts to whistle softly as he moves further into the room, unhurried. He knows I'm good and trapped. I can feel the ghosts cringe. It hurts my skin. His whistling scares them more than anything else. What had he done to them while whistling a jaunty little tune? Their fear presses in on me, and for a moment it's hard to breathe. The cold invades me, invades my lungs.

The whistling stops and he turns in my direction. My eyes widen when I realize what caused the reaction. He can feel the cold. It's centered here, around me. Oh crap. The ghosts are going to get me killed, the little buggers. I feel bad almost as soon as I think it. They have been doing everything they can to help me. Still, though, they need to stop with the freeze-fest.

He stops about ten feet away and cocks his head. I can make him out between the cracks in the stacks of boxes I'm hiding behind. The knife is clearly visible in his hand and my breathing quickens at the sight. I'm terrified at just the thought of it on my skin. I hate my mother more than I ever have in this moment. *She* caused this terror and it's going to get me killed. I giggle. I can't help it. What she failed to do when I was five, she'll accomplish now.

Oh, crap. He heard the giggle. He's coming this way. How stupid can I be? Eric is right. I am going to get killed because I'm doing everything wrong. I've seen enough scary movies to know better than to let my emotions get the best of me. You forget the basic rules of a scary movie and you die. I could so be Rose McGowan in *Scream* right now. I remember thinking 'How stupid can you be?' when she went out into that garage And here I go and giggle, of all things.

Before I can blink, the boxes I'm hiding behind go flying in all directions and I stumble back, falling. The ankle I'd sprained twists at an odd angle and I hear a crack. Pain lances up my leg and I cry out. Tears spring to my eyes, but I force myself to focus on getting away from that knife coming down at me. I roll away and land against an old chest. I use my forearms to maneuver my way up. My ankle is broken. Each step tells me that. I push the pain to the back of my mind and concentrate on moving one foot in front of the other.

Icy waves of cold wrap around me, trying to comfort me. I want to snarl at the stupid ghosts. It's *their* fault he found me to begin with. I don't, though. The cold actually helps. It gives me strength. Dr. Olivet said my energy was a beacon to them, that my aura was made up of ghost energy. Maybe theirs can give me strength? Could mine give them strength too? Can I use that? My mind races with the possibilities.

Hands catch my hair and yank hard. I fall,

screaming as my ankle can't handle the fall. It isn't a pain I can push back this time. The knife catches me in the shoulder and sinks deep. My throat closes off as panic seeps in. The knife is ripped away and I try to roll, but it catches me in the side as I try to escape. I can see my Mom bringing a knife down toward me, stabbing me over and over. Her face takes the place of the man standing above me. I see her bright blonde hair and blue eyes smiling as she tries to kill me. I hear her humming and telling me she loves me.

"Please, Mamma," I whisper. "Please don't. It hurts."

The knife stops mid-air. It hovers over me, but I don't see it. All I can see is Mamma smiling while she kills me.

"That's it, Mattie!" Eric shouts in my head. *"Keep talking, it's making her think."*

Her? I blink at Eric's screeching in my head. Her? I look up and see him standing over me, knife in hand. Why has he stopped?

"Mattie! Keep talking like she's your mother!"

"Mamma?"

I hear a choking noise coming from the figure above me.

"Why are you doing this, Mamma? Wasn't I good girl?" I whisper, inching backward just a bit. "Why do you want to hurt me?"

The man shakes his head, almost like he's confused. I can see him inhale deeply then the tension drains away. He brings the knife down. I moved far enough away that the blade misses me and sinks into the wooden floorboards instead. He yanks, but it's stuck. I don't waste time. I roll and roll. There's no point trying to get up. Best I can do is roll away from him. I roll into something and items rain down on me. I flinch, but I see a baseball bat. It's an old wooden one made for a child. It's small. I reach for it and grit my teeth as the pain swells up. I can't get a good angle, so I'll wait for my chance. I turn away, close my eyes and listen.

It only takes a moment before I hear the footsteps. Closer and closer they come until he's right behind me. There is a movement in the air and I can guess it's him raising his arm with the knife. I waste no time in rolling and swinging as hard as I can. It's not my best work, but I hit him squarely in the kneecaps. He grunts and falls forward, landing on me. My breath goes out in a whoosh, but I notice two things at once. One is that the person on top of me is not a man. I distinctly feel breasts squished against me. It is not Mr. Olson who is on top of me, but *Mrs.* Olson. The hoodie has come off and her muddy brown hair is falling around her face.

Mrs. O? No way. I knew she was seven kinds of crazy, but never did I think for a second that she was the killer.

The second thing I notice is murder in her eyes. My death. I try to push her off, but it's no use. What little strength I had left was in that last-ditch effort with the bat.

Mrs. Olson gets up slowly, glares, and grabs my hair. She uses it to pull me along. I know I'm crying at this point, but can't help it.

"Mrs. O., stop, please." I beg her as she drags me toward the attic door. "Why are you doing this to me? Please, stop, please."

"You!" she snarls. "Shut up! Be a good girl and shut up. You are going back to the chair. She won't let you up again. I'll make *sure* of that."

I frown. What is she talking about? Who is 'she'?

She starts down the stairs, dragging me with her. Each step causes agony. I blink back tears and fight the darkness around the edges of my vision. If she gets me back in that chair, I am done for.

"Eric, help me!'

"How?" he screams back.

"I don't know, do something ghostly!"

It's as if every ghost there just pauses and says 'Huh?' and 'Duh.'

We are on the second floor by now. I can hear them whispering, but there are too many of them talking all at once. The air around us gets colder and colder; I see my breath in front of me as I exhale. Within seconds it is so cold, I am freezing. I wouldn't be surprised if my lips are blue.

Mrs. Olson stops and stares at me. She's frowning, but feels the cold. I remember how scared she was earlier. *I* can help too.

"Can you feel them, Mrs. O? They are all here, all of the kids you killed. They are standing right here with us."

Her eyes move around the hallway and she snarls something incoherent before giving me a swift kick in the stomach. I grunt, but am not deterred. I look up and see the walls weep with a steady stream of what looks like blood. So cheesy. Eric sighs, but hey, if it works, I'll take cheesy. She stops trying to drag me away when she sees the walls.

A boy about sixteen or so is standing a few feet from us. His ebony skin is marred by puncture wounds, big gaping holes. There are hooks in his chest, abdomen, arms, and legs. I get the distinct feeling he was suspended from those hooks. He grins at Mrs. O. This is Ricky. I know it without having to be told. He walks toward Mrs. O and she backs up. Whoa, she can see him! He winks at me and I know he is using a lot of energy to make her see him.

"You remember, Ricky don't you, Mrs. O?" I ask her softly.

Another form flickers to our left. She swings in that direction, and probably twisting my hair out by the roots, but I don't care. I see Tina this time. I know it's her just like I knew Ricky. She could have been pretty once, but her face has been carved up, a pattern embossed in the skin. I shy away from it. It's almost as bad as Eric's face. She walks toward us. Her movements are jerky and disjointed. That's because her legs are bent at an odd angle. Even *I* cringe away from the walking nightmare and I know she means me no harm.

More and more kids flicker in around us, their mangled forms converging on us. I close my eyes. I can't take it. If I thought I'd reached my scary threshold, I was wrong. I know they don't want to hurt me, but I'm so scared, I'm shaking, never mind Mrs. O ripping out my hair.

Then I hear Eric's familiar screeching start up, like a chainsaw cutting through a wall of nails.

"That's, Eric," I whisper and flinch at the pain in

my head. My nose starts to bleed. It's almost unbearable. "Was Eric your first? You remember what you did to his face, don't you, Mrs. O?"

Mrs. Olson lets out a whimper and I know this is working. She's afraid of him, but why?

"Why are you so afraid of Eric, Mrs. O?" I whisper, opening my eyes to look up into her terrified ones. "Why does he scare you more than the others?"

"He's dead," she hisses. "Dead, dead, dead. I killed him. He's dead!"

Eric's screeching gets worse. *"Ask her who I am,"* he orders.

Right. "Who is he, Mrs. O? Who is Eric and why did you choose him first?"

"He had to pay," she growls. It's Mrs. O's voice, but not. It sounds deeper, almost masculine. "He made us do this."

"What did he do?" I ask. "Who is *he*?"

"She was a good wife to him, did everything for him, but he couldn't keep it in his pants." Mrs. Olson lets go of my hair and brings the knife up, slashing at the shapes around us. It goes right through them and I hear their laughter. They are laughing and it makes Mrs. Olson insane. She screams.

"She couldn't give him children." Mrs. Olson is panting, rage burning in her eyes. "That other woman could. I couldn't let him hurt her like that. I had to make the whore pay for her sins."

Who is 'she'? My mind is whirling.

Eric's face swims up in front of us. The broken, twisted mess of flesh and blood snarls at her. I swallow, my throat on fire. The blue eyes are glittering with their own rage. Blood seeps down, falling onto the carpet.

Mrs. Olson lets out a yelp and moves backward again. Eric pushes at her, his rage is making me hurt everywhere.

"You had to die," Mrs. Olson says. "She saw you that day, knew who you were. We thought you had died in the fire with her. But there you were, laughing! How dare you!"

Mrs. Olson takes a shaky breath. She blinks and I see reason return to her eyes, then fear. She's staring at Eric like he is the Death Angel come to collect. He now towers over her, blood oozing down his face, dripping onto the pudgy form.

"No," she whispers. "I had to help him. He wouldn't listen to me. We had to kill her, had to kill you. Then I couldn't make him stop killing. He had to have them, had to hurt them. I didn't want to, but I couldn't tell him no. He means everything to me. Please, please, I'm sorry, so sorry."

"You killed my mother," Eric hisses. His voice fills the house. It echoes off the walls in octaves not meant for the human ear. I can feel the blood dripping from my ears. *"Then you killed me to make sure my father never found out I lived."*

His father? My eyes widen and then it all makes sense. *Mr. Olson* is his father. He has to be. Mrs. O killed Eric's mother and Eric ended up in foster care. When she saw him and realized he didn't die, she took him and tortured him before finally killing him. Oh dear Lord.

"You're dead!" Mrs. Olson's voice once again

has that deep, masculine quality in it. The madness is back in her eyes. She walks back toward us, swinging her knife. "You are dead, and you can't hurt me, you little son of a…"

I get to my knees and throw myself at Mrs. Olson. She staggers back. I keep pushing, rolling as hard as I can. She hits the banister. Her hands clutch the railing and the knife falls from her hands. I catch it and turn, stabbing her right above the left knee. She screams and Eric and every ghost in the hall runs at her. She jumps back and in doing so, falls over the banister. I hear the sound of her body hitting the floor below. It's a unique sound, one hard to describe, and one I'll never forget.

It's quiet.

I shiver and work to pull myself up to look over the railing. She is sprawled below us, unmoving. Is she dead? God, I hope so. I don't know how much more of this I can take. I let myself slide back down, resting against the bars of the banister. I'm woozy from blood loss. I hurt and don't think I'll last much longer.

At least she didn't kill me. If I'm going to die, then this is a good way to go, fighting.

"Mattie?"

I blink and try to focus on Eric. His face is back to normal. He looks so worried. I smile at him. *"Thank you,"* I say. *"Thank all of you."*

"Come on, Mattie, you need to get downstairs and outside. No one can find you in here."

I can hear them all murmuring sounds of encouragement, but I can't move. I have no strength left. All my aches and pains are going away. I'm numb. I often figured dying really hurt. I know people say it doesn't, but you don't really feel anything. The pain is unbearable at first, but the human body is equipped to only handle so much pain before it shuts itself off. I'm grateful for that.

The sounds of whispers seem fainter and fainter, but I fight to keep my eyes open. I don't want to miss the light. It's beautiful. One of the bedroom doors is filling up with the most beautiful golden light I have ever seen. There is joy in that light and I want to cry. It so full of love. I can see people standing at the end of that light. Ha, it really does look like a tunnel.

"Do you see it? I see my dad. Look, there my brother Matt! Granny?"

"No, wait!" Eric is back to hissing. *"It's dangerous in there, I can't protect you!"*

I groan, but must help them. They helped me and it's my turn.

"No," I tell them. *"That light is for all of us."*

"All of us?" Eric whispers brokenly. *"No, Mattie. Not you. I promised I'd save you. I'm sorry."*

"You did save me." I reach up and for the first time in a long time, there is no pain in my hands. I cup his cheek and smile. *"You got me out of that basement, you helped me hide, and you helped me kill her. You saved me, Eric, and now it's my turn to save you."*

At least I don't have to talk out loud to do this. *"The light is your doorway to the next life,"* I continue. *"There is joy and peace there. You don't belong here anymore. You belong there. Those people are waiting to guide you through the Between. They will keep you safe. I promise, there is nothing to be scared of. It's time to go home."*

"Mommy!" Michael Sutter. I remember him from the whiteboards, the little boy I'd seen in the bathroom when all this first started. His puppy-dog eyes shine with happiness. He hurtles himself into the light and then is gone. After that, they all drift in, calling out to their loved ones. I watch every ghost I'd seen since the little girl in the bathroom, to Rick, go into the light and it makes me happy. As much pain as I am in, I am happy I could help them.

Sally squats in front of me. I haven't seen her since she showed me Mary's bike. I hadn't expected to, though. Sally is not brave. She runs from the things that scare her. The fact that she brought me here is more than I would have hoped for. She looks at me uncertainly, as if asking for my permission. "It's okay, Sally," I tell her. "You were brave and helped me find everyone. It's time to go. Your grandmother is waiting for you, isn't she?"

A quick look toward the light has Sally nodding. "Then go. I'm okay." I watch her stand and then walk into the light.

Only Eric and I remain.

"You should go too," I tell him, blinking. I'm so tired.

"You can't get rid of me that easily, Hathaway." He smiles and sinks down beside me. The cold surrounding me is safe and strangely enough, warm. *"I'll wait for you."*

"Did I tell you how cute you are when your face isn't all Texas Chainsaw Massacre*?"*

Eric laughs softly and I feel his fingers brush against my cheek.

My head falls forward and my eyes close. I just want to sleep.

Then I hear a crash.

"Mattie!"

Chapter Thirty

The ever-growing familiar beep, beep, beep pulls me out of a blissful darkness. I try to move and can't. Panic sets in. Am I still there? Am I still trapped? Still strapped to that table? I force my eyes to open. Good. I can see. Relief sweeps through me. It's dark, but the IV machine is all lit up.

There are several other machines I don't recognize, but I'm in the hospital. Again. The smell alone should have alerted me, but I'm tired. My blurry eyes do a frantic search of the room, looking for ghosts, but again, they are strangely absent. Why do they leave me alone when I'm here?

I shift my head slightly and wince at the pain, but am glad I moved. Dan is asleep in the chair beside my bed. He propped his feet on the bottom of the bed and is slouched down. He looks exhausted. His police uniform is wrinkled and stained with dark patches. It has to be blood, whose I don't know. It could be mine or it could be Mrs. O's.

Thoughts of Mrs. Olson make me shudder violently. Never in my wildest dreams could I have imagined she was the killer. She took care of me, stayed with me, and made me feel safe. How can I have been so wrong about her? Usually my instincts are much better than this. I never saw it coming. The things she did to those poor kids, to me. I can still feel the knife tracing over my skin even now. The shakes start in as soon as I think about it. The monitor attached to me starts to beep wildly. My breath comes in short, panting gasps and in a heartbeat I am back in that house, strapped down, crying and begging for it to stop.

"Shh, Mattie, you're safe now, shhh...."

Eric? I open my eyes and find his blue ones staring at me. He is sitting beside me on the bed. I thought he'd gone into the light. What is he doing here?

"If you don't calm down, you're gonna wake up your friend. He hasn't slept in days."

"Eric? Why are you here?" I ask in my head, mindful of Dan asleep in the chair. *"Why didn't you cross over?"*

"Trying to get rid of me already, Hathaway?"

"What? No! I just don't understand...why didn't you go into the light?" My breathing slows, calmer now that I know I'm not alone in that basement again.

"I said I would wait for you, Mattie, and when you didn't go, I stayed. I needed to know you'd be safe, that you were okay."

His eyes have lost their teasing light and he's serious. He is looking at me the way I'd always wanted a boy to look at me, and I want to scream at the unfairness of it all. Why does he have to be dead? Fate is cruel. She gives me someone I could really come to trust, to maybe even love, and I can't have him. That is not his fault, though. He did his best for me, now it's my turn to help him.

"I am okay, Eric, because of you."

"When I first saw you, you were so outrageous." He laughs softly. *"I knew they'd want you. I thought if I scared you, you'd stop looking, but you just got more determined. I swear I didn't mean to hurt you, Mattie. I didn't know I could."*

"You and me both," I tell him wryly. *"I thought you guys could just pester me. I didn't know you could physically harm me. I'm glad, though. Without that screeching of yours, I don't think I could have taken Mrs. Olson."*

"I do not screech. Girls screech, not guys. Guys yell."

The outraged expression he wears makes me laugh. Why does he have to be dead? Why do I have to convince him to cross over? I don't want him to go.

"Eric...."

"No." He puts a finger to my lips to shush me. *"I am not going into the light, Mattie."*

I shiver at the cold that seeps into me. *"Why? You don't belong here anymore. Everyone you were protecting is safe now. They are on the other side waiting for you."*

"Not everyone. There is still one person I'm waiting for."

My eyes widen. Does he mean me?

"Who else is going to keep you out of trouble, Hathaway? Besides, the other side is overrated."

"Eric, you can find peace over there…"

"I said I'd wait for you, Mattie, and I will." He leans down and presses his cold lips to my forehead. *"Get some rest now. I have to go find a girl down in the morgue scaring the attendants with her moaning."*

"Eric!" He's gone. Just like that, I blink and he's gone. He's supposed to cross over, to find peace. He deserves it after all he's been through, but secretly, I'm glad he didn't go. I'm so messed up. Here I am wanting something I can't have again. I don't think I'll ever find anything normal to hold onto.

Then I see Dan. He's about as normal as you can get. And he found me. God only knows how, since Eric had issues trying to get through to him. Dan is here, sitting in bloody clothes, waiting on me to wake up. He hasn't left me despite my attempts to push him away. I don't know what I'd do without him. I'd be dead right now if not for him. Leave it to Officer Dan to save the day.

The slow steady beeping of the machines lulls me back to sleep. When I wake up again, I am not as afraid as before. I know where I am and I also know Eric is around. If anything spooky tries to hurt me, Mirror Boy will eat them alive. Maybe he's the reason the spooks are leaving me alone this time.

The blinds have been drawn and sunlight streams into the room. I blink, but my eyes aren't nearly as sore as they were before. At least it gives me a chance to take stock of my injuries. Both my hands are bandaged in some kind of splint. Most likely so I can't move them. My leg is raised slightly in one of those contraptions you see on TV to elevate it in a makeshift sling. Another splint is secured to my ankle. Multiple stab wounds are stitched and bound. They itch. I also notice I'm restrained. Maybe it's so I can't move and hurt myself, but I don't like it, not after what I just went through. They are going to take these off right now, even if that means I have to scream bloody murder to accomplish it. No one is ever going to tie me up again. Ever.

I hear the toilet flush and a sink turn on. Dan emerges from the bathroom after a minute. He's taken off his uniform shirt. The white t-shirt he'd worn under it is just as stained. Big, dark, brownish spots decorate it. Funny how blood doesn't dry the color of red. It can be black or brown, but I don't think I've ever seen it red.

"You're awake," Dan whispers when he sees me looking at him. The look of relief on his face is almost comical. He rushes over and then stops, unsure where to sit. I'm all wrapped up.

"Dan," I whisper hoarsely. My throat still hurts something awful. It was bruised, swelling, and I thought for sure it was gonna close up on me last I checked.

He grabs the water pitcher and pours some into a cup. Carefully, he helps me to take a few sips. Oh, God, that feels so good against my throat. He only lets me have a few more sips before he puts the plastic cup down. I glare at him, but he only shakes his head.

"Just a little, Squirt. Give it a few minutes, and I'll give you more. I'm going to let the nurse know you're awake."

He runs out and after a few minutes I am bombarded with nurses and two doctors. The next twenty minutes are spent being poked and prodded while trying to answer questions. I do manage to get them to remove the restraints. Dan made them, once he understood how upset I was about them. Once they leave, Dan pulls up the chair and settles himself in.

"Don't you ever scare me like that again, Mattie. If you do, I swear I will kill you myself."

The anger radiating off him is surprising. He is so pissed. My eyes go round. I've never seen him this mad before. He looks a little scary. His brown eyes are almost black in their fury.

"What in the hell were you thinking, running off like that without your phone?"

A lecture is not what I was expecting. I know he's right, so I get mad too.

"Why would I have called you?" I whisper back angrily. Or at least as angry as I can be, sounding more like a mouse. "You said you didn't believe me!"

He runs a hand over his face and I can see him counting to ten in his head. "Mattie, just because you get your feelings hurt is no reason to run off looking for a serial killer on your own!"

"My feelings hurt!" The beeping on the machine starts to rapidly increase. "You think I ran off alone because my feelings were hurt?" Well, maybe I did, but I was running from Mirror Boy too. I hadn't been about to lose my only lead. It isn't my fault I forgot to bring my phone.

"Mattie, you could have died. Don't you

understand that? You almost did die." His face loses its angry expression. Fear replaces it. "You were so cold when I found you…I thought you were dead." He takes a deep breath to steady himself. "I thought I was too late. I've never been more scared in my life than when I saw you broken and bleeding in that hallway."

"I did try to call you," I tell him, "but I forgot my phone at the house. I saw Sally and she was willing to take me to where she was. She showed me Mary's bike…oh God, Mary! Did you find her? Is she alive?"

"Yeah, we found her. She's two rooms down. She's pretty messed up too, but you saved her. Her mom wants to talk to you when you feel up to it."

I nod, grateful she's okay. I thought for sure she was a goner when I didn't hear her anymore. At least I can say I saved someone.

"Mattie, promise me you won't ever go off following a ghost again without telling me. Please. Don't do that to me again."

I swear I think there are tears in his eyes, but he's not looking at me so I can't tell. Typical guy move. It strikes me then how much this boy cares. He cares if I live or die. He cares if I'm safe, if I'm happy, if I'm okay. He cares about me. I admitted to myself how much I care about him, but I didn't let myself think about if he felt the same. He does. Tears spring to my eyes. I am not much on crying, but I can't help it. Once I start, I can't stop.

Dan looks helpless, but then he jumps in the bed and just holds me, careful of my injuries. It hurts like nobody's business, but I wouldn't tell him for all the world how much pain I'm in right now. I need him to hold me. He and Eric are the only two people in the world who can make me feel this safe.

"I was so scared," I whisper. "When I woke up tied down to that chair and I couldn't see..." Shudders wrack me. "No one knew where I was, and I felt so helpless."

"It's okay, Mattie," Dan soothes. "I found you."

"The knife scared me more than anything else," I confess, a sob ripping from my throat. "I hate knives. She strapped me down to a table and...and...cut me."

"You're safe now, Mattie. She can't hurt you ever again. You're safe."

"How did you find me?" I ask him to try to distract myself from the memories of the table. "You didn't even know I was missing."

"I got called into work and my phone died. I didn't get your message until I plugged it in to charge on the way home. I swung by your place after that stupid message to set you straight. Mr. Olson had just come in from work. He said you were probably still asleep, but he'd wake you up. He was making coffee and hit play on the answering machine. That's when I heard the message on the machine."

"You thought he was in on it too?" The message on the machine had convinced me Mr. Olson was the killer as well.

"When I couldn't find you and your phone was still in your room, I took him down the station for questioning. This time, no one even hinted that you were just a runaway. Having a friend on the force is a good thing sometimes. Once my captain heard the tape he came to the same conclusion I did. We've had your foster father in custody since Sunday morning."

"He wasn't involved."

Dan sighs. "There was no way he wasn't, Mattie."

"He wasn't. Do you remember when I told you Eric was the key to all of this since he was the first?"

"Yeah?"

"Mr. Olson cheated on Mrs. Olson."

"So?"

"Mrs. Olson can't have kids, the other woman could. Eric was their son. Mrs. O killed Eric's mother. She thought Eric died in the fire that took his mother. When she saw him at the basketball game, she knew who he was. He looks like his mom. That's when she took him. There's something wrong with her, Dan. She flips from one mood to another."

"We had our psychologist talk to her." Dan settles me back against my pillows and gives me a little more water.

"She's not dead?" I squeak. She has to be dead. I saw her fall.

"No, Squirt, she's not dead. She broke her arm in the fall and has a concussion, but other than that, she's fine."

"Where is she?" There's not a chances in Hades I'm staying here if she's here. No way.

"She's in county lock-up. We moved her there after the doctor cleared her. You're safe, Mattie."

"Okay." I calm down, breathing deeply. She's not here. I can deal with that. "So what did your shrink say?"

"Do you know what Dissociative Identity Disorder is?"

I shake my head no.

"It's basically multiple personality disorder. She had two separate identities. One was hers and one was that of her brother. The kid was brutally murdered when he was about nine. The doctor doesn't know how long she's been sick, but the brother's identity was the one doing all the killing. She just cleaned up after him."

How did I miss that? I know crazy, all foster kids do. It keeps us alive. What is wrong with me these days? Has to be the ghosts. Not that I'm not grateful for their help, but they cause more problems than anything else.

"How did you find me, Dan?" I ask again. "Mr. Olson couldn't have told you where I was. There's no way you would have even thought to look for me there."

"It was the strangest damn thing." He shakes his head and shivers at the sudden cold in the room. "Every time I went to my computer that old article about Hartford House was pulled up. Every single time. I'd close out the browser, take a phone call, and when I looked at my computer, it was right there again."

"Ask him why he finally checked it out," Eric laughs.

"Why did you finally come check it out?" I ask him, trying not to laugh at Eric making bunny ears above Dan's head.

"Just figured I should."

"He closed out the page and I dumped his coffee onto the keyboard," Eric says smugly.

"Wouldn't be because a whole cup of coffee spilled onto your keyboard the last time you tried to close out the page?"

Dan's eyes widen and then he frowns. "How do you know that?"

I laugh and then wince. Laughing is not good. "Who do you think sent Eric to tell you where I was?"

There is such a look of horror on his face, I forget it hurts to laugh, and I giggle. A coughing fit sets in and I do my best to try to control myself. It's so comical. Eric is cracking up, which is making me laugh harder. Dan is glowering at me.

"Sorry," I wheeze.

Dan rubs his eyes and frowns at me. "No, I'm sorry, Squirt. Just because I can't explain something doesn't mean it's not true."

"So, you're willing to admit I might be able to see ghosts?"

"I'm willing to admit you can see ghosts."

My eyebrows shoot up, and even Eric looks impressed. Dan looks extremely uncomfortable.

"Oh my gosh."

"Mattie, I'm really, really sorry. When I got that message, it hit me like a fist in the gut. Then you were gone and I…I went a little insane thinking about what might be happening to you. I had all those drawings you did of the victims and…and…" He stands up, his fists clenching. If he could have, I think he might have smashed something.

"I'm okay." It's my turn to soothe him.

"No, you're not!" He turns back to me and I understand the rage I'd seen before had been directed at him and not me. He blames himself for what happened to me.

"Dan, don't do this to yourself," I whisper. My throat is hurting from all the talking, but I need him to understand it's not his fault. "I would have found a reason to push you away with or without the ghost stuff. It's something I always do. I ruin things that are good in my life. You got too close,, and I was afraid."

"If I had believed you, you wouldn't have gone off on your own!"

"Yeah, I would have," I disagree. "I'm not used to depending on anyone and I would have followed Sally with or without your help. That's just me. It's my own fault I ran out of the house without my phone." I fail to tell him I couldn't have called him anyway because I got knocked out as soon as I found the stupid bike. "There was nothing you could have done. The important thing is you found me. You found me with a ghost's help, but it was you who found me and got me to the hospital before I died."

He and I are going to disagree. I don't think there's anything I can say right now to convince him this isn't his fault. It's going to take a long time before he gets over the guilt.

Dan sighs and walks over to the thermostat. "Why is it so cold in here?"

"That would be Mirror Boy, a.k.a. Eric."

Eric grins and goes over to stand beside Dan. He grins at me and then the temperature gets colder and colder. I can hear the water turn on in the bathroom. Eric is using the moisture caused by the running water to ice up the windows right next to Dan. I would have freaked out a couple days ago seeing this, but I know Eric is only playing a joke this time. He doesn't mean any harm.

Dan stares in fascination at the windows as ice covers them. He turns to give me a look of utter disbelief. No way can he explain this away. He looks as terrified as I felt the first time I saw a ghost with a nasty mangled injury. At least he's spared seeing them on a daily, sometimes hourly basis.

"Isn't he the one who hurt you?" Dan asks at last.

"Yeah, but he didn't mean to," I tell him. "He was trying to warn me, but I didn't listen. It was because of him and the other ghosts I survived long enough for you to find me. They helped me with Mrs. Olson."

He nods and comes to sit back down, his face serious again. "Are you going to do this a lot?"

"Define 'this.' I do a lot of stupid stuff."

"Leave me voicemails breaking up with me."

"Officer Dan, we can't break up 'cause we were never together."

"Mattie," he growls.

"Maybe."

"Well, get over it because I love you, Mattie Hathaway. I'm not sure what that means right now, but I do. You're stuck with me, Squirt. I'm not going anywhere."

The truth of that statement is shining in those liquid brown eyes of his. I can get lost in those warm brown depths if I let myself. I think I love him just a bit too. I don't know if it's the way a girl usually loves a boy, or if I love him like a friend or like a brother, but I do love him. I think he's as confused as I am. My heart clenches in fear at that admission. I've never let myself love anyone, ever. Not since Mamma. This could be very bad.

"Or it could be very good," Eric whispers by my ear.

"Are you eavesdropping?" I screech silently at him.

"Sure am," he replies unrepentantly. *"Don't push him away, Mattie. Let him in. Let him be there for you like I want to and can't. Let him love you. Don't be afraid. Love doesn't hurt, not always."*

"Are you talking to Ghost Boy again?" Dan asks suspiciously. "Your eyes are a little unfocused."

"Be quiet, Officer Dan," I whisper, staring at Eric. He looks so sad, but he's smiling at me with his one-hundred-watt smile. "Eric…"

"Shhh, Mattie. Trust yourself, trust him. It'll work out. Now, I am going to go roust out a rather pesky ghost terrorizing the surgical floor. Poor guy keeps trying to get people to watch him throw a football."

Just like that, he's gone again. I shake my head. That boy moves fast. He's also hurting. He is watching me live while he's stuck as a ghost. It's so not fair.

"Why are you crying, Mattie?" Dan asks, alarmed.

"Because everything is so messed up," I whisper. "I'm messed up." Dan tries to interrupt me, but I don't let him. "I didn't want to let you get close, Dan, but you got past every wall I have, and that terrifies me. You see *me*. You don't care about my snarky attitude. You see me. And as much as you scare me, I'm glad you didn't give up on me. All I wanted to do was to take back everything I said in that message while I was down in that basement. I...I...I love you too. You're my friend and that's all I need for right now."

"Then that's what I'll be, I'll be your friend for as long as you need me to be." He gives me a kiss on the forehead, much like Eric had done. I don't get any butterflies in my stomach this time, though. Dan's kiss only makes me feel safe, warm, and loved. Maybe that's all I ever really needed.

Maybe for once, I can be happy.

Chapter Thirty-One

It's not the cold that wakes me up this time, but something else. I know there's a ghost here even without opening my eyes. I feel not just the cold, but an energy. It surrounds the bed, almost suffocating me. I know who it is. Why has she waited this long to come to me?

My mother is sitting at the foot of the hospital bed. She's wearing the same stained pink tank top and blue jean shorts she wore when she died. Her blonde hair isn't stringy or messy. It's the one thing she kept up. I remember she used to sit and brush it for hours on end. Sometimes she'd even let me. It looks as soft as ever. Her blue eyes are sad, but I expected that. She always looked sad. My mother is beautiful. The drugs aged her, but only a little. She hadn't been hard core when she died. She might have been doing heroin for maybe a couple months.

"My beautiful girl," her voice sighs through the room.

"What are you doing here?" I ask her. My hand automatically searches for the nurses' call button, but I realize with a start, I can't do anything. My hands are bound. She could do some serious damage to me before anyone found out.

She reaches out to me and I flinch away. Her hand drops and there is regret in her eyes.

"You were such a beautiful baby. I loved you the minute I saw you. You were smiling before you were a month old. There was this joy in you even as a baby. I only ever wanted to protect you. Please remember that. I love you more than life itself, my sweet baby girl."

"Then why did you try to kill me?" I hear no fear in my voice, no emotion at all, really. Honestly, I think I'm just tapped out for the day. After what I went through, my Mom doesn't scare me all that much anymore. Not that I'm gonna let go of the nurses' call button, though. I'm not stupid. I'll figure out a way to use the darn thing.

"To protect you, but I can't anymore. You are shining like a lighthouse. I can't do it anymore."

"I don't understand." Protect me from what?

The light I'd seen before at the house opens up in the window. My mother stares at it and then looks back at me. The light is for her.

"Forgive me, Mattie."

"For trying to kill me, Mamma?" I wasn't sure I could.

"No, not for that."

"Then for what?"

"Just remember everything I did, I did to keep you safe, sweetheart."

"You're not making sense, Mamma."

She smiles at me and then goes over to stand in front of the light. She tells me one thing before she walks into that glowing warmth.

"I'm not your mother, Mattie."

About the Author

So who am I? Well, I'm the crazy girl with an imagination that never shuts up. I LOVE scary movies. My friends laugh at me when I scare myself and tell me to stop watching them, but who doesn't love to get scared? I grew up in a small town nestled in the southern mountains of West Virginia where I spent days roaming around in the woods, climbing trees, and causing general mayhem. Nights I would stay up reading Nancy Drew by flashlight under the covers until my parents yelled at me to go to sleep.

Growing up in a small town, I learned a lot of values and morals. I also learned parents have spies everywhere and there's always someone to tell your mama you were seen kissing a particular boy on a particular day just a little too long. So when you get grounded, what is there left to do? Read! My Aunt Jo gave me my first real romance novel. It was a romance titled "Lord Margrave's Deception." I remember it fondly. But I also learned I had a deep and abiding love of mysteries and anything paranormal. As I grew up, I started to write just that and would entertain my friends with stories featuring them as main characters.

Now, I live Huntersville, NC where I entertain my niece and nephew and watch the cats get teased by the birds and laugh myself silly when they swoop down and then dive back up just out of reach. The cats start yelling something fierce...lol.

I love books, I love writing books, and I love entertaining people with my silly stories.

Acknowledgements

As always, I have to thank my girls: Susan, Mags, Sheree, Ang, and Ann. You guys keep me on pace and never let me by with stupid stuff.

Special thanks to Mags and Lawrence. Mags, what can I say? Without you, this book wouldn't be where it is. You believed in it when I didn't. Lawrence, you made sure my facts were straight and I needed that help with the forensics. Grazie, my friends.

The cover of this book is near and dear to my heart. We searched and searched until we found the perfect image. It took a bit of work to actually get the image. So I want to give my personal thanks to the people responsible for the artwork itself. Thank you to Gemma Wright and Tugba Sevinc, and Aelathen from Deviant Art. Tirzalaughs—you took the image I gave you and created a cover that has inspired so many to read the book. Your work is as always gorgeous. Thank you so much for all your hard work on it and for putting up with my constant nagging.

Most of all, I have to thank all the fans at Wattpad—you guys inspire me every day and I love you all.

My favorite band, Fall Out Boy, deserves a thank you as well. Your song "My Songs Know What You Did In the Dark" helped me write the last few chapters of the book.

Last, but not least, thanks to my family for putting up with me during my writing spurts. I know I zone out when I write. I hear you…really…

Facebook:
https://www.facebook.com/authorAprylBaker

Twitter:
https://twitter.com/AprylBaker

Wattpad:
http://www.wattpad.com/user/AprylBaker7

Website:
http://www.aprylbaker.com/

Blog:
http://mycrazzycorner.blogspot.com/

TSU:
http://www.tsu.co/Apryl_Baker

Goodreads:
http://www.goodreads.com/author/show/5173683.A
pryl_Baker

Linkedin:
http://www.linkedin.com/pub/april-
baker/44/6b9/3a4

Made in the USA
Middletown, DE
23 May 2018